ISBN: 978-1-54394-951-3 (Paperback)
ISBN: 978-1-54394-952-0 (eBook)

Cover Design by StudioJasmineMalia
Cover photo by Grace E. Castle
Author Photo by Ty Cary

First Edition 2018 (Softcover)
Printed in the United States of America

Chittum Tree Publishing
501 Roper Rd
Eugene, Oregon

"A TIME TO WAIL is a marvelous novel, written with unique empathy and authenticity. Grace Elting Castle uses her first-hand knowledge of both PI work and the reservation life and customs of the Siletz people to create a compelling and insightful read that will call to mind the great Tony Hillerman."

--Michael Koryta
New York Times bestselling author

"...I foresee a series in the future."

—Marie Girard, Retired
Masters Level Clinical Psychologist
Mohawk (Canada) Descendant

"Had it not been for her writing and being one of our strongest support-ers during our Restoration era, 1970's through the 80's, very tumultuous times, we may not have succeeded. She's so deserving of acknowledgement and credit of this huge feat. Our family is indebted to her contribution. Our tribe is enjoying the labor of love today of this great writer, woman and friend."

--Selene Rilatos
Siletz Tribal Elder

"Former private investigator Grace Elting Castle gives us a unique and har-rowing story set on the Siletz Indian Reservation in Oregon. With first-hand knowledge of this tribe, Castle quickly moves us into a mystery of family loss and regrets, grave robbing, Native customs, and destruction of a heritage. She introduces us to the ills and hopes of 1970s reservation life, still under attack from ignorance, prejudice, and greed. A story that must be told and is told with wisdom and compassion."

--Valerie J. Brooks, Author
Revenge in 3 Parts

"This is some of the best descriptive stuff I've ever read":

--Paul Ciolino, Author *Dead in Six Minutes*

A TIME TO WAIL

AN INDIAN COUNTRY NOVEL

By Grace Elting Castle

For Nancy K. Cary and Tari A. Messman

---daughters extraordinaire

WAIL: *a mournful, prolonged cry or sound expressing grief; a Native woman's honoring of a deceased person*

"My Aunt Phonola (Van Pelt) Smith, a Hupa tribal member, died in a tragic automobile accident far from her California homeland. Walking from my Siletz, Oregon home to her sister-in-law's house a street away, I heard heart wrenching sobs that became louder as I grew closer.

I rushed through the door without knocking, certain my Aunt Clara was injured. 'What's wrong?' I shout. Aunt Clara sat straight in her rocking chair, turned to me and said, 'Someone has to wail for her.'

This was my first experience with traditional wailing to honor the dead. In many following years in Indian Country, where death is a constant, the sound has pierced my heart far too many times."

--- Grace Elting Castle

Foreword

As you begin your journey into the world of Ellie Carlisle, a fictional Siletz Indian woman, it may be the first time you hear about the government-mandated Indian reservation on the Pacific Coast of Oregon. In the 1850s, over a million acres, stretching north to near present-day Tillamook County, south to near the California border, and inland to the western edge of the Willamette Valley were reserved for the Indian tribes and bands defeated by state and federal troops. The U.S. government deemed the land, the ocean, the bays and rivers, and beautiful stands of spruce, fir, and hemlock to be unfit for human occupancy or use, then relocated the Indians there to become farmers. Extermination failed and so the survivors became targets in an assimilation project.

Gradually, the worth of the area became evident to white soldiers and settlers who lobbied for ownership. And, oops! The government never signed the treaties, so it was easy for the land to be sold to non-Indians. It is a sad story of mistreatment and racism based on a national plan to drive the Indianness out of the survivors, including the children sent to schools far away from their Siletz homes.

A compatible community developed among the survivors and the non-natives who moved onto the land made available by nefarious government edicts in the late 1800s and into the 1900s.

By the 1950s, the U.S government was making plans again. *Termination* became the buzzword across Indian Country. It was a complicated and frightening time for Indian people. Some tribes survived, however they could, on their reservations, but some chose, or were schemed into choosing, termination. In 1956, all rights to be Indian were extinguished for the Confederated Tribes of Siletz Indians.

Imagine, as a child going to bed as an Indian, then waking in the morning to be told, "We are not Indians anymore. The government has terminated us." It was yet another kind of genocide. Many elders went to their graves in the ensuing decades never knowing their identity would be restored. Many families left the Siletz Valley in those years.

Early in the 1970s, the generation that had been young and heartbroken during termination was now raising families of their own. Most were not sit and take it personalities.

One of the most Warrior-like of my Indian friends came to my office at the *Lincoln County Leader* newspaper in nearby Toledo, Oregon to say, "What are we going to do about this?" I wasn't sure what *this* was, but I knew the following months would be interesting. When Robert Rilatos decided on a project, it happened come hell or high water. The project was a determined drive to ensure restoration of the tribe. Robert gathered friends and relatives for a long, often sad, battle. On November 18, 1977, the Confederated Tribes of Siletz Indians became the second tribe in the nation to be restored. They were officially Indians again!

A Time to Wail, An Indian Country Novel, is fiction. The people are from my imagination, as are the conversations and activities. The history, the places (except River City), are real, based on my personal experiences and interpretation of the primary documents, books, and videos I have studied, and my conversations with descendants of those brought to the early Siletz Reservation. The problem of desecration of Indian graves is also very real.

Please remember this story takes place in the 1970s in a tiny town of 500 people. Some of the words used then are not considered appropriate today, especially by the younger generation—some the descendants of the people who fought for restoration, for the right to be Indian. To be true to my story I chose to use words we spoke and heard in that era. Some of the elders in my early years spoke English in short, incomplete sentences, but were more comfortable with using the old trade language or their original Native language. In my story on the following pages, Grandma Kline will be a good representative of those elders.

1

November 1975

A HEAVY OREGON COAST FOG FALLS OVER THE HUSHED RIVER
valley. It's a harsh November day for my son's burial in our Siletz tribe's
cemetery on the old reservation's Government Hill.

I shiver in my traditional dress of fringed and beaded white buckskin. Always too warm during summer pow-wows, it gives little comfort
today even with my late mother's beautiful embroidered shawl around my
shoulders. Logan loved the shawl almost as much as he loved Grandma. I
wore it to honor them today and tucked a beaded feather into my braided
hair, though these symbols of Siletz culture don't mean as much to me as
they once did. The fog soaks my hair and trickles down my face.

Logan's service at the tribal center is long. I watch through tears and
memories. I don't know what is said. Someone brings me in a car to the
cemetery across the way while pallbearers, relatives all, carry my son in
his casket. Friends and more relatives follow. Most of the town's residents
trudge silently, urged on by the rhythmic beat of native drumming. They

huddle together near the gaping hole as the sodden ground transfers the icy cold up through my body. Majestic evergreens drip tears onto the crowd.

I stand away from the burial site in the northeastern corner of the Kline family section. Sheltered by some of the oldest trees on the hill and surrounded by the gravesites of many of Logan's grandparents, aunties, uncles and cousins, some he knew and loved in his short life, he will lie next to his great-great-great grandma. My Grandma Kline, our tribe's senior elder, approved the site. Some men of the tribe, more close relatives, dug the hole.

A local minister offers a prayer. Then the tribe's spiritual leader offers a blessing before the drummers begin the honor song.

I can't concentrate. Don't want to hear any of it. My heart turns to stone as the casket bearing my only child, dead at 17, is lowered. The drums, usually a solace, can't penetrate my agony. I see Logan beside me in another place and time. I feel him engulfing me in his love. I feel the thud as his casket hits bottom. I fall to my knees in the mud. My mouth opens and the ancestors sob through my wailing to honor my dead son.

Now, through clouded eyes, I see dim shadows and know the movement is my uncles and cousins scooping dirt with shovels. They will stand in line beside the hole where I'm supposed to lead the others in a final goodbye. I can't do it. I don't want to say goodbye. I hate this place. Never should have let him come here. I should have made him go back home to Chicago with me. Should have warned him.

A man helps me to my feet, guides me along, puts my hand into the freshly dug dirt heaped on a shovel. I must sprinkle the dirt into the hole as generations have done before me.

The soil warms in my hand, drips through my clenched fingers. I can't let go. I can't make the final move to release my son's spirit to the afterworld. I want to fall into the hole, to go with him, but strong, young arms hold me, pry the dirt from my fingers so it drops onto Logan's coffin.

A voice whispers, "Hold my arm, Ellie." It's the young man from Marge's house. Can't think of his name.

Ka-thump, ka-thump, ka-thump. My heart keeps pace with the sound of the dirt clods as the relatives shovel the remaining dirt into the grave and make our traditional mound to hold the flowers and gifts.

When the burial is finished, I watch my people begin the walk back to the tribal center for a potluck dinner organized by the aunties. There's no set time, only Indian time where things happen when they happen. It's what my Logan would want. As Grandma Kline reminded me yesterday, "It's tradition."

Grandma couldn't come. She's 92. Too frail to be in this dampness and cold. I know she's in her little home on the other side of the cemetery, wailing for my lost son she loved so much.

I struggle to walk away. Someone helps me. The young man again. Chance, that's his name. Jean's son. The one we thought was dead. He walks with me to a car and suddenly an older, gray-haired, white man steps from behind a tree. He holds out his arms and calls, "Ellie!"

Oh, no. Not Russ.

I move away from him, into the car, and ask to be taken to Grandma's house. As we drive away, the side mirror captures the mist falling over the gray-haired man--the father for whom Logan yearned throughout his brief life. Russell Carlisle kneels in the mud at the grave of our son.

Weeks later, Grandma Kline asks me to go to Logan's gravesite with her. I have made numerous trips to talk to Logan since he was buried. Never with Grandma.

As I drive up the hill toward Grandma's, I feel sad at how tiny her house is. As a child, I didn't notice there were only three small rooms heated by a too large wood-burning stove in the kitchen. Now seeing through adult eyes, I worry she may not be safe or comfortable here.

She's not my straight as a hemlock tree Grandma now, with a powerful voice eager to share memories of our people's history and culture. She's hunched over and walks with a stick, the result of years of doing and grieving for her families, her community, her tribe.

Once noted for her youthful beauty, her brown face is now weathered and wrinkled, the harsher look of a revered elder who has spent too many hours outside tending gardens, feeding animals, picking berries and walking into the hills to peel lucrative chittum bark to sell to laxative producers, and to gather fragile fern fronds for the floral industry.

When I left Siletz as a rebellious, frightened and angry teenager, Grandma was still agile and famed throughout Indian Country for her artistic baskets created from materials gathered in the nearby forest and on the river bank. She competed as a traditional dancer in pow wows across the Pacific Northwest.

She's excited for the next Siletz Pow Wow, one of the first here since termination. Says she will wear her regalia but can't dance. I once hoped to inherit her beautiful buckskin dress, the traditional woven basket cap and her dentalium shell necklaces. Strange I haven't thought of this in years.

The house sits on the eastern edge of tribal property beyond the cemetery and about a hundred feet from her outdoor toilet. The outhouse has been moved numerous times and now is much too far for an elder to walk in the night. It's also a long trudge in the rain or snow to empty a chamber pot in the morning. I should ask someone to find a solution. It's the last occupied home of all the houses built on the Hill in early reservation days, still drafty when the wind blows through single board walls and thin, single pane windows--one in the kitchen and a larger one in the living room.

It is early morning for me but when she opens the door, Grandma says she was up before the sun. I wonder why she wants to go to the cemetery today. It's raining and cold. Christmas looks to be a typical no snow day here. I was taught from early childhood to act respectfully when Grandma makes a request, no matter how miserable I am. Some things one never forgets.

I learned the importance of wailing in this very house when my cousin Jean, young, alone and pregnant, was murdered up on Dewey Creek. The community still grieves for her, for the baby boy who we were told died with her, and for cousin Mark Thom, convicted of killing Jean, who spends his life locked in prison.

Death is not uncommon in Native communities. Grandma says it often comes in threes and far too often to the young. Her words from long ago burn in my heart and mind today.

There's a faint knock. When I open the door, no one is there. On the porch is a large, lacy, fern frond I pick up and bring inside to Grandma.

"Katie," Grandma says and smiles.

"Who's Katie?"

"My friend."

I wait for further explanation as Grandma gives me a plate and motions for me to sit at the table. Soon a platter of cold, smoked salmon is placed near my plate. Grandma returns to the kitchen and comes back with blackberry pie and a small pitcher of thick cream. Visions of my childhood are quickly replaced by thoughts of my teenaged son sitting at this table devouring Grandma's treats.

"Where did you get blackberries, Gram?"

"Katie bring me all kind of berries from the woods. I have pie ready when she come to ask questions. I put berries in Marge's freezer because Katie brings them every day when they ripe--until no more in her favorite place."

I almost expect Grandma to revert to the old Chinook Jargon trade language. She speaks in more broken English now that she's older. Years ago, she spoke proper English learned at the boarding school. As she ages, she alternates between jargon, English, and this current broken English.

Once, when I came from Chicago to visit, I asked about the change in her speech. She laughed and explained, "Old woman is elder. People expect ancient woman to have trouble with English. I do what I want now. Lazy talk."

As I wash the dishes, I notice Grandma putting on a new pair of tennis shoes from a company she says the tribe should buy. Now, snuggled in a warm coat, gloves and a furry hat, she's holding her walking stick, ready for our walk to the cemetery.

"Chance bring new shoes for old Grandma, say Merry Christmas."

Grandma's pleasure with the gift from her 'new' grandson makes me smile despite the ache in my heart remembering the dreadful holiday without Logan. Who would guess a woman nearing a hundred years old would love a pair of runner's shoes?

Walking to the cemetery, I ask, "Why is this called Paul Washington Cemetery, Gram? Who was he? I always heard it called Siletz Cemetery."

"Boy killed in war. World War I they call it."

"Was he a tribal member?"

"Yes, he Siletz. Die in France. Some say brother Andrew die in war, too. Some say Paul buried in France. Family have funeral here for both boys. Grandma points to the tombstones for Paul and Andrew. "Sad time in Siletz."

At Logan's gravesite, I notice a bench that wasn't here two days ago. Grandma points to the bronze plaque and says, "Girl read."

Grandma still sees enough to read the words, so I know she has an ulterior motive for making me read the inscription. A whiff of fresh cedar lumber shocks my nose as I bend down to read.

"Out loud," Grandma orders.

In loving memory of Logan Carlisle
November 1975
Ellie M. Carlisle and Russell L. Carlisle

"Who did this? Why is Russell's name here? He never—"

"Hush, child. Russell is dad. You chose him. Can't change that now. Words don't say he was good Dad."

"Did he do this? I'll make the tribe take it away. I'll chop this thing to bits." I shout and try to push the bench over. "What the hell? Concrete pads?"

"Old woman know girl have temper, so ask for sturdy bench put in at night while you sleep."

"YOU did this? Why did you put his name on it, Gram?"

"Russell call me. Ask if he could pay for nice bench for us to sit on when we visit Logan. He not ask for his name on it. I did."

"Why, Grandma? You know he beat me when he was drunk. You know how sad Logan was that he didn't know his father. Wait. Are you the one who called Russ when Logan died?"

"He call me sometimes to ask about you and the boy. Last time he called he was older, no drink anymore. Feel bad. Say he coming to see Logan while you live in Chicago. He came two days before wreck."

The reality of her words sinks in as I grasp the edge of the bench and sit down.

"Two days before? He saw Logan, didn't he? He snuck into town and this whole damned reservation knew it. Secrets. This place is a cesspool of secrets."

"Old woman say keep mouths shut. Don't tell Ellie. You hurt and angry. Don't need more."

"Why tell me now? I'm still hurt and even angrier."

"Boy heard. Came to Grandma to find dad. He really mad. Sound like you. Said he will cuss man out and won't call him 'Dad'. He walk toward cemetery and I never see him again."

"And people wonder why I didn't want Logan to come to the rez. There it is. He learned to drum and wear feathers. Drums and feathers, really? That's our culture, Gram? What we have is a culture of secrets and lies. My son is dead! We buried him with all the cultural nonsense expected. All the witchy hullabaloo can't, for a second, protect his dead body from grave robbers. Too freaking funny, Chicago folks would say."

The sadness in Grandma's eyes stops my tongue. Why did I lash out at her? This poor weathered old soul, no longer the physically strong Grandmother of my youth, who welcomed me and loved me from the moment of my birth, who claimed me as her granddaughter though her son had been dead for two years, is now bent from the cold, and suffering from my words. She walks with great difficulty, hunched over, dressed in a tattered house dress created years ago from the patterned feed sacks popular here in times of little income. Worn out from years of doing for her family, her community, her tribe—me, Grandma Kline sits on the bench and motions for me to sit beside her.

"You have lost contact with your soul, Ellie. You must heal, or you will die, too."

"Not my soul, Grandma, but I have lost touch with much of what you taught me. Since Logan's death I am so angry with everyone, especially myself."

"What you do wrong to be angry at self?"

"I should have warned Logan about this place. Should have told him the truth about my father, about his own father. Worthless men. I let him come here innocent and defenseless. Should have told him the real reasons I ran. Should have told him what I saw. Instead I followed your lead and taught him to be proud of his Siletz heritage and culture.

I am broken by the betrayal of my grandmother and her teaching, yet I pull her into my arms. I'm tense with anger. She's tense from my harsh words.

Grandma's goal throughout her life has been to keep her family together, for all of us to be happy and loving. Sometimes her efforts cause deep hurt, anger and tension. I know this and can't hate her but could strangle her for bringing Russell Carlisle back into my life, and Logan's.

Back at her house, Grandma's exhausted, so I heat milk to make a cup of cocoa for her. When she's tucked in for her afternoon nap, I stoke the fire and close the front door as I leave.

I drive off the Hill, down Logsden Road to Gaither Street, turn left toward Marge's house. I glare at the few walkers, an unspoken accusation pounds in my head, "You knew, you bastards!"

2

I LEAVE MY BAGS INSIDE THE DOOR OF MY CHICAGO APART-
ment and fall into a chair, exhausted and hollow. Everything will be better
here, I tell myself. But a quick glance around the room reminds me otherwise. Logan is not here. My son will never again be in our home. Tears flow
again as they have since I answered the phone on that awful November day
to news my son died in a car wreck near our rez in Oregon.

The past two months in Siletz are a blur. I probably have few friends
left and fewer relatives still speaking to me. The rage within me burst
through on too many occasions when I strayed from the tiny bedroom at
cousin Marge's home. I blamed everyone, raged at the secrets and the people who keep them and then, when there were no more tears or screams,
no wails or sobs, I packed my bags and came home. Away from the pain.
Or so I thought. One step inside my door and I knew it all came with me.

I try to ignore the doorbell, but it keeps ringing. I brush my hands
over my face to wipe the tears. When I open the door, the building manager, her arms full of mail piled up in my absence, pushes past me and goes
through the living room to place the bundle on the dining table.

Perhaps if I stand here holding the door open, she'll take a hint. No, with her usual attitude, she sits on the couch and begins to ask questions. Not the best move in my current state, but that's how she is. Always pushy. Always nosey.

"Going back to work soon?" she asks.

"Don't know."

"Come, sit down and tell me all about it."

"It? My son is dead. That's it." I wipe my hair back from my forehead and glare at her. "Sorry, I don't feel like visiting."

She leaves, grumbling "Bitchy Indian."

I close the door behind her and head for my bed.

It's morning. I drag out of bed, hoping the sight of trees twinkling in the morning frost will make me feel better. I forgot. There is no window in my bedroom. Opening the blinds on the window near the dining table where my mail is piled, I look out onto traffic. No river, no trees, though there are icicles hanging off the building across the street. My mind whirls and finally settles enough to realize I am back in the city. Back home. At least it was home before my son walked on in death.

The phone rings and I moan. I forgot to call Marge. "Hello?"

"Ellie! So, you are home. You were in such a nasty mood when I dropped you at the airport, I didn't know what you might do. Anyhoo, I'll let Grandma know."

She hangs up before I can respond. No wasting of her limited income on long distance charges. I haven't been very kind to her. I can't forgive or forget she let Logan go out with those boys. We didn't say much on the way to Portland yesterday. I appreciate her inviting me to stay longer at her house, but there were so many reminders of Logan. The only place to sleep was in the bedroom where he had slept. Agonizing nights left my throat and eyes raw from silent crying.

With a cup of tea to calm my nerves, I tackle the pile of mail. Catalogs, a package from the Book of the Month Club, some magazines, bills, and a card from Mama's only living white relative. I don't know many of her family, but this great auntie has always kept in touch with me. Can't bear to read her card now. More catalogs, the tribe's newsletter and---Oh, my God! A letter from Logan!

I freeze, unable to open the envelope. I sit and stare at his handwriting. My heart pounds. My face is wet again as I carefully open the envelope postmarked "Siletz, Oregon. November 15, 1975". The day he died.

My hands shake as I remove the letter, unfold it, then squint to see through tears.

"*Mom,*

Hey, so much to tell you when you come for Thanksgiving. Hope you get here in time to see your favorite son in action against the Jefferson football team. Big guys, but we're the 'Warriors' so no problem. Movie tonight with the cuzins and then we meet with a guy who says he can help with a project I started. We need your help, Mom. Things are out of control. You won't believe what's huppening in our graveyards. We'll talk when you get here. Saw Mr. Carlisle today. Tried to be bossy 'Dad'. Kind of late for that. Love ya.

Later, Logan"

In the bathroom on my knees, I vomit into the toilet until there is nothing left and then my stomach jerks and tries some more. How do I live with this? How do I go on knowing, completely knowing, it is my fault my son is dead? I may as well have picked up a gun and shot him. I kept secrets from him. Oh yes, I learned lessons on my reservation, didn't I?

"Don't tell. Don't tell. Don't tell." That's what the man said to little girl me long ago when a grave robber saw me in a tree. I told my mother and she said, "Don't tell. Don't tell. Don't tell," so I didn't. Then I didn't tell my son before I let him move to the rez. Now he's dead and his grave could be vandalized.

I feel a blackness coming. Swirling things surround me. Gray faces swirl above a hole. Crying, wailing, screaming faces look at an open coffin halfway out of the hole. Sometimes Grandma Kline's face tries to join, but they push her back, back until she's gone. No Grandma face, just swirling ancestor faces. I'm so cold. A face speaks to me, but I can't hear the words, only see the lips moving. A freezing, powerful wind comes in and makes the faces bob and twirl, dip into the hole and out again. They are angry and sad. Sad and angry, changing faces so fast I can't keep up. I can't stand. Too much pressure from the wind and sorrow keeping me down. Something is coming. The faces turn to watch. The wind slows and grows quiet. No more twirling. Staring faces, staring at me. And then a word, "You!"

I wake with a jerk. Covered in sweat, in a wet bed, I am so exhausted I must struggle to move my legs and arms to push up into a sitting position. How did I get into bed? When did I get into bed? I try not to think of the dream, but I know the ancestors have spoken. Maybe not to me. Maybe the vision was for some other "You". What can I do, anyway?

It isn't that I don't know what I should do. I don't want to do it. I don't want to move back to the reservation. I don't want to quit my job here in Chicago but what I've learned as an investigator here would serve our Siletz people well. I don't want to deal with the ugliness of grave robbing. Not my job. But I could, of course. As I struggle with myself, always in front of me is the possibility Logan's grave will be robbed. And now, Logan's message, *"We need your help, Mom."*

He wins.

3

I'VE COME ONCE AGAIN TO MY RIVER.

The Siletz River guides the lives of my people with its seasons for vital foods like eels, salmon and trout, with placid waters for swimming and rafting, and frantic, boulder-knocking rapids to avoid during spring and winter fishing. It shares a name with our tribe, our town, our schools, and again, after more than twenty years of the U.S. government declaring us 'non-Indians', our tribal name and rights will be restored.

There are stories about the word 'Siletz'. Some based on science, others on romantic legends. No one knows for sure, though everyone thinks someone must, and newcomers always ask.

Sitting here on a cold, wet rock, filled with loneliness and guilt, I stare into the dark waters. It's been four painful months since Logan's death. Often, I sit huddled on these rocks in the sheltered cove near his favorite swimming hole where I taught him to fish the summer he was five and watched him splash the water to capture his first tiny trout. There's a photo of him with his first fish on my bedroom dresser. The blue feather he picked up on the rocks is tucked into the corner of the picture frame.

"An angel dropped it, Mommy. He wants us to know he loves us."

I feel the tiny brown hand squeezed tightly in mine.

On a later trip, Logan explained he was a big boy and didn't need Mama to sit by him. I sat in the car with a book. When he caught a fish, he held it up for me to admire. Sometimes, during the magical afternoon, he'd turn to wave at me.

These memories, and Logan's letter, convinced me to move back to Siletz. I made the return trip to Chicago, but I couldn't stay there. I took some time to transfer investigation cases to my attorney clients and to cancel my apartment lease. Then, I hurried back to Siletz and Logan. Only he isn't here, nor is the old me.

I don't *want* to be here. Who would? I can't stand the sounds. Can't bear the sights. The endless thumping of drums. The sad faces of our elders. Restless young girls in their jingle dresses with nowhere to dance. Ceremonies and more ceremonies. Praying to God, to Mother Earth, to Grandfather. And, dear god, the mournful wailing for the dead.

I didn't hear those sounds in Chicago. I ignored the genetic draw which summoned me home. No one ever really leaves the reservation. It follows you until you recognize it, succumb to it. Maybe later, I sometimes thought. But I didn't think my son would die. Now, I am here again but if the river hears me, not for long.

I know this river. Life revolved around it for my first seventeen years. Now it offers solace of a different kind. A temptation. A solution. It releases from the earth, bubbles up in the mountains and surrounds our valley after winding and twisting, tumbling and growing as it slithers its way along a hundred-mile journey to the Pacific Ocean. At the eastern border of the city of Siletz, the river encounters the small valley the soldiers chose for their agency headquarters to imprison the tribes as they arrived by government command from Southern Oregon, Northern California, and the Willamette Valley. This is where the community, the little city, later came to be.

Our river takes things that don't belong in it. Logs lying too close to winter river banks. Fishermen wearing heavy clothing and boots against the winter rains, unable to keep their boats from colliding with hidden boulders in the upper reaches near the Gorge. Our murdered loved ones whose killers too often go unpunished. Children. Too many children. Oh, the agony of the families of the lost. This agony now controls me, but not because of my river. A car took Logan into the water, but it wasn't the river's fault. My river will rid me of this agony. Now, my boy and I will be together again.

Today, I'll go back to a place where I once lived. On another hump. This little hill, only a slight incline, flattens out into a nice field, a vantage point for watching the greens of spring move over the valley below like a gentle paint brush working its magic. There's a pool in the river, directly below where our house stood. A dark, deceptive pool, so deep the coldness grabs one's breath on contact.

I find my trail to the river is overgrown with blackberry vines sprouting green and thorny in the first days of the new season. I fight my way through, slipping and sliding on the muddy path. The other part of the river has been uncooperative. Perhaps here, away from Logan's favorite spot, the river will grant my wish.

I wade in, hoping the weight of my wet clothing will pull me down into the frigid pool. I've done this before, waited for death, longed for it. Today my river will hear my plea.

Filled with melted snow, the roar of the swift moving water crashes over the ancient, rocky, riverbed deadening the sound of my death knell, though I feel the knell's power as it escapes my throat. Peace comes, invites me to sink into the finality. My head enters the water. My nose burns.

In the sudden hush I hear crying, my child's cry. I push against the icy current, raise my head above the water, shake it hard and gasp for breath. There, on a large rock, is a little boy, crying. I struggle, unknown strength pushing me toward the sound. When I reach the rock, there is no child, no little boy who sounds like my Logan, only a blue feather. Sobbing, I clasp the message from my son to my bosom and leave the river.

Dragging my body up the slippery trail to the car, I know I will not attempt to take my own life again. My son has asked me to live, to help fight the grave robbers. I feel the tug of a smile despite the guilt of my terrible secret.

Back at the house I've bought down the street from Marge, I throw open the living room curtains for the first time since I moved in. I see a young girl sitting on a bike near the end of the path to my door. I've seen her at the store a few times. Once, at the cemetery, when I replaced the dried and dying flowers on Logan's grave mound, I saw her perched on a tombstone watching me.

I want to talk to her, but before I can open the door she moves away on her red bike, a boy's bike, her long, tangled brown hair flying behind her. She seems to be everywhere. Like me when I was little. There was no one I didn't know, no question I didn't ask. The memory makes me smile.

It's evening now. Leaning back in a lawn chair outside my back door, I watch through lacy cedar needles as storm clouds march across the sky much like the battle raging in my mind over how to ensure my son's grave is not disturbed. I know what I must do, but I continue to fight it, dissect it, to search for another solution. If only Sheriff Kramer would do his job. He isn't interested, I'm told, nor are the state police who consider it Kramer's job to respond to Siletz complaints. The Feds have forgotten us.

I used to be eager to tackle a big case. I didn't hesitate. The more complicated, the better. That was Chicago. This is Siletz. A world apart.

Since Logan's death I haven't felt like doing anything, not even stopping the digging in our family graveyards. But, I must do this. Who else will step forward? Who in our community has the training and experience to find answers? Whose son is dead because of my secret?

I remember the grave robbers who visited our valley during my childhood, especially the one who threatened to bury me in a hole like the one he had just dug, if I told anyone what I'd seen.

I remember when Auntie Jean was murdered. Now Grandma wants to know who killed her. Who is this young Chance guy who says he's Jean's son? I thought her unborn baby died with her.

Wiping tears of frustration on a blanket wrapped tight around my shoulders, I walk into the house, my decision made. I will talk to Chance about investigating the grave robbers. I heard he's the tribe's economic development manager and he also prepares the agenda for tribal council meetings.

I want to speak to my tribe during a public forum like the meeting of the General Council. There is an important meeting scheduled to discuss the tribe's restoration efforts. Many will attend. Most of my people understand grave robbing must stop. Poor Grandma Kline is afraid to die 'cause the diggers might steal her old bones.

4

"I'M SURPRISED TO SEE YOU."

Chance smiles at me standing in his office doorway. It's been months since he helped me at Logan's funeral and I haven't visited around at all. He stands and motions toward a chair on the other side of his massive oak desk.

"Come on in. Sit."

I hesitate, fight the urge to leave, wonder if this decision will ease my guilt.

"I am worried about the robbing of our burials and think I should get off my butt and do something,"

"Great. Every meeting of the Council somebody asks me to get you to investigate. I always tell them, 'You know her better than I do.'"

"What do they say?"

My solitude and sour demeanor since I returned to the reservation has scared away most of my relatives. Death is such a reality here my people seem able to shut away their sorrow and move on. I'm trying to learn how by focusing on something else, like grave robbers.

"The council members don't want to bother you, but most are worried about grave robbing. Except the chairman. He doesn't live here. Doesn't understand the impact of ripping the bones of our ancestors out of the ground," Chance says.

"Though you do. Why?"

"I don't know. I feel the sadness. Don't know much about our beliefs and culture yet, but Grandma Kline is taking care of those problems."

The sound of my own laughter surprises me. Why do I laugh so much, even in the midst of sadness and sorrow? Grandma says it became our medicine. Her Grandma Annie said laughter kept the ancestors from going mad in the early reservation days.

"Guess it's about time I mended some fences."

"You might want to start with Marge."

"Yeah, I know. I shouldn't have blamed her for Logan's death. Not her fault he went against the rules, hers and mine. I lashed out in my pain. Poor Marge. It'll be tough to approach her, but I will."

"There's a council meeting Saturday morning. Want to be on the agenda?"

"Sure. I'll need about fifteen minutes. If they don't agree to my terms by then, I've lost my touch. Had lots of practice negotiating for major investigations for the Chicago firm."

Heading for the door, I say, "By the way, you can't waltz into my life believing you're the son of my Auntie Jean Kline without some explanation. Some proof would be good, too!"

As I expected, he doesn't answer. I hear his life story is already convoluted. I'll need the details.

5

"HEY, MARGE."

She doesn't respond, backs away from her front door to let me escape the soft spring rain. I grab a chair at the kitchen table and wait for her to say something. Anything. The uncomfortable waiting reminds me of how the years away robbed me of many native ways, just as Grandma said. In the old way, people didn't introduce themselves like Chance does. Our people aren't usually the first to start a conversation, either. Makes it difficult when there are only two of us, like right now. Someone must speak first.

During a long silence while Marge prepares coffee, I glance around the little house, so typical of all our rez homes. It was in this house my son spent his last days and nights. Not fancy at all, with a tiny living room, maybe ten by twelve feet with one large window facing the Siletz River and a smaller window in the front. Both windows are covered with heavy green drapes. The old couch sags to the middle, and there is a matching chair with a few springs remaining. The wooden chest serves as a coffee table and is covered with magazines. Every available wall space and table top is covered with family photos. Here and there are beautiful Siletz baskets made by our elder women. The large color television, perched on a wobbly table directly across from the couch, blares away, program after program. Comfortable, I wait.

Marge finally hands a large mug of coffee to me, so I reach out to take her other hand in mine.

"I don't know what to say other than I'm sorry. I was so desperate in my sorrow I wanted everyone, especially you, to suffer with me."

Oh no. I didn't mean to start crying.

"I loved him too, you know."

I stand to embrace her, both of us sobbing. I notice potatoes in the sink and take advantage of the opportunity to move past this uncomfortable situation.

"Here, let me help you start dinner."

Happy to be busy with the never-ending dinner making tasks of rez women, I move to the sink to peel the potatoes.

Marge tries to tell me about finding the wreck. It's too painful to talk about. Better left until later. An occasional comment brings a fresh torrent of tears, sometimes only a dribble down a cheek. I have questions about the wreck, but I'm not ready to hear the answers.

The cold chicken sizzles as Marge puts it into the hot, cast iron frying pan on the old wood cookstove that has served the house for generations.

"What's the story with Chance, Marge?"

"He's Cousin Jean's boy. Here's a pot for the potatoes."

"Yeah, so I heard. We all heard Jean's baby died with her after the attack up Dewey Creek. Why do you believe him?"

The silence lasts too long. My potato peeling speed increases dramatically as I struggle to wait for Marge's answer. Another culture thing. Patience is inbred, the result of decades of my people waiting for life's essentials. Grandma says I'm too impatient to be an Indian.

"Sit down. The potatoes can wait."

Uh oh.

I put the knife down, turn to pull a chair away from the table and watch Marge move the frying pan off the heat. When she turns toward the table, I am surprised to see the intensity of her gaze.

"A few years after Jean's murder, my Rose was a tot, a lady called me."

Marge pulls a chair out and sits across the table from me.

"Said she saw my name in the newspaper article about Jean's murder. She asked if I was Mark Thom's sister. Surprised, I admitted I was. She had something to tell me. I told her to talk to the police and hung up."

"Why the police? You knew they wouldn't do anything," I ask.

"Yeah. I was scared. I figured she *was* the police. Why would anyone call about Jean after all that time? Anyhoo, she called back a few weeks later. Insisted she didn't mean to upset me. Said she had information the family needed to know. Wanted to meet me somewhere. I said, 'No. Hell no!'"

"And?"

"She cried," Marge continues, "Explained she was a Mom and what she had to tell me was important to her son. She begged me to meet her. I told her I'd talk if she came to my house. Figured she wouldn't come here."

"She came? From where?"

"Yeah. The next day she came down from Portland. Shocked me."

Marge rises to refill our coffee cups while my stress headache worsens in the waiting.

"So, then she, Vivian Andrews, came and sat on the couch. She wiped her tears and told me Jean's baby didn't die at the hospital. She adopted him in some underhanded scheme her husband was involved in. Now she felt guilty about it and wanted the boy to know his mother's people, to learn about his own culture."

"Wow. What did you say?"

"'Why now? If you knew who he was, why didn't you bring him home when they gave him to you? Whoever 'they' is?' She wanted a baby for a long time and when her husband brought this beautiful little boy to her, she didn't care how he found him."

"So, what changed?"

"Boy started school. Got teased about his dark skin and hair. She didn't know what to tell him. Her husband yelled, 'Tell them you're a Siletz Injun.' It was the first she knew he came from here."

"Why didn't the husband tell her?"

"Apparently, he never wanted kids. Got one for her. She demanded the paperwork to prove Chance was Indian. He didn't have any. Said he bought the baby from a Portland attorney. They have a birth certificate with their own names as parents."

"Why didn't you tell anyone?"

"I did. After she left, I told the aunties. They put him on the tribal roll. Before they needed all that proof, you know. It was enough to tell one of the aunties."

"And Grandma? Did you tell her, Marge?" I dread the answer. I hate the lies and secrets.

"No."

"Just what I thought. Why? How can you live with that?"

"The kid had a good home." Marge leans over the table, inches from my face. "A mother who loved him and a father who made enough money commercial fishing to get him educated. Who could take care of him here? Grandma was too old. I was a drunk, barely able to take care of my own baby, livin' on welfare. If he lived past his teen years, how would he get... Oh, I'm sorry Ellie."

"It's OK, "I say as I wipe tears with a dish towel I picked up from the counter. "What did you tell the woman to keep her from contacting Grandma?"

"I told her if anyone knew about him, they would take him away from her. If they couldn't do it legally, they'd steal him. Scared her to death. It was true." Marge looks a little defensive, or maybe worried. She rises to put more wood in the stove.

"Anyhoo, I was going to ask you, Ellie, have you noticed how much my Rose looks like Jean did at the same age? Kind of spooky."

"Now you mention it, she does. I don't remember Jean like you do because I was mostly around you and Mark. Sometimes I saw her at Grandma's, but for a long time Mama wouldn't let me go to see Grandma because Jean was there."

"Right, Your Mama didn't want you asking questions about Jean's belly or where the daddy was. You would have, you know."

"I wish I had been able to ask those questions. Wouldn't have all this work to do now."

"I'd better get this chicken to frying or we won't have any supper. How are those potatoes coming?"

I resume peeling potatoes. Can't endure the silence. I have so many questions.

"How did this Portland woman connect Chance to Jean?" I ask.

"Oh, forgot to tell you. She hired an investigator out of Portland. Paid him big bucks. All she knew was the baby was Siletz. He reported there were no births at the Toledo Hospital the week she received Chance. A murdered Siletz girl had a baby during the same time frame, a little sooner, so she thinks Chance is older than his birth certificate states."

"Marge, there had to be nurses and other people who saw a living baby."

"Yep. Nurse on duty told the PI she saw the doctor deliver a baby boy. The doctor took him away and later told them he died."

"What did they think happened to the body?"

"Why would they think about it, Ellie? Maybe you were too little to remember, but Mark had been arrested for Jean's murder. The police were not our friends. We were scared. Anyhoo, we knew no one would help us. We warned Jean not to get involved with a white guy when she went to work at the mill office. Then she got pregnant. Everybody knew she wasn't seeing a 'skin. People were mad at our family because Jean brought trouble to Siletz. When the cops took Mark, we all forgot about the dead baby 'cause we were worried about Mark. ...and other stuff."

"What other stuff?"

More silence. After all those years away, I'm relearning the patience it takes to get information on the rez.

"I do remember being scared, Marge. I hid behind Grandpa Thom's old truck when the police dragged Mark out of the house. This house! A little girl can see a lot while hiding behind things."

The sizzle of the frying chicken mingles with occasional sighs as I struggle to connect the pieces of our family puzzle. I finish the potato peeling, fill the pot with water, add salt and hand it to Marge. I notice the rain has stopped and catch a glimpse of a little girl riding her bike into the driveway.

"There's the little girl again, Marge. I see her all over town. I think she's coming here."

"It's probably Katie. Yep, it's her knock. Come on in, Katie."

The door opens and the girl races through the living room. As she enters the kitchen, she slides to a stop, her brown eyes opened wide, long brown hair wet and dripping.

"Hello, Ellie I've been waiting to talk to you. Do you like your new house? Are you staying here now? Grandma Kline says I'm like you when you were little. She says we ask too many questions. Maybe I'll grow up and make money asking questions like you. Do you still ask questions?"

"Wow. Hello, Katie! Grandma is right. And yes, I still ask lots of questions. I'm an investigator."

"Logan told me you. …" Her eyes open wider as she clasps her hands to her mouth.

"It's okay. So, you knew my Logan? Tell me. Please."

"He told me you helped people get out of jail in Chicago because the cops were bad and put the wrong people in jail and I asked him lots of questions and made him laugh. He and Grandma called me Ellie Two. You know like number two? I showed him how to pick fern. He liked it. I take a new fern to him every other day. Okay? I miss him a lot."

Suddenly, I feel tiny arms hugging my neck. Warm tears wipe against my face. I reach out to hold her, but as quickly as she bounced into the room, Katie is back at the door, telling Marge, "I'm going to Grandma's now. Do you have anything to go?"

"No, Honey. I went up earlier. Be careful now, it's wet out. …"

The door slams shut before Marge finishes her sentence. A blur of bicycle speeds past the kitchen window.

"Isn't she a sweetie, Ellie?"

"Yes, who is she? I mean, who are her parents? Do they know she's all over town every day?"

"Oh, yeah. She lives on Bagley Street. Katie knows everybody and tries to take care of our elders even though her family is white. She goes to Grandma Kline's on Tuesday afternoons to watch "Batman" with her. On other days, you'll see her walking Old Joe Logsden home, listening to his stories. Or she might be up on the Hill cleaning dead flowers off a gravesite. Nothing gets by her."

"I wondered who put ferns on Logan's grave. I thought maybe he had a girlfriend. So sweet. She's not a tribal member?"

"No, only in her heart. She told me I'd feel better if I went up on the hill to talk to Logan. She tells him everything. Picks those ferns from a different place each time so she can tell him where she got them. I imagine her mother had her hands full after Logan died, but Katie's a strong little girl and her work keeps her busy."

"Her work?"

"She calls all this buzzing around spending time with the elders her work. She's not Siletz, but Grandma says she's definitely got Indian blood in there somewhere."

So, Logan had his little follower, like I followed Mark all those years ago.

"Her mother helped with the push for restoration. There are good people here, Ellie. Not just Indians. Many white neighbors. Good friends."

"It's sad we have to say white grave robbers, but history seems to support that. Although there could be a tribal problem on this rez."

"Ellie, I'm almost finished with this chicken. Can you bring those ears of corn in from the back porch?"

She ignored my comment. So irritating.

"Sure." I reach for the doorknob, then turn back. "You know, I have a difficult time believing Grandma didn't know Jean's baby lived. She always knows everything. How could she miss one of her own was not dead, but living and growing up away from the reservation?"

"She did know."

"What? I thought you didn't tell her."

"I didn't. When Logan took Chance to see her, Grandma opened the door, looked at him and shouted, "Welcome home. I wait long time to see you."

"Ohhh. How could that be? And why was Logan the one to take Chance there? How did he know what to say to her? Not that he had to say anything, I guess, the way it turned out."

I'm trying, without much success, to not judge Marge's way of handling things.

Ignoring my tone, Marge explains, "Chance had been here a few days when he and Logan jumped into Chance's Corvette and roared out of the driveway without saying where they were headed. Logan loved the car and it was his first excuse to ride in it. When they came back, way after dark, they chattered away. I kept shushing them, so they wouldn't wake my old man."

She laughs when I poke her in the back to get her to speed up the story.

"Anyhoo, Logan told me about Grandma's reaction. Apparently, Logan wondered all the way up there how to tell Grandma who Chance was. But Chance was more worried about his car getting stuck in the muddy ruts of the road to her house."

"I'm surprised he would take his Corvette on such a road. Logan probably didn't warn him."

"Grandma baked eels for them. Chance was horrified as he watched her prepare the slimy things, though he knew he had to eat them. Logan told him no one could fix eels like Grandma. Chance wasn't buying it."

"I forgot about eels. I haven't eaten them since I left home the first time. Geez, being seventeen seems like a long, long time ago. How did she get eels in October?"

"She freezes them when people gift her with fresh eels in the spring. There aren't as many in the waters now. No one knows why. Rumor is they were poisoned. Before Logan ate his first bite, he asked Grandma, 'Did my Mom eat these things?' Grandma told him you not only ate them, you hooked them in Rock Creek and brought them home to her."

"There's a side of his mama he never saw."

"I gave him an eel pole. Still several out in the shed. I think his might have been one of Mark's. He wanted to take an eel back to Chicago. Ellie. I'm sorry," Marge says as she sees my tears again.

"No, it's okay. I want to hear, to treasure every detail about my boy, even though it hurts. He wanted to know our people and our ways. Thanks to you he got to do some. But I was wrong. Should have kept him home in Chicago, away from the evilness I knew lurked here."

"You had the hard part, allowing him to stay to play football and spend his last year of high school with his cousins. Grandma spent hours doing what she called 'Turn city boy into Indian.' He chopped wood, repaired the outhouse, tried to fix the road to her house which amused everyone because the next rain always washed away all his hard work."

"I guess Grandma had a terrible time after the wreck. She spent so much time with Logan. I should have thought about her more, you know?"

I am so ashamed. I've been so deep within my own grief I seldom thought of Grandma's pain. The poor dear is already afraid to die until someone stops the ghouls who might dig her up. Now she's probably as afraid as I am someone will violate Logan's grave.

"He was the champion fisherman, Logan was. Grandma has enough fish in my freezer to last all year."

"Did you know I'm staying in the little house by the old swimming hole? Right down the road."

"I heard. You know that's where he caught all those fish, don't you?"

"No. But doesn't surprise me. Right where I taught him when we came here to visit. He always loved to swim and fish there. I bought the house."

"So, you're stayin' this time?"

"Yes. Yes, I am. I released the apartment and left my job in Chicago. There's work to be done here. Speaking of work, Chance put me on the agenda for the council meeting Saturday. I'm ready to investigate the grave robbing. We must stop the desecration of our loved ones."

"I'll be there!"

6

———————

THE RINGING TELEPHONE INTERRUPTS MY CONCENTRATION ON what I might say at tomorrow's council meeting. A man's voice returns my greeting.

"Ellie Carlisle? Sgt. Roger Wood here. River City Police. Got your number from the editor over in Toledo."

"And?"

"I got a case here in the River City area may fit in with what you're doing for the tribe. Wondered if we could compare notes."

"I'm not doing anything for the tribe. Yet. What are you working on?"

"It's kind of convoluted. Miss Carlisle. Rather drive over there to talk to you, if you don't mind, but I can tell you it includes serious allegations about Chance Andrews' father."

Guess he doesn't know Chance changed his last name to Thom. But I'm curious, so why not hear him out?

"You're welcome to come here if you're not nervous about being on the rez. Monday, 1 p.m. Come on 229 from Highway 20, left at the first bridge, third house on the left."

"See you then."

7

I AM UP INTO THE EARLY MORNING HOURS, ALTERNATING between doubting myself, remembering my new resolve following my attempted suicide and being angry at the violation of two more graves on the Hill.

I ponder what to say at the tribal council meeting as I stroke the feather Logan left for me on the river rock. I always go through this. New case, new headaches, new doubts, wondering what I'm getting myself into. I utter a prayer to Jesus, and for good measure also plead to Grandfather, my Native god, for strength and wisdom. Haven't figured those two out yet, but a double dose of blessings can't hurt.

Now, at the meeting in the Siletz Grange Hall on the corner of Gaither and Metcalf Streets, I feel stronger, prepared to answer any questions my relatives have about my Chicago work, and how I plan to discover who is violating our ancestors. No regalia or beaded jewelry today. They all know how I feel about 'Looking Indian.' Probably snickered at me during Logan's funeral when I wore the traditional dress and shawl. I don't care what they think. I'll do what it takes to save my son from the diggers and give Grandma the peace she needs. Deer hide dresses and fancy jewelry can't accomplish anything.

I choose a chair near the front of the room, at the end of a row, and search the agenda received at the door. I am scheduled to address the council under old business.

"Probably about 11 o'clock," Chance comments as he walks past to sit with other staffers.

I watch with interest as the various council members take their seats at the front table. Some I know from childhood, many are relatives, a few I have never seen before. It would be good to compare them with photos and occasional comments in the tribe's newsletter about grave robbing. Wish I had more closely read the monthly newsletters while living in Chicago.

The man, sitting on the middle chair, must be the chairman, Henry Parsons. I've wanted to meet him. He's a new Indian who came here recently, gained enough political clout to oust the original chair. Chance says Henry doesn't understand the grave robbing issue. I hope he isn't a problem. I should have asked Grandma Kline about him.

Henry grabs the gavel, then pauses and looks toward the door. At the sudden hush, I turn with the rest of the crowd and am surprised to see Grandma Kline being led into the room by Katie, who whispers to Grandma and guides her straight to the row where Marge and Rose have joined me. Someone at the end of the row near the council table moves to a seat farther back. The rest move down, leaving two seats for Grandma and Katie.

"Welcome, Mrs. Kline," the chairman says. "It's good to see you here."

The old woman pretends not to hear him. After an uncomfortable wait, he gavels the meeting to order, exactly at 10 a.m. Guess tribal council has done away with Indian time since Henry took over. The room is full of tribal members so there is no reason to wait. They move through the preliminary agenda items and by 11 o'clock are ready for me.

"We've had this discussion before, so it's on the agenda under old business, I guess," Henry begins. "Some of the council considers this grave robbing business a problem and have suggested we hire an investigator, perhaps Ellie Carlisle. Do any of you council members want to speak on this?"

One of my cousins speaks up, "We've had our say. Ellie's here. Let's hear her."

"Let Ellie speak. We came to hear what she can tell us." I don't recognize the voice from the back of the room, though it tickles my memory with a faint recollection I can't capture.

Looking around the room, the chairman says, "I haven't had the pleasure of meeting Mrs. Carlisle. If she's here, let's have her come up front and talk to us."

Before I can respond, Katie stands to point at me, "She's right there, Henry."

The crowd erupts in laughter as she sits down, but Grandma pats her leg and says, "Girl be quiet. Let Ellie talk."

It is the comment I've waited all my life to hear. I giggle and stop to touch Grandma's cheek as I walk to the council table and pick up the microphone from the edge of the table where Henry left it. I look out at the faces of my people, try to remember if this is a time for respectful silence, then realize this time silence is the role of the audience. I can speak to my heart's content. I look at Henry, then begin.

"Mr. Chairman, your comment about 'this grave robbing business' couldn't be a more apt description of what occurs in our cemeteries. Do you know there is an international market for the tiny finger bones of our dead children?"

I hesitate as a communal gasp ripples through the room.

"Do you know those little bones are used in Europe and other areas of the world, mainly for satanic purposes? They are believed to be magic, to have special powers. They also want our skulls. Both adult and child."

I pause again and note the shock register on younger faces.

"So those men, maybe even women, who come into our family and tribal cemeteries to dig up our ancestors, even our recently deceased family members, are making big bucks selling the bones they collect. They still look for beads and trinkets, perhaps a gun or knife or gold coins from older sites. Mostly it's our *bones* they want.

"Though there are some new federal laws proposed to require museums to return their collections of thousands of native bones and sacred items, we still find them on display across the nation and here, in Oregon. There are ads in magazines offering $1,250 for human skulls, $4,500 for a full skeleton. There are ads for human leg bones for training dogs. It's a lucrative market. There are few laws against disturbing Indian graves, and only minor penalties if they are disturbed. It becomes worthwhile for these looters to disrupt the final journeys of our loved ones. Last night men dug in the tribe's Paul Washington Cemetery. I'm told a deputy answered the phone in the sheriff's office and laughed as he gave the standard response, "It's not illegal to dig up Indians."

Again, I pause to let the rumble die down, and take a small sip from the glass of water Chance brings to me.

"We may believe in the old way that digging up our graves disrupts the loved one's journey to the other world. We may believe that we should pray to Grandfather or to Jesus, or maybe to both. Either way, grave robbing is wrong. It's disrespectful. It's ghoulish. It must be stopped. It's our responsibility to find our stolen ancestors, to bring them home for reburial. It is also our responsibility to protect more recent burials from the modern thieves who have somehow identified all our burial sites."

Coming from a newly-deepened conviction, my words are louder and more forceful than I intended. The crowd bursts into applause and surprising shouts of support and agreement.

"You may not know, Mr. Chairman, I ran away from Siletz when I was seventeen. I thought I would escape to the big, wonderful world where people had plenty, where a child might know her father, where Indians could be Indians without the government terminating their identity. Where I wouldn't have to watch the police haul my loved ones off to jail. Where alcohol wouldn't tear my life apart. Where a grave robber wouldn't notice me sitting in a tree watching him."

I hear a tiny gasp and see Katie's eyes grow wide as her hands fly to her mouth. Our eyes lock for a brief second and I know we must talk. My knees nearly buckle when I realize what I've done. I didn't mean to say I'd seen grave robbers at work. My secret is out. I collect myself and continue.

"I found the big world quite different than I imagined. I got a good job, raised my baby after Russ, my drunken, abusive husband abandoned us. You know what? I found the police dragged innocent people off to jail in those big cities, too. What I didn't have there were the legends, the stories, the drumming that hold our people together in bad times. I didn't have my Grandma nearby to help me through the rough times. Often, I desperately missed my people, but fought against coming back, against honoring our culture. I finally agreed to let my young son stay here. He came. He died in a wreck. I hope you young people understand alcohol took his life. Alcohol drove the car into the river and broke many hearts in this town."

There is some whispering, but I can't make out the words. I wonder what I don't know. Secrets. Always more secrets.

As I reach out to take the tissue Marge offers, I wipe my eyes and explain, "I wanted to die since I've returned. I tried to die, but a little blue feather, a message from my son, saved my life."

Heads nod in the crowd acknowledging the age-old symbolism of guardian angels who watch over a feather finder.

"I had to move on, find a new purpose for my life. Everywhere I turn on this reservation, families suffer from the tragedy of disturbed graves. For those, especially the elders who truly believe the journey is interrupted and won't be completed until the bones are returned, there is a feeling of hopelessness the damage will never be repaired. Our younger tribal members search for life's meaning, how to relate to tribal ceremonies. They feel a soul-wrenching disturbance they can't interpret."

Taking another sip of water, I let my words rest on their minds.

"No council member has asked me to use my investigation skills and knowledge though I've heard rumors some of you have talked about me."

I wait for the laughter to die down.

"I must warn you, investigating this issue will be the most difficult task I've ever encountered. It will be emotional, frightening and dangerous. Diggers can make more money than most of us will see in our lifetimes and they are not going to give up easily. We can't do this the usual 'Siletz way' where no one knows anything no matter how many times they're asked even though most know everything. This will require the cooperation of each of you. Believe me, if I'm hired to find these people, I will do my absolute best. It may take a long time and may get expensive. I truly believe we must act against this horrific business. There is also the case of my aunt, Jean Kline's, unsolved murder. We all know her cousin, Mark Thom, took the fall for it. Some wonder if it's tied to the grave robbing. Chance has been told Jean was his mother. Is this true? There are many unanswered questions here--and some of *you* know the answers."

I turn back to the council to conclude:

"So, Mr. Chairman, members of the council, I offer to be your retained investigator. That means a signed contract will include our agreed upon retainer fee and hourly rate. I would also like the contract to include the name of the tribal official or staff member with whom I'll work so it won't take a council decision every time I need something from the tribal records or contact information for a member. I'm ready to begin when... IF...you are."

As I lay the microphone on the table and return to my chair, the crowd again applauds. Katie claps with enthusiasm. Grandma doesn't move a muscle. Three of the council members join the applause. Others, including the chairman, seem nervous. Finally, he gavels and begins to speak. "Thank you, Mrs. ...Ellie. I am astonished at this information. Guess I never thought about our ancestors, our relatives, being dug up. Thought it was amateur archaeologists collecting. ..., you know like they've always done. Arrowheads mostly. I didn't think anything about it. I didn't have any family graves where I lived. They were all over here and I didn't come here often."

I can't decipher the mutterings, probably best since anger seems directed at the chairman's comments.

"What do you council members think?" Henry continues. "Are you ready to vote?"

"I certainly am," one of my cousins answers. Her comment is followed by a council member I don't recognize. "I don't feel comfortable voting on a contract we haven't seen."

I stand to explain they should vote on my proposal; the contract can be written and approved later, but the voice from the rear calls out with those very words, adding "We need to get started on this. It's been going on for a hundred years already."

"That is the thing. If it's been going on for so long and you haven't stopped it, why should we think one woman can do it now?"

The chairman's opposition seems stronger. As he finishes, I notice movement down the row and see Grandma Kline is on her feet.

"We don't try to stop 'em all these years. We stay in houses. Cryin' all time. I get old and want to go with Grandpa. I scared my bones get dug up.

Some people born to do one special job for their people. Let Ellie do her job." She sits as quickly as she stood, belying her advanced age.

Can anyone, even those as powerful as the council, disagree with Grandma Kline, their oldest elder? Finally, the chairman looks at me and asks, "If we vote to do this, who do you have in mind to be the tribal contact for your work?"

I am surprised. I expected the council would tell me who they would authorize to provide information. Sure didn't anticipate having to name someone. In my hesitation, a tiny voice says, "Henry, Mr. Chairman, Grandma says Chance will do it. He will help Ellie."

I gasp and lean over to look down the opposite row of seats where Chance sits looking back at me, eyes and mouth wide open. I know Grandma didn't consult him, either.

"Does this suit you, Ellie? Should we appoint Chance to be your contact person, if we approve your proposal?"

I hope I can hide my confusion at Grandma's choice.

"I learned a long time ago never to question Grandma's decisions. If she thinks a tribal woman, an experienced investigator who has been in the so-called white world for a couple of decades, and a young man who arrived a few months ago from the same world, are the ones to do this, that's what we'll do."

A motion to approve follows, with nearly unanimous support. The young girl leaps to her feet, clapping, her example followed by most in the room. I make a mental note as Henry Parsons remains seated and there in the back of the room I see a stocky Indian man, a friend from my childhood. I won't need Katie to explain who spoke up for me, after all, but I'll need his help.

8

On Monday afternoon, Sgt. Wood arrives in a black Ford pickup. No markings or police signage. Jeans and a blue shirt. I am impressed. Not only is he quite handsome, but he may have a touch of common sense. Many cop egos demand a well-marked vehicle, and full-dress uniform. Better to show up in Indian Country in a truck, wearing casual clothes.

I grab the teapot and a couple of coffee mugs and lead Sgt. Wood to the tiny wilderness area outside my back door. I choose the smaller, wicker chair in the corner of the yard beneath a massive cedar tree and reach over to remove a stack of magazines from the lounger. It is a loveseat, but I think lounger seems more appropriate with a cop about to sit in it.

He tramples the sturdy salal brush edging the seating area, his movements more like stomping than pacing. He's full of questions and an attitude. Exactly what it takes to anger me. I set him straight after the first two minutes, emphasizing I am doing him a favor inviting him here to discuss his questions.

"You know, Miss Carlisle, you can't refuse to answer my questions or prevent access to the information I need. You wouldn't be the first person I've put in jail for interfering with an investigation."

"Call me Ellie, but if you want a professional discussion about the information you believe I have, do not *order* me to answer under threat of arrest."

He avoids the flying tea as my finger pointing causes me to lose control of the cup. Disgusted and frustrated, I sink back into the chair, regretting those first, lustful thoughts when I opened the door to this man. Wish I'd never agreed to meet with him. Why do the best-looking men often turn out to be devils? But I am curious what he has to say about Chance's parents.

"Okay, how about the questions you had?" I ask.

"Yeah. It's all about Chance Thom's Dad. Hank Andrews. I had a weird visit from his ex-wife a couple weeks ago. Made a lot of accusations. In fifteen years with the Department, I have never met another person who leaves me as confused. Vivian Andrews is a strange one with what I think, hope, is a wild imagination. I wanted to run some of her stuff by you just to get a local take on it."

"I'm listening, but I barely know Chance. Don't know much of his story yet. I have never met his parents, adoptive parents," I explain.

Sgt. Wood looks confused, but finally begins.

"I know her ex-husband, Hank, from our high school days in Newport over on the Oregon coast, and I've known her since they married in the '50s. I see Hank at the docks when he is in port on his salmon troller, but I avoid Vivian as much as possible since their divorce. She's one bitter woman. Friday, she began with 'He stole our son, Sergeant. Stole him and never told me!'"

"She meant Chance?" I ask.

"Yeah! I told her when I talked to Hank a few weeks ago he mentioned Chance has a great job with the Siletz tribe. He's okay."

Vivian said, 'Yes, so I'm told. I'm not talking about now. I'm talking about when Hank brought Chance home. He went to Alaska to buy a baby and never told me the truth about any of it. He's a liar, a cheat. He's robbed me of my own son.'"

I am interested now, but don't want to show it so I just say, "Hmmm."

"I tried to calm her by saying, 'Whatever happened, Hank found the baby you both wanted. Let your suspicions go, Vivian. Move on with your new life. Chance loves you. Be happy for him,' but she snapped back, 'You are wrong, Roger. Your friend is not the man you think he is. You should investigate Hank. There's more money made on his boat than any other fisherman makes. He's running a scam buying and selling babies, Indian babies.'"

Now, he has my attention, "Did she give any other information?"

"Hell no! Sorry, excuse my language. Vivian hurried out of the office without another word. Last Friday she showed up again with a lot more details, so I decided to call you."

"In my office," he continues, "she pulled a chair as close as possible to my desk and sat directly across from me before she asked, 'Roger, did you investigate Hank's activities on the boat like I told you to?'"

"No. I told her. I've been a little busy."

Sergeant Wood stands suddenly and heads into my house. "I have something to make this easier for you. I get confused trying to keep her accusations straight, as I tell it."

He returns carrying a bulky recording device. We go inside the house to use a plug in. When he inserts the recorded tape, I hear a woman's voice and then Roger's.

"Oh bull! You didn't believe a word I uttered. The wonderful Hank Andrews could never do anything wrong. Everybody loves Hank. I may change my last name, you know. Whatever he's doing, I don't want anyone to know I was married to the. ..."

"Whoa, Vivian. Your accusations seem a little far-fetched. As far as everyone loving Hank, you know it's not true. He has some enemies, including your son, who would be happier never to see him again."

"Let's leave Chance out of this."

"Ok. You told me Chance was a stolen baby. How do we leave him out?"

"Roger, remember you're a cop. Don't go running to Hank, certainly not to Chance, to tell them how crazy I am. This is confidential information. Give me your word."

"OK, start from the beginning, Vivian. Do you mind if I tape this conversation?"

"You'd probably tape it without my permission, anyway. I'm telling you the truth. You'll need this information to arrest Hank. Some of this doesn't make sense or fit together. It's driving me crazy. It's your job to make the pieces fit, Roger. I trust you to do it. First, though, Chance is not only a stolen baby, he's Hank's baby."

"Vivian, you told me already. Hank stole Chance and brought him home to you."

"When I talked to you before I thought it was true. Still partly true. Now I know he didn't bring Chance home to me, to be ours; he brought him because he was *his*. His own natural son, born to a Siletz Indian woman."

"What? How do you know?"

"Long story. When Hank brought the boy to me, I thought he'd been out fishing. He denied it. Said he arranged to pick up our little boy. Cost him a lot of money for the deal with a doctor who specialized in finding homes for the babies that Indian girls couldn't keep. We wanted a child so badly he didn't mind the cost. He gave me a birth certificate with our names as the birth parents. Part of the deal. No one could take him away from us."

"I've heard that went on years ago," Roger says.

"I was ecstatic. Didn't care where the baby came from. I loved him from the moment I saw him snuggled, sound asleep in Hank's arms. When he opened those big brown eyes, my heart melted. It was strange. Hank didn't seem to want anything to do with him. Very seldom picked him up. When I questioned him, he muttered he'd never been around kids and didn't know what to do with Chance."

"Some people don't, Vivian. I know they haven't been close through the years."

"Yes, you do know that. The records prove it, don't they? How many fathers spend time in jail for beating their teenage son, Roger? I don't know where Hank's anger comes from. Chance didn't do anything to deserve the way he was treated."

"Go on. Where are you going with this?"

"One day he yelled that Chance is a Siletz Injun. Got me to thinking the paperwork was probably illegal. I asked a private investigator to see what he could find about a baby boy born in the Siletz area on Chance's birth date. He brought back an interesting bit of information. No babies born on Chance's date. Earlier there had been a murder on the reservation. The woman died. The news reported her unborn child died with her. The dates didn't match. I often wondered if the baby lived and the doctor lied and sold him to Hank."

"Seems like a stretch, Vivian."

"I know, now listen. The murdered woman's name was Jean Kline. She worked at the office in the mill where Hank worked before he bought the boat. Sometimes in his sleep Hank muttered and I'd hear something like 'Jean.' I convinced myself it was my imagination working overtime."

"You and Hank were married then, Vivian."

"Yes, I was. Apparently, he forgot because one day when I opened the mail, I always opened the mail even if it was addressed to Hank, because he was gone so much on the boat and bills had to be paid. Inside this envelope was another birth certificate. Same name, Chance Aidan Andrews, different birth date, and the parents were listed as Hank Andrews and Jean Kline."

Roger turns off the tape and looks at me.

"You have my attention now. Is that all she said?" I ask.

He doesn't answer but turns the machine on again.

"There was no note. The address on the envelope was typed. Postmarked in Newport, Oregon. I was hysterical, angry, afraid for Chance."

Same female voice Roger told me is Vivian's.

And now Roger's voice again, "What did Hank say?"

"Chance was very young at the time. I couldn't tell Hank. What if he acknowledged it and wanted to take Chance back to the reservation, give him to his relatives? So, I didn't mention it. I hid it away in a box at a bank. I got a special post office box, too, so bank notices wouldn't come to our house. The bank and the post office are in different towns.

"From then on, I dedicated my life to Chance. I didn't care what Hank did, said or believed, so long as he didn't take my son away from me. I taught Chance to hate him. Told each of them the other one disliked him, didn't want them around, whatever it took to keep them apart, so Chance wouldn't get taken to Siletz."

There is a long pause in the taped conversation, so I fill our cups and choose a comfortable chair. Sgt Wood remains standing and Vivian's story continues.

"Once I re-read all the newspaper clippings the PI brought to me, I felt guilty about Chance's birth family, apparently half the reservation. They didn't know he existed. I contacted one of the cousins or aunts, who was listed in the newspaper articles. She wouldn't talk to me on the phone. Wouldn't meet me anywhere. Seemed very scared. So, I went to her house."

"To Siletz? By yourself, Vivian?"

"Yes, I was terrified. Almost didn't go. Then I thought, 'These are my son's blood relatives. How bad can they be when he's such a sweet, loving child?' I went. I told her the story as I believed it. Took photos of Chance to show her. She seemed interested. Didn't talk much. I'm not sure she believed me."

"How did she react?"

"It was weird. Almost like she never wanted to see or hear of me or Chance. It is her brother who is in prison for killing Jean Kline. She told me never to tell anyone. If anyone knew, they'd try to get Chance. If not legally, some of them would kidnap him. I never contacted her again. Never heard from her even though she had my phone number. I wished over the years I hadn't made the calls or the trip. Every time Chance was late I was sure he'd been kidnapped. Most of the fights between him and his father were over his being late and my being irrational. I have a lot of regrets."

"It seems if Chance was really Hank's son. ..."

"I know. I know. Like I told you, I have a lot of regrets. Should have put Chance first in my thoughts instead of focusing on the fact Hank cheated on me, lied to me. I wanted to punish him by keeping Chance to myself. I thought I was being reasonable. Now. ...Oh God. Now it is inevitable Chance will discover Hank is his birth father. He hates Hank because it's what I taught him. I am so worried."

"Yes, might be a tough thing for Chance to hear. Probably tough for Hank to face up to the truth, too. When Chance finds out, I guarantee there will be a confrontation. Hank won't win this one."

"It's even more complicated now, Roger. I don't know what to think. I've stewed for months. While Chance worked on his master's degree in Eugene, I divorced Hank to let each of us get on with our lives. There had to be something better than what we endured all those years. I kept the house. He lived on the *Lost Lady* most of the time. I packed everything of his, so he would have no reason to be in the house after the papers were served. There is a closet in the basement where we kept old jackets and coats. In the pocket of a heavy fishing jacket I found two pieces of paper that changed my life. Again."

"What? What papers, Vivian?"

"An airline ticket to Anchorage, Alaska in Hank's name, two weeks after Chance's birth date. Return trip dated the day he brought Chance to me. And a little note with pinholes in it. Someone had written, 'Forever grateful.' The last straw. I drove to the dock and climbed on board the *Lost Lady* without Hank hearing me. I shouted and when he turned to look at me, I shook the papers at him and yelled, 'What the hell are these? What did you do?' He didn't take the papers. Probably recognized the note. He sat on an overturned bucket, put his head in his hands and whispered, 'It's too late to explain now, Honey.' As usual, I couldn't get him to talk. I left, still clutching the papers. As I climbed back over the boat rail to the dock, I shouted that the divorce would be final next week. Haven't seen him since. Our attorneys are battling over the financial settlement."

"What do you think the papers mean?"

"I think someone bought the baby from the doctor, then Hank heard about Jean's murder and the baby hadn't died. He has a friend over there from high school. You probably know him. Last name Kramer. He's the sheriff now, so Hank always can find out what's happening in Lincoln County. I think he bought the baby in Alaska but was too cowardly to tell me the truth."

"I can see why you're so upset, though there's nothing I can do about any of this without proof something illegal occurred. Even if there was a law for any of it, the statute might have run by now."

"What's that mean?"

"Statute of limitations. Length of time the law allows before a person can't be charged for a crime. Nothing here to include in your divorce papers. No custody issues."

"Uh-huh. Except there are financial issues. My attorney found too many discrepancies between what Hank lists on tax papers and the kind of money he's had through the years. It was nothing for him to hand me cash when I wanted a new car, or when it was time to pay for Chance's college tuition and expenses. Always cash. Lots of it. When I went to Spain with some girlfriends, he handed me $10,000 and told me to have a good time. We barely spoke, yet he threw cash at me as if he was a Rockefeller. He paid cash for the Corvette Chance drives. How he's always been. However, the attorney says our tax papers show only a modest income. Roger, I think all these clues show he's been buying and selling Indian babies."

I try to maintain a professional face. If Vivian's story gets any more complicated, my head will explode. We are silent for a few minutes when the tape ends. When the cop continues to stare at me, I ask, "So, how much of this do you believe, Sergeant?"

"I want to check some details, Ellie, but it seems to make sense. Except it is Vivian telling it. Makes me uncomfortable because this would destroy Hank, probably put him in prison which I think may be her goal."

"There are plenty of questions to ponder," I say. "Questions about Jean's murder, questions about selling babies."

"It has always been quite the mystery why Hank chose to be a commercial fisherman in River City when his father held a major interest in Lincoln County's largest paper and timber corporation. Why not follow the money with a mill-related career? If he wanted to fish, why not stay in Newport? But, I suppose he may wonder why I'm a cop when my family owns a large, Newport fishing fleet."

"There are always reasons why people leave their hometown and all the expectations." That's all I can add. My mind whirls with the possibilities in Vivian's story, but talking too much is not a good idea when I don't know this cop.

"After Vivian left my office, I sat glued to my chair, scribbling notes as I played and replayed the tape", the cop said. "The pieces of her story don't fit together, but there is enough to assure me I must do something. The money is a big issue. It could lead to federal tax problems. But selling babies? I doubt it. Too risky. He has other money she may not know about."

"Tax evasion doesn't interest me, Sergeant. Let the Feds handle that. It. But I do want to know if Hank Andrews is really Chance's father, and especially if he's selling Indian babies," I tell him.

"The newspaper articles Vivian left for me were interesting. One quotes the sister of the convicted Siletz guy. She says he's innocent. Do you know who she is? Where she lives?"

He's not as smart as I first thought. Give him names and addresses? Not in this lifetime.

"There were copies of both birth certificates, the plane ticket and decades' worth of tax filings, too. A trade?"

Keeping a stone face, I tell him, "I thought we might work together to solve this mess you mentioned on the phone. Maybe solve the one or two we face here in Siletz. I have the trust of my people. I'm a private investigator. You are a cop, so you have public recognition. Working together might be easier."

"Yeah, right! Like I need help from a so-called PI. You may think you're somebody, lady, but I won't work with a wannabe cop."

He grabs his briefcase and stomps through my house in his fancy cowboy boots. I don't follow him. The door slams and gravel crashes against the side of my house as his truck speeds away.

Abrupt, but predictable. He thought he could share an interesting tape-recording and then sneak in a few questions. Now what? I do hope he finds out he can't get answers in this town without my help. So much to think about. So many decisions. Those accusations about Chance's dad sound horrific. They may only be wild imaginings and accusations from an angry ex-wife, but they are too serious to ignore.

9

As soon as Roger left, I dialed Chance's phone number. Now, I hang up the phone and make a quick note on my afternoon calendar. I'm irritated at what I just heard but I'll meet Chance at his office at five, so we can visit Grandma Kline.

My first call must not have rung in at Chance's desk. I could hear him talking to someone. "Hey, Chance! You look confused," the visitor said. I heard the door close and the scratching of a chair. He's probably pulled it up closer to the desk, nearer the errant phone.

You always seem to know what I'm thinking, man." Chance says.

"It's in the blood, Chance. We both belong to Grandma Kline."

"I hope one of these days all this Indian stuff will make sense to me. I struggle to figure out what people are talking about. Sometimes I manage to laugh at the right time."

"And sometimes we say things to confuse you, Mr. Bigshot Tribal Official. Good thing we all like you. Usually new Indians aren't so popular when they take the best jobs on the rez."

"I know. I appreciate the way I've been treated. Grandma has explained some of it to me, but some people. …"

"Hey, don't pay any mind to the bitchers. Are you doing OK?"

"Mostly. One thing bothers me. Nothing to talk about."

"Ha. Not getting any, huh, Chance? Tough part of coming home. These women are relatives. I grew up on a rez over east of the mountains, so I came over here to look. My Dad was from here so that didn't get me any women."

"When I meet someone interesting, I ask Grandma and it always turns out she's a cousin. I will never understand this confusing relations thing. So complicated. Everyone is a cousin—unless they are past fifty and then they become 'aunties' or 'uncles', except Grandma Kline who seems to be 'Grandma' to the entire Western hemisphere. Oh, Chance, I almost forgot. Ray wants a copy of your report on your first meeting at Ellie's."

"I'll get it to him tomorrow."

I heard more than I should have.

Ray wants a copy of the report on a meeting at my house? We'll see how that goes.

When I call again, it is transferred from the receptionist and Chance answers.

"Hey, Ellie. Just sittin' here staring out the window. Watching traffic disappear down the Hill. Thinking about my murdered birth mother, Jean."

Still the 'Jean is my mother' thing.

"I thought we'd go see Grandma in a couple of hours."

"Sure, about five then?"

The mystery of who Chance's birth mother is has morphed into another Siletz 'fact' that he is the baby we were told died with Jean. Chance is fixated on calling Jean his mother. Even told the reporter.

Lots of people here are uncertain of their family line. Grandma says throughout the history of our rez some white people have been eager to adopt Indian babies and young children. She says many of the soldiers, government agents and employees, all white men, took Indian wives without the benefit of a legal marriage. Interracial marriage was illegal in Oregon, providing a ready excuse for those men. When they were no longer employed by the government, most moved back to their homes in other states, their women and children left behind. She told me a few even took their children away from the Indian 'wife' and gave them to white families. Oregon finally allowed whites and Indians to marry in 1951. Couples usually went into the state of Washington until then.

As I gather some food items, a *Reader's Digest* and a *Life* magazine to take to Grandma, I try to put the sad history out of my mind.

When I arrive at Chance's office, the door is ajar. I walk in and see he's there at his desk staring out the window. Must have seen me drive up the Hill but he seems far away.

"Chance!"

"Ellie, I didn't hear you come in. Lost in thought. You said five o'clock."

"It's five. What is going on? You look like you've seen an ancestor."

His loud laugh rumbles in the room.

"Great description, El. Better than seeing a ghost."

10

THE DIRT ROAD TO GRANDMA'S IS LONG AND BUMPY. THE TRIBE plans a new subdivision for the elders, modern homes with electricity, running water, and inside toilets. The cozy homes will be warm in winter, cool in summer--pure luxury for the men and women who have known few of life's pleasures.

This evening, we're not on our way to a future subdivision. We are going to Grandma's, the only old reservation house still occupied by a tribal member. The others are hangouts for small forest creatures. One crumbling shack serves as an occasional flophouse for guys hiding from the cops.

"Grandma still firmly refuses to leave the only home she has known for the past sixty years," I tell Chance.

"Why, Ellie? She could live in one of those new houses when they're built. Probably have her pick"

"She could live with me right now, but she won't. She returned from Portland to this reservation with her two children after her first marriage failed. When she remarried, her husband, my grandfather, was crushed by a giant Douglas fir log dropped on him when a choker cable snapped. Grandma never lived anywhere else after he died."

"She's over 90 years old."

"She claims to be comfortable and content right where she is near Grandpa's grave. Do you know anyone who would dare to suggest otherwise?"

"Only Logan. She told him, 'Not boy's business' when he took me to see her."

It makes me smile to know my boy was concerned about Grandma.

Chance gazes out into the ancient firs, holds onto the door frame of my topless Jeep as we bump along the dirt road. I wonder what he thinks. I know he hates my driving, so I go too fast just to irritate him. He won't drive his precious Corvette on this road anymore. I don't mind being his chauffeur. I'm enjoying this favored auntie status. He considers me an auntie since he's only a few years older than my son was. Having Chance here takes a tiny bit of the edge off this awful ache, yet his full-of-life attitude sometimes makes the pain cut deep.

He turns to stare at me with large dark eyes. I'm used to dark eyes; most everyone here has them, but Chance has those piercing black eyes that see into your soul. Like Grandma's and Mark's.

He finally speaks, "Today something reminded me of when Mother told me about Jean. About my birth mother. It was like I relived the day all over again. Weird."

The intensity softens in his eyes and I hear the same confusion as on his first visit to my home several months ago. Being a new Indian is tough. He looks Indian, is by blood, but he's still learning the culture and ways of our people.

Now he blurts, "I think I'll ask Grandma about Jean again to see if she knows who my father is."

Thrust forward, Chance hits his head on the windshield as I swerve the Jeep off the road, lumber across a grassy patch and slam to a stop beneath a stand of towering hemlocks.

"Ellie! What the hell?"

"Chance Thom, you are making me crazy!"

I jump out of the Jeep and motion for him to follow. Walking toward a huge rhododendron bush covered with pink blooms growing beside a barely visible tombstone, I feel him following me. I don't turn back or acknowledge his presence. At least he knows how to walk quietly on the forest floor.

It takes a few minutes to find Grandpa's gravesite and I feel guilty at how long it has been since I've paid respects to my relatives. I have made numerous trips up the hill to this cemetery, to this very section, but only to visit Logan.

I sit on a stump, taking in the mingling scents of early summer flowers and foliage that are almost overpowered by the sharp aroma of the needles on the overhanging branches. The ground beneath my feet, a carpet of dried, brown spruce needles, releases a pungent odor of their own when shuffled underfoot. I watch Chance walk slowly, silently, stopping to read the tombstones as he moves nearer. Soon he pauses, crouches in respect at the tombstone of the man he thinks is his great-grandfather.

When he sits on a decaying log near me, I explain, "I try to be patient with your comments, Chance, and I realize you don't know not to ask certain questions. I'm trying to help you find yourself, to find your place. You simply cannot barge into Grandma's house asking questions about her dead daughter. It's disrespectful. She seldom mentions Jean's name. You might kill Grandma with your questions. Do you think of these things?"

I harbor enough of the rough and tumble Kline attitude to want to slap him around. The thought is so amusing I smile. Chance stands a foot taller than me and is built like a two-hundred-pound prizefighter. My hundred ten pounds is stuffed into a short five-two. I might be that tall when I stretch upwards as far as possible.

"Nope," Chance answers. "I look like an Indian, but I think like a white man. I haven't learned how to think Indian yet, if there is such a thing. It's frustrating; especially when I act like Andrews."

. His constant smile is what I most admire about Chance. When he mentions Andrews, his face hardens. He doesn't smile.

"You were raised by Hank Andrews so some of him could have rubbed off on you."

He glares, while Grandma's words slip easily from my mouth, "You will have to work to find your natural self. In the meantime, if you could think before you open your mouth, it would be helpful."

Silently, I plea, "Please, God, don't let him ask ME how to do it."

"What did I do to make you drag me over to these graves?"

"Weren't you listening? You don't ask an elder like Grandma a question about a loved one who has died. Wait for her to offer her stories. Now let's hurry. She'll be worried about us."

We are back in the Jeep before Chance asks, "You told Grandma we were coming?"

"Nope." Then, eager to get to the house where I expect Chance to tell his life's story, I ask, "Tell me when you learned you were adopted, Chance. Who told you?"

"What's that got to. ..." he begins.

I hope the look I shoot back reminds him I am not in the mood for questions.

"I don't remember when I realized I was different from my family. I was pretty young."

"Different how?"

"Look at me. Does anyone here look more Indian? My adoptive family is full of blue-eyed blondes. Didn't take a genius to see that."

"How did you find out?"

"One day sitting around my mother's house doing absolutely nothing with my degree, I confronted her about my special story."

"You had a special story?"

"Yeah. As a kid, I used to bug her to tell me why I looked so different from her and the old man. She promised to tell me my special story when I was older. I couldn't wait any longer."

"What happened?"

"Mother told me she had some papers to review and she'd talk to me in the morning."

Grandma's house is in front of us. I swerve hard right and create a large dust cloud to avoid running over the chickens scratching in the dirt.

"Here we are. You can continue your story inside. Grandma is anxious to hear what your mother told you about all of us. I think she's more interested in your reactions."

"You can't expect me to tell her my reaction to finding out I was named after a jailbird! She won't be happy."

"Doesn't matter whether she likes it. She wants to know the story. C'mon, she'll wonder why we're standing out here with the chickens. Watch out for the dog. Remember he gets excited and pees on strangers."

The warning comes too late. I look up in time to see Grandma's ample belly moving up and down in rhythm to her laughter as she points at Chance's wet pant leg.

"I'll go in the bathroom. ..."

"No bathroom," Grandma gasps, still pointing at Chance as she walks into a room at the rear of the little house.

Chance stands helpless in the living room, too near the woodstove that quickly warms his wet pant leg and releases the nose burning odor. When Grandma reappears with a pair of jeans and points toward her bedroom, he gratefully accepts them, dashes through the kitchen and pulls aside the hanging blanket door. From inside the bedroom, he reaches out to grab a warm, soapy washcloth and a towel from me.

When he re-emerges in perfect fitting dry pants, he asks how she happened to have pants his size. Grandma and I exchange glances but don't answer. He puts the washcloth and towel in the basket on the back porch then carefully opens the front door, lays his rolled-up pants off to the side on the top step. He goes into the kitchen to wash his hands and after an interminably long silence, Grandma asks, "You hungry now?"

When he assures her, she asks, "What you come to tell me?"

"Me? I didn't come to. …," he begins.

"He will tell you his story now, Grandma. How he heard about us." I wink and assume Chance's scowl means he hates me at this moment.

"You tell story. After story, we eat food Ellie make," Grandma commands.

Now it is Chance's turn to laugh. I am surprised to be ordered to the kitchen while he tells his story. He claps his hands and points toward the kitchen even though I will hear every word from there. It obviously feels like payback to him.

"Girl always talk too much. You tell story without her help," Grandma shouts. She waits for my protest, smiles broadly, then points to the stuffed chair by the door and settles herself on a rocker near the woodstove.

"Grandma, that's not fair. I don't talk all the time like I did when I was little. I think you. …"

"See? Girl talk too much. Tell story, boy."

"I don't know where to start," Chance says.

"Start with mother who adopt you. What she tell you about us? About Jean?"

"The first time, when I was in grade school, she explained I was from the Siletz tribe of Indians over by the coast and she thought my mother's name might be Jean. That was all she knew. She promised to find out more. That was after my adoptive Dad, Hank Andrews, called me a Siletz Injun."

"She not want to tell story, I think."

"Yeah, you're probably right."

"Bad choice of words, Chance. Grandma doesn't like being told she's probably right," I say, while standing in the kitchen doorway.

He apologizes. I see Grandma smile and motion for him to continue.

"Mother had trouble starting so I touched her shoulder and said, 'Once upon a time.' We laughed, and then she began to cry. As she grabbed my hands, an album slipped off her lap spilling newspaper clippings and photographs on the floor. Some of the photos went under her desk."

I look at Grandma to see if Chance should hurry with his story. She seems satisfied. A tattered blue shawl covers her shoulders as gnarled hands softly stroke her ugly old cat. I don't like the cat and he barely tolerates me.

"So, I picked up her pictures," Chance continues. "Had to crawl under the desk to get one that slid all the way to the wall. I sure didn't fit under her desk like I did when I used it for a play fort."

"You play cowboys and shoot Indians?"

Now I'm out of the kitchen and staring at Grandma as I twist one of my braids into a knot.

Chance is too embarrassed to answer until Grandma says, "Ellie always wanted to be cowboy, too. She ride her stick horse and shoot at Indians she see behind trees in the woods. Mark tell her she's Indian but when she on a stick horse, she is cowboy."

Back in the kitchen, I crash some pots and pans in protest.

"When I settled back into my chair," Chance tells Grandma, "I was concentrating on what Mother had to say and I didn't look at the photos in my hand. When she couldn't think where to begin, I suggested, 'Start with me,'"

"Story not start with you," Grandma says.

"I know. Learned later. Anyway, I asked where I came from. Where I was born. Who my parents, birth parents, were. She decided to tell me about my birth mother. Jeannie Thom."

"Jean Kline," Grandma corrected.

"Yeah, she told me it was her name. She spelled Kline for me. Explained Jean was a member of the Siletz tribe over by the coast. Me, too."

"What you think?"

"I was excited. I kept asking her, 'They know about me? I'm an Indian? From where you and Hank grew up, right, on the Oregon coast? All those questions tormenting me for so many years spilled out as I got answers.'"

"You not ask about old Grandmother?"

"Oh, Grandma! I didn't know about you. As soon as I heard from Marge I had a grandmother living right up here, I jumped in my car and came to see you. Remember?"

I peek around the doorway again to see the toothless grin spread across the aged, wrinkled face as she remembers the day.

"What she tell you about real father?"

"She wouldn't tell me anything. Said it wasn't her right."

"Not Mother, Marge. What she tell you about father?" Grandma asks.

"Marge says she doesn't know."

"Hmmm."

"Mother said Marge knew about me. She visited Marge a long time ago, here in Siletz. When I asked where I was born, she said Portland."

"Tell story."

"She said Mama was young, unmarried and planned to give the baby up for adoption. She didn't want to do it, and it wasn't something she would talk about when she got home. She made up the story she was going to Portland to work."

"Enit?" Grandma said.

"That word seems to be important here, but I don't understand what it means, Grandma."

I decide to jump into the discussion.

"Elders seldom explain what enit means, Chance. Children learn its many meanings as they hear it used in different ways. The questioning way Grandma just used it could be compared to a person asking 'Really?'"

"Thanks," Chance said, and then continued answering Grandma. "So, I asked more questions. Where is my birth mother, Jean, now? Who is my father and where is he? Mother explained Jean was murdered by her own cousin, Mark Thom. Then she told me to look at the photo in my hand. It was a newspaper photo of this person who killed my mother and nearly killed me in her womb."

"What you think?"

"I nearly dropped the photo. I knew the face. Saw it in the mirror every day. Then I got mad. I didn't know where my middle name came from. No one in our family was named Aidan. I yelled at her, 'You named me after a damned murderer?'"

"You make Mother cry when you yell," Grandma says.

"I did. Seemed to be all she knew, except Hank, my adoptive father had already named me before he brought me home. Chance Aidan Andrews. He needed a name to put on the birth certificate before he paid the doctor."

"Doctors like to sell Indian babies," Grandma tells Chance.

"That's weird, I think, don't you, Ellie?"

"Yes, Chance, I do." More crashing of pots and pans. I so want to be in this conversation.

"Mother gave me papers she received from a private investigator and refused to talk more. When I got to Siletz, Marge explained Mark was wrongfully convicted. Said he was tried in a 'white man's court'. Made me mad. What's a white man's court? Did he kill her or not?"

"He didn't," I shout from the kitchen. Grandma doesn't respond.

"Marge talked about Mark. Claimed there were strange circumstances. She said 'they', the white people, I guess, needed a quick conviction. Marge remembered one of our relatives saying it was an 'any Injun will do' kind of conviction. They found her body up Dewey Creek outside of town. Someone had tied her. …"

When he stops, I hurry to the door and see Chance staring at Grandma rocking back and forth, arms folded across her bosom, eyes closed.

"Ellie," he says softly. "Ellie, I can't do this."

"You must."

"Grandma. …"

"She's fine. Tell the story like she asked you to."

"Okay." He begins again, "Marge told me someone tied Jean's hands behind her, tried to strangle her. Left her on the ground. Probably thought she was dead, but she was only unconscious. Someone came by in time, I think. So strange. I remember shouting, 'Good Lord! What kind of place is this?' Marge said, 'Bad things happen here sometimes, most of the people are good.'"

He grows quiet again, probably recalling his mixed feelings as the story progressed.

"Story not done," Grandma says.

"No, it sure isn't, Grandma. "She said they rushed Jean to the hospital, I guess in Toledo. The old doctor was drunk, and Jean died."

"Marge say baby live?"

"Yes, she did. Mother did, too. Of course, it's true. I'm here. But, I didn't buy the wrongful conviction story. I asked why they blamed Mark. There had to be some evidence, a LOT of evidence, for him to get a life sentence. If the guy wasn't guilty, the jury would have said so. Acquittal, they call it."

"You still think so?"

Chance is trapped. The old woman expects a truthful answer and his won't match hers.

"Still struggling with what I've heard about the courts in this county, Grandma. I can't believe a person can be convicted without any evidence. Besides if everybody was Indian, why weren't they in an Indian court?"

I try not to groan.

"No Indian court here. You know now?"

I am not staying in the kitchen now, so I see Chance nod his head in response.

"Maybe boy need to go to jail then he know he guilty of being 'Injun'. You fit in Mark's pants, maybe you fit in his cell. Sheriff like to put this one in jail, I think."

Chance stiffens when he sees Grandma's stern look.

"I plan to find out what happened to my Mama. I hear about all these young people being stopped for no reason. There *are* problems on this rez. Are these really Mark's pants, Grandma?"

Nodding, Grandma asks one final question.

"What else Mother tell boy?"

"That's pretty much it, Grandma. Right after that I packed my stuff and headed to Siletz."

"To Grandma," she says, and holds out her arms.

He crosses the room, draws her up from the chair causing the old cat to screech and jump down. Chance hugs her tightly as she says, "Remember old Grandma when you tell your special story. Tell people she wait many years to feed you."

They come to the kitchen where they fill plates with fried salmon steaks, salad and cornbread, some prepared by Grandma before we arrived. I place a large pitcher of lemonade in the center of the table. My mind races. There are so many holes in the story Chance told Grandma. How does his adoptive mother know Chance is Jean's son? How did Hank Andrews get the baby? Why did Hank move to Portland if he grew up on the coast? Did he know Mark, Jean, Marge? Is Marge telling the truth? Too many holes. Too many questions.

Why did I become an investigator? My other braid is in a knot now.

Grandma's face is radiant as she takes our hands in her own to ask the Lord's blessing on the food and for His protection as we face the tasks ahead of us. After dinner, when the dishes are clean, she sends Chance out to bring in more wood. When the door closes, she turns to me, "Boy not know truth."

11

Rose is in my kitchen helping prepare the evening meal.
Indian tacos! I am so excited. Never have mastered the trick of making
good fry bread. I'm hoping Rose has her mother Marge's knack. She looks
like she knows what she's doing. I have the lettuce and tomatoes chopped,
and elkburger fried. I'll put some black beans, shredded Tillamook cheese,
chopped onion, salsa and sour cream on the table so we can build our
tacos just the way we like them. After we eat, we will begin to formulate an
investigation plan.

Chance is asleep in a chair near my fireplace where he was reading
the *Oregonian* newspaper. I marvel at how easily he captured my heart. I
wonder if he misses his former home and life.

"What's going on, Ellie? He falls asleep a lot. I worry about him."

"He has a lot to figure out. He'll be fine. Just needs time. He's Indian
but doesn't know yet what that means. His mind will crash back and forth
between the world he was raised in and our Indian world. Every person
must find their own way. I sure know the struggle. Trying to find my Indian
self again after so many years away from the reservation isn't easy.

"I don't understand. Lived here all my life. But I wonder what is happening to my Mom."

"What's wrong with Marge? Your Mama?"

"She's so different since Logan and the other boys were killed in the wreck."

"How?" I ask and clutch my chest. Every mention of my lost child is excruciating.

"Indians don't really say 'how' you know," Rose says as she slaps me on the back and bends over in a fit of giggles.

"Mom quit drinking when Logan came to live with her. Never gets drunk anymore even with the awfulness of the wreck. Spends way more time with her little grandson."

"That's all good, isn't it?"

"But if she isn't doing stuff with him, she's cleaning house. Peculiar. It was never a great concern for her in the past."

"Maybe she has more energy and pride in her home since she's not drinking."

"Maybe. I think she has secrets." She leans close to me and whispers, "Do you think Chance might be my brother? Mama was raped a long time ago, you know."

I shrug my shoulders. I've wondered myself.

"Why would you think that, Rose?"

"I found a cedar chest in our attic. You know the kind some girls fill with linens and household stuff for when they get married. So, I opened it and found it filled with letters and photos of Chance. Tiny baby photos, copies of his degree from Oregon State and his master's from the University of Oregon. The letters are postmarked from Alaska. Bundled and tied with ribbons. No return name or addresses on the envelopes."

"What do the letters say? Are they signed?"

"Ellie, I didn't dare untie the ribbons. Mom is always home now so I can't go to the attic and snoop again."

"Hmmm. I thought the woman who came to visit your Mom about Chance all those years ago was from Portland. But the letters are from Alaska?"

"Yep. The postmark on the top one is Seward, Alaska."

We carry our dinner plates and drinks into the living room where the blanket chest provides the perfect table and we can enjoy the heat from the stove. Rose shakes Chance's shoulder and waits until he seems awake enough to hold the plate of food she hands to him.

I pull a green velour swing rocker closer to the heat. This will be a long evening of discussion and planning. I want to be warm and comfortable. The wood box near Chance's chair is nearly overflowing. Chance's chair. How quickly I've changed from thinking of it as Logan's chair. The hole in my heart will never heal, but this young cousin has given me hope life can go on.

With the fire blazing and our stomachs filled with tacos, it is time to formulate a plan. The phone rings as I start to speak. Chance grabs it before the second ring. His terse responses and look of concern make me impatient for information.

"Call from a guy in the office. Someone was messing around in the cemetery when he made the rounds a few minutes ago. He noticed them as he drove up the Hill. They drove away before he could ask what they were doing. It's barely dark. They're getting braver, showing up earlier. He didn't recognize the truck, an older, black Ford. '65 or so. Couldn't see the plate."

"Are they ever going to stop?" Rose asks.

"Not until someone stops them."

"Chance, why don't you call around? Start with Noel's Market. See if anyone noticed a strange truck in town. Maybe some strangers stopped at the store. Or the gas station. They might be at the tavern, or maybe there this afternoon before they went up to the cemetery," I tell him.

Chance grabs the phone again and dials Noel's Market.

"No use to call Bensell's Store," he says as he hangs up the phone. "Strangers don't go there."

"Call them, anyway, Chance. They'd be the first to notice someone new in town."

"Called, but no one saw anything, anywhere, Ellie."

"Of course, they didn't," Rose says.

In unison, we say, "It's Indian Country."

"Oh, Ellie, the city cop, Roger Wood, still comes around. I saw him at the store the other day when I was filling in," Rose says as we carry our dishes back to the kitchen. "He seems nice. Pretty nice to look at, too. A little old for me, though."

"Hah. Buying beer, wasn't he? Heard he buys beer every time he comes to town. Probably drunk by the time he heads back to River City. He'll kill himself on the highway and maybe somebody else, too."

"Ellie, listen. Those are rumors. Just because a guy drinks a little doesn't mean he's going to die on the highway."

I pull away as she touches my arm.

"If you'd lost a child, ..."

"I know. I'm sorry. I think people exaggerate about the cop's drinking. You know how it goes. If he bought one bottle, it will grow to be cases, probably to 'every time he comes to town' like you heard."

I keep my eyes down and don't respond.

"Actually, the cop asked if I knew a woman named Ellie. Mentioned he talked to you once. Thought you were very pretty but had a sharp tongue."

"I have a sharp tongue? He called me a wannabe cop."

I see Chance turn back to the window. Probably wants to laugh.

"I said I might know someone like that. Then he asked if you were an actual investigator or a local busybody."

"The jerk!" I hate the lean, muscular man with the thick, graying hair and tempting mouth who inhabits my fantasies.

Chance turns back to us. The twinkle in his eyes makes me uncomfortable. Maybe I protested too much. He grows serious again. I'm happy when he says, "Now, we've decided we don't need the drunken cop's help. Are you ready to sign the contract with the tribe tomorrow morning?"

"Yes, I am." I sound much more confident than I feel and giggle to hide my nervousness. I keep my emotions hidden just as I learned as a child.

"So, we have the grave robbing, Jean's murder, a cold case that could lead to proving Mark was wrongfully convicted, plus some other little issues we want to resolve. Like determining who Chance's birth parents were," I explain.

"Yeah, only a few minor problems." Chance returns to his chair by the window while Rose and I find our comfortable spots on the couch.

"The tribe assumes I will solve all these issues, even though they only agreed to pay for the work on the grave robbing."

"Some people have suggested we find one thief, shoot him, and the others will get the message," Chance says.

"So, I've heard. I wish all of them were dead. However, I don't want murder as one of our investigative goals. We can't take any of this lightly. Investigating people who steal human bones from burial sites is dangerous. Such people, with the money involved, would kill anyone in their way.

"Chance, the tribal council will pay for the search for the robbers, and they did agree to put a provision in the contract to cover the investigation of Jean's murder if I find a connection to the diggers. I must keep a separate accounting of all the work and can submit a bill at the end for anything done on Jean's case if it connects to the grave robbing."

"It's good they put that in the contract."

"Yes. They also included you are available as my contact person at the tribe but beyond providing any files or information available from the tribe's records, you are only to work on a volunteer basis after regularly scheduled work at your office, unless there is an emergency involved with the grave robbing case."

"Henry came in and explained all of it to me. He didn't seem too enthusiastic."

"Nor at the contract discussion, either. I think he's stuck on dreaming of the casino. So, about your search for your birth parents. How serious are you?" I ask.

"Totally serious. What if my father is the one who killed my mother? We have to assume it's possible, don't we?"

I think we might assume Jean was not your mother.

"Perhaps. Numerous parts of these stories don't make sense. We have a complex puzzle to solve and it's not clear if any of the pieces will fit. Chance, do you have a pistol?"

"What? No. Why?"

I rise from my chair, walk over to the teapot, reach into the cupboard for cups, fill them, stir in some honey and carry them to Rose and Chance. Carrying my cup to the couch, I say quietly, "I have received a death threat."

"A death threat? When? What did they, he, whoever, say?" Chance leaps from his chair and grabs my arm. Somehow neither of our cups spill.

"He told me to stay out of this. Wouldn't bother him to make it a family affair."

"Ellie, why the hell didn't you tell me?"

"I just did," I say as I sit again to sip the hot tea.

I feel Chance's heightened sense of urgency now he knows about the threats. He demands to know more.

"Look, Chance. I am grateful you are willing to work with me, to find the people who are targeting our family, the living and the dead, if this threat bothers you so much. ..."

"If you are threatened, so am I."

"Comes with the territory. This isn't my first threat. One tough case in Chicago caused a political stir and someone wanted me gone. Never amounted to more than nasty phone calls. I do have to be careful with this one. You, too."

"Do you have any idea who this guy is? Where he is?" Rose asks.

"I didn't recognize his voice."

Too soon to discuss my terror that it might be the grave robber who threatened me so many years ago. There was something about the disguised voice on the phone. I'm not sure yet.

"I don't have a gun. Only my hunting rifle, no pistols."

"Get one and learn to use it. Oh, and don't buy it from a cousin. You can't tell where a rez gun has been or what it's done. Keep it legal."

"Yes, ma'am."

"Now the good news is I have a copy of the transcript of Mark's trial. I was reading it when you arrived."

"Where did you get the transcript?"

"Magic. I tell you. I have magic in my bones. Things appear when I need them."

"When did this amazing information magically appear?" Rose asks.

"Katie's mother called to ask if I could stop by her house real soon. I thought she might be upset about the girl spending so much time with Grandma, so I went right over."

"She had the transcript? Why?"

"She was in grade school right here in Siletz when Jean was murdered. She had a crush on Mark, one of those little girl things. She was like

Katie, knew everybody and everything. Lived in the housing project down behind Bensell's store. I don't remember her. She remembered me because I was always with Mark and Marge and she wanted to be. I usually stuck with my cousins and didn't have many other friends."

"If she was so young, how did she get the transcript?"

"She always believed Mark was innocent. Later, as a clerk for a judge at the courthouse in Newport, she was assigned to clean an office to create space for a newly-elected judge. When she found a stack of old trial transcripts in a closet, the court administrator told her to toss them in the trash. She was shocked to find Mark's. She's had it ever since."

"Enit!" Chance and Rose shout with excitement.

"Exactly. It's amazing the trial record was transcribed and saved. Unusual unless someone specifically orders it. I suspect someone anticipated an appeal, or knew he was innocent. Were they preparing to defend the appeal, or was someone hoping to save him? I don't know. Someone who is or was in the courthouse, might have the key to this murder."

"Now you're losing me, Ellie. How did we get from the transcript to thinking the legal folk are involved?" Chance asks.

I avoid an answer because I don't have one. Not yet.

"When I began investigating, I asked my mentor how he found the answers, the solutions. He told me, 'There is always someone who knows. It's your job to find that person.' Perhaps this transcript will help us find our person."

"Have you read the transcript?"

"Some of it."

"Let's look through the information my mother got from the PI. Maybe there will be answers there, too, and you can compare them," Chance says.

I pull a newspaper clipping from the package. "The victim," I read aloud, "was Jean Kline, a young Siletz Indian who was found stabbed. ... Stabbed? That's new. I haven't heard she was stabbed, have you?"

"No. All I know is what I reported to Grandma the other day. Someone tried to strangle her and left her for dead," Chance says.

"I do remember knowing Jean didn't die right away. Once on a visit back here I heard an auntie talking with Cousin Marge. She cried and said her sister must have suffered so much, been in so much pain. Maybe she read the papers and knew about the stabbing. They wouldn't have told me when I was a kid. I always eavesdropped, even as an adult."

"All we know for sure is she survived long enough for me to be born."

We don't know any such thing, but no use to argue without facts.

"Listen to this, Chance. It says a fisherman spotted the murder scene after daybreak. He first noticed a bonfire, then found the girl crumpled on the ground, gasping for breath, blood running from a stab wound to her chest. This guy could be a good witness--or the murderer. Make a note to check the trial transcript for his testimony."

"Okay, it's on the list."

"What list?"

"The list I just started, the 'look in the transcript' list."

"Oh, sorry. I was thinking out loud. Good to know you're so obedient." I smile at him and offer to read some of the trial transcript to help him understand what happened in the courtroom.

"Lincoln County Circuit Court, State of Oregon versus Mark Thom," I begin. "Transcript of Proceedings of September 22, 1951. Judge John Upton presiding. District Attorney Vance Morgan representing State of Oregon; Attorney Charles Hinkelrod representing the defendant."

The scent of fresh tea fills the air as Chance pushes aside a stack of papers and places a filled cup near me.

"Listen to what poor Mark went through in the trial. They didn't understand him at all. I don't know why his useless attorney didn't tell him he didn't have to testify."

I pace beside the table, to and fro, as I read aloud.

"Clerk: Please state your name and address and spell your name for the record.

Thom: Mark Aidan Thom. T-H-O-M. I stay in Siletz.

Morgan: What is your address?

Thom: I live in my grandfather's house on the reservation.

Morgan: What is your address? Your honor, this man is uncooperative. I demand he answer.

"Oh, like any of our people would know their address then." I groan.

"The rez didn't have street names for years and it was only a few years ago the Jaycees figured out a house numbering system, so the new phone system could be installed in town."

"You didn't use street addresses?"

"No, we picked up our mail at the post office, like we do now. Who needed a street address? We all knew where everybody stayed."

I begin to read again.

"Hinkelrod: Let me try, your honor. Mark, where do you live? What street? What town?

Thom: In the house by the corner where the road goes to the bridge. In Siletz.

Morgan: Your honor..."

I push my hair away from my eyes and skip through the pages until I reach the questions about Mark's alibi. Exasperated, I slam the pages on the table.

"That's what they missed. He lied about no one being with him. He was protecting Ruthie. He went to prison rather than tell them she spent the night with him."

"Keep reading out loud, Ellie. I don't have much experience at this---none, in fact. Maybe if you. ..." Rose says.

I resume reading, louder, hoping Chance and Rose will see the problem.

"Morgan: Where were you on the night of May 15, 1951?

Thom: With my grandfather at our house. He was sick.

Morgan: With your grandfather who was sick. Did he go to the hospital?

Thom: No.

Morgan: He didn't? Did a doctor come to your house?

Thom: We didn't have a doctor.

Morgan: Why didn't you take him to a doctor in Toledo?

Thom: We didn't have a car. My uncle had the old truck. He was somewhere, probably drunk.

Morgan: Will your grandfather testify you were with him that night?

Thom: My grandfather is gone.

Morgan: Gone? Where'd he go?

Thom: He has gone over to the other side.

Morgan: The other side of what? Your honor, again I demand this man be made to answer my questions.

Judge: Mr. Hinklerod, please instruct your client to be cooperative.

Hinkelrod: I think I can help here. Mark, is your grandfather dead?

Thom: That's what you would call it, I guess.

Morgan: Dead? Your grandfather is dead? So, you have no alibi? No one to testify to your whereabouts on the night Jean Kline was murdered?

Thom: No sir."

Chance interrupts, "So, a newspaper clipping and a few pages of a transcript that proves Mark had no alibi are supposed to tell us, you, how to help Mark? I don't get it. What do you mean he was convicted because he was protecting Ruthie? Who is Ruthie and why would he go to jail for her?"

I know more questions are coming. He drinks his coffee and keeps his dark eyes focused on me. When he can't stand it any longer, he slams his cup down and asks, "Why are we reading trial transcripts, anyway? I don't understand why the hell everything is about Mark. What about Jean, my mother?"

"It isn't all about Mark. He was convicted of Jean's murder. We must find what led the cops to a false conclusion. What did the jury hear besides their probable racist attitudes, that convinced them he should spend his life in prison? Please get that look off your face."

"What look? And don't tell me I look like Mark. I don't want to hear it."

"You do look a lot like him, silly. He is supposedly your cousin, but I was referring to your anger."

"The day you came here," Rose says, "the aunties all got sick because they relived the day Mark was arrested. They say he looked then exactly like you look now, Chance. Only he didn't have a fancy red car or a nasty scowl."

Chance's clouded face tells me we've failed to lighten his mood. He doesn't respond or look at me. I feel the discomfort of being the waiting half of an Indian-time conversation, grow restless under his penetrating gaze, so I walk into the kitchen. I point at Chance's cup, but he ignores me.

I feel his gaze while I tidy the kitchen, take out the garbage and bring in wood for the stove. I run out of busy work and still those eyes watch, wait--for what I cannot guess. He's picked a bad time to practice being Indian. Back on the couch, unable to stand the silence any longer, I take charge.

"Okay, young man. Let's get this over with. You obviously have a problem. I'm not going to sit here for six months while you try to figure it out. What do you want?"

"Answers!"

The ferocity of his reply startles me. I notice Rose, who has been sitting patiently, jerks to attention.

"Help me, Ellie. I have pieces of the stories. It's all so confusing. When Marge said I had a cousin who was a PI, I thought, Great. Someone to tell me how my relative got convicted if he didn't kill his cousin. Why no one from my mother's family claimed me at the hospital. Why my adoptive father brought me home if he hates Indians. The puzzle gets more complicated by the hour. And all anyone wants to talk about is Mark. I can't do my job while I'm trying to figure this out."

"The first day, do you know how much your arrival changed the lives of our family, Chance? No, of course you don't. It did. Marge recalls it was like a breath of fresh air, of hope, had arrived. Someone with new ideas."

"Yeah, I can't go anywhere in this town without hearing, 'The day you came home,' or 'You look like Mark.' Never mind I was never here in the first place and many of the people are too young to remember Mark," Chance says as he flops into the brown chair by the woodstove again.

"Chance listen to me. This may be difficult for you to understand. Society has changed since Mark was convicted. People are more integrated now. It was a mean world in those years. Indians were treated like pond scum. Some white kids were taught to hate us. We were taught not to trust white people. Few white parents let their kids date us. We could play together as little kids; forget about dating when we got older."

His look is quizzical, full of curiosity, like he is waiting for the punch line of my joke.

"Marge played volleyball on the high school team. She was good. Very good. The only girl in the county who compared with her was over at Newport High School. One afternoon, the two teams played at the coast and a girl got hit smack in the face with one of Marge's powerhouse serves. There was an instant of complete silence, according to the story the aunties tell. Every person in the room knew Marge could place a ball anywhere, at any time, as softly or as viciously as she wanted. This wasn't an accident."

Chance listens. When he doesn't comment, I continue. "Blood flew as the girl ran to the bathroom. An auntie said she saw Mark, sitting above midcourt in the bleachers, stand up as Marge and the girl exited the bathroom. The girl held a paper towel to her face, looked up at our side of the stands, waved and returned to her team. Marge walked back onto the floor, flashed thumbs up and served the ball. Ever after, the white girl and Marge were best friends. The girl was here on the rez as often as she could get here. They never told anyone what they said in the bathroom."

"Who was the girl? The one from Newport?"

"Ruthie. Mark's girlfriend. Or at least she was until he got arrested."

"She met him when she came to visit Marge?"

"No. I heard Ruthie and Mark knew each other long before that day. They met on the beach near Newport. Mark was a wanderer. Grandpa Thom could not keep him home. Ruthie was forbidden to date Indians, but they managed somehow. Lots of kids did. Guess Marge figured it out when she gave Ruthie a bloody nose."

"But why did Mama hit her on purpose?" Rose asked.

"Only way she could talk privately with Ruthie. She knew if the girl's family found out about Mark, he'd be in trouble. The sheriff would find some way to put him in jail to get him out of the way. Marge wouldn't stand for her brother to be strung along."

"Anyhoo, as Marge always says, Ruthie knew Marge was Mark's sister and figured out why she got hit. And why she hurried into the bathroom, besides the blood, and insisted she didn't need help from her team."

"Sneaky girls. I can't see Marge as a teenager."

"I thought Mark and Marge were magical people, Chance. So good to me when I was a little brat always following them. Especially Mark. He was my hero."

"What happened to Ruthie?"

"When Mark got arrested, he told Marge to keep Ruthie away from him. He knew he was being set up; knew he would be sent to the pen, probably forever. He didn't want Ruthie connected to any of it, so he sent her away."

The intensity has returned to his black eyes again. I know Chance's mind is whirling. I hope he's listening. He doesn't respond.

"So, Mark was convicted and sent to prison. The uncles blamed Ruthie. The aunties didn't. When she came to visit Marge, I saw the aunties sitting with Ruthie, helping her through the loss. Many of them knew what it was to lose a man behind the iron bars in Salem."

"Why did the uncles blame her?"

Incredible. His anger seems directed at the uncles rather than toward the court system that convicted an innocent man. He still doesn't get it.

"Probably because they thought white girls always bring trouble."

"So where is she now?"

"I'm not sure. Marge wrote in a letter about Ruthie living with relatives in Alaska and married a commercial fisherman. Later, Marge reported Ruthie's husband had died. I don't know what happened to her. I'll ask Marge."

Chance leaves the chair, walks to the living room window and braces his left hand against the top of the window frame. As he stares out, he brushes his right hand through long, dark hair left unbraided today. I wonder if he wore braids before he came to Siletz.

"Who the hell is my father?"

His question startles me.

"Um…I don't know, Chance. I've never heard anyone say."

"Everyone I ask hesitates and then says, 'I don't know.'"

"I really don't know. There were rumors Jean was dating a man at the mill where she went to work as a secretary after high school, but no one. …"

"A white guy?"

"Maybe. Must have been. There weren't any Indians working at the mill. She was a beautiful girl. Wild and fun-loving. Someone may have noticed."

"I wonder if any of those aunties in charge of the tribal rolls know. They seem to know everything about everyone." He smiles.

"Maybe. They might have tried to find out if you had a white father. Because of the blood quantum to see if you qualified to be a tribal member under U.S government rules."

"No one has questioned it. … at least they haven't asked me about it," Chance says. "Spent my life being Chance Aidan Andrews. Came here and learned I am Chance Aidan Thom. Thom was Marge's maiden name, right?"

"Yes, she says she gave you her surname when she enrolled you because she didn't know who your father was. This is a valley of secrets, Chance. Everyone thinks they're keeping their own secrets secret, when most secrets are known by many other people. If anyone knows who your father is, we'll find out. Someone will slip."

"Are your parents still living, Ellie? I didn't see any grandparents listed when. …"

"My father is still living, though I supposedly don't know who he is, so I couldn't list him in Logan's obituary. Logan didn't know, anyway."

"You supposedly don't know. How does that happen?"

"We're in Indian Country, remember? I thought my father was the late John Simpson. When I was a teenager, I noticed on his tombstone he died two years before I was born. No one bothered to tell me."

"So, you're not my cousin, hm?" Now he's relaxing a bit, searching through the cupboards for snacks.

"Sorry, buster. I am your cousin. Seems John's brother was teepee creeping. He's my father. Since he was married, it was never talked about, at least not publicly."

"His brother? I thought Grandma only had two sons, John Simpson and Uncle Oscar Kline," Rose says as she refills my coffee cup.

She hasn't said a word for so long, I forgot she was sitting in the kitchen.

"Exactly, Rose."

"Uncle Oscar is your real father? He has a jillion kids."

"Yep. And I'm one of them. There are more than you know. A couple of wives, lots of women, and kids. Figure I have at least thirteen brothers and sisters."

"How did you find out? Does he know you know?" Chance asks.

Ah, the endless questions. This must be how Grandma felt with all my questions.

"One of my cousins thought I knew. It happens. People forget who knows and who doesn't."

"What did she say?"

Chance leans forward in his chair again, anticipating the rest of the story. His curiosity will serve us well in our work if I can teach him how to ask the questions and not look too interested in the answers. That's my best investigative skill.

"She referred to one of my other cousins as my sister. I asked Mama, but she said it wasn't important. Guess it wasn't. Didn't change my life, knowing or not. Didn't have a Dad either way."

"Doesn't he know?"

"He must. He was there at conception, or so they say. He's never mentioned it and neither have I."

"Maybe he's my father, too," Chance says.

"Sick, Chance. Jean was his little sister."

"You saying it wouldn't happen here?"

"No, you're right. We should consider the possibility, sick as it sounds. Would cast suspicion on a lot of men. You planning to say, 'Hi, Dad' to all the guys until someone admits it?" I tease.

"I think I will. Next time I give a report at general council meeting, I'll ask, 'Will my real father please stand so I can get on with my life?

"You will learn in time. Right now, we have a huge task to catch you up on tribal history. What do you know about Mark?"

Chance doesn't appreciate my starting point.

"Mark!" He comes up out of his chair, then settles back again. "Okay, okay. We'll do it your way. Not much choice."

"Chance, you might have been created right here in this town. The life waters of your body come from here. You're home. Do you feel it?"

"Sometimes. There's so much confusion. I don't think it's only me, either. Everyone seems confused and sad here."

His connection is deep if he feels the blackness left over from this valley being what I consider a concentration camp. Will he ever question whether Jean was his mother, and the story he's been told doesn't make sense? I pull my turquoise Chief Joseph Pendleton blanket across my lap and begin again.

"Much of the sadness and confusion comes with the history of this old reservation, Chance. That's a politically correct word for a concentration camp. Even back then they hid the truth with special approved words. It is a way to manipulate the masses to do what seems right, sounds right and becomes so implanted in the public mind they support the idea, though they may not recognize its reality."

"You lost me."

"Think of it this way. If the government had stated publicly, 'We don't want these Injuns here on this valuable land. We want to take the gold, everything of value, and the best way to do it is to make false promises and herd the people to a desolate part of the territory. We'll create a concentration camp from which they can't escape. We'll take their weapons, forbid them to hunt or fish to feed their families, and we'll make sure hundreds of them die from starvation the first winter. Then we'll put the children in boarding schools. We'll beat the Indianness out of them.' Perhaps some white people would have objected. Maybe enough to keep it from happening."

"Didn't our people know what 'reservation' meant?" Rose asks.

"They only knew they were leaving their homeland that held the graves of their deceased loved ones. They believed the soldiers and government men who came to negotiate with our leaders who said they represented the Great White Father in Washington, D.C. Most of our people believed the U.S government's word was good and true--until they began to starve to death."

12

———

Sneaking off to the cemetery to sit on the bench at my son's grave is a brief respite from the deeply tangled web of misinformation. Every day has brought more questions and fewer useful answers. I need to get away to concentrate on what we know, to separate fact from rez fiction. The pressures of this case, combined with the deep ache of losing Logan, is taking its toll. Nagging headache, rising blood pressure and jangled nerves are my constant companions.

"Ellie can I. …"

"Oh, Katie. I didn't hear you coming." I slap my right hand on my breast to calm my racing heart, catch my breath, then point for her to sit on the bench.

"What are you doing here, Katie?"

"We need to talk. If I talk to you here, people will think it's about Logan. At your house, or Mama's, people will get nosey about what we're saying. Can I talk to you?"

"Yes, of course. What's bothering you?"

"Crazy stuff!"

"Where did you hear crazy stuff?" I smile, so she scoots closer.

"In my tree. It's right by those graves, you know. Only tree in the cemetery I can climb up and just sit there. No one ever sees me."

"Yes, the tree has been there for many years. I used to sit up there and hear things. What did you hear, Katie?"

She speaks in a hushed voice even though there are no other living souls visible in the cemetery. "I saw the grave robbers once. It was almost dark. I was supposed to be home, but I couldn't get down or they would catch me. Before Logan died, he told me if I ever climbed in the tree again, he'd spank me. I still do it sometimes."

"You told him about the grave robbers?"

"Yes! He said he would make them stop. He and his guys started a group to fight them, but a guy came to talk to Logan. Then they all died in the wreck."

"What man, Katie? How do you know a man talked to Logan?"

"I heard them yelling over by the office the afternoon before the wreck. The guy said, 'No, you have to stop, Logan. This will get you killed. Everyone knows it's you. They may already be looking for ways to hurt you.' I heard Logan say before he walked away, 'It's a little late for you to tell me what to do, isn't it, Mr. Carlisle?'"

Struggling to stay composed, I hug Katie close and thank her for the information. "Mr. Carlisle was Logan's father, Katie. I didn't know he was here until I saw him at the funeral."

"Yeah, but they were fighting about the grave robbers. I heard the man, Mr. Carlisle, tell Old Joe Logsden if the tribal council didn't get their act together Logan would be killed by the grave robbers."

My mind whirls back to the council meeting when murmurs from the crowd left me feeling there was something I didn't know about the wreck that killed my son. Now Russ and Old Joe are involved in this mess. Was Logan murdered? Have I blamed the wrong people for his death?

"Katie, do you know who the boys were who wanted to help Logan stop the digging?"

"Sure, the guys in the wreck. All of them. His cousins. They played football and Logan wanted the team to stop their next game and ask the crowd to help them fight, but the coach heard about it and said, "No way!"

Oh my God! The secrets in this place. I wonder if Chance knows this?

"Chance doesn't know," Katie says, assuming I would ask. "Most people don't know. Logan made me promise not to tell. I didn't tell my Mom."

"Did you know any of the men you saw under the tree, Katie?"

"No. One, but I can't say his name. Didn't see his face, just heard his voice and remembered where he lives. Down by the old jail."

"Why can't you say his name?"

"I don't know it. He told them to quit digging, but they laughed at him. One of the guys said, "Too late, old man, you already told us where to dig."

I must find the man. But I must be calm, so I don't frighten this little girl. Much as I hate to do it, I will warn Katie's mother to keep her at home. Oh, how I would have hated the restriction at her age.

"Katie, thank you so much for telling me. Don't you worry about anything. Stay out of the tree like Logan told you. Grave robbers are dangerous. And you must tell your mother. I will speak to her, too."

"OK. I keep hoping the Little People will stop the grave robbers, but the wrong people keep dying." Her face twists as she struggles not to cry.

The Little People. Forgot about them. Must have been the Little People who whirled in my dream world in Chicago. They made me pay attention. Some believe they are a merely a myth, a legend, or just a story. I wish. Never seen one of them other than in my dream but their power is undeniable. I'm here because of their demand, and Logan's plea.

13

"Carlisle Investigations. This is Ellie."

"Uh. I was going to leave a message."

"You called, but you don't want to talk to me?" I feel my face redden as I recognize the voice.

"Uh, um...this is Roger Wood, Ellie. I need to talk to you."

"The infamous Sergeant Wood. Still tripping the rez trying to get answers? Last I heard you weren't having much luck."

"Can we keep this civil, Ellie? I need your help. Been wasting time there. Your people won't talk to cops. Especially ones they call city cops."

"You're right. I think we discussed this the first time. You told me you didn't need a female, wannabe cop messing up your case, as I recall. Even threatened to arrest me, which you had no authority to do. What's different now?"

"Insulting women is my specialty these days. Finding out whether Hank Andrews has sold Indian babies for decades isn't. Can we meet somewhere? Soon?"

"Sure, but let's start over. We have no hope of finding answers for either of us if we continue on this path."

He arrives the next morning.

I'm glad Chance has a meeting in Salem. I haven't told him about his adoptive mother's allegations against her husband, nor am I ready to deal with two testosterone driven hot heads in the same room. Not yet.

Chance and Rose were here last night, so I told them the sergeant called.

"We've agreed we won't work with him," Chance says.

"He can be a jerk, but we'll find some way to get the information we need to prove Mark's innocence if the cop's case is tied to finding the killer," Rose says.

"And Grandma wants me to help you bring Mark home, Ellie."

I have not forgotten it, but he's trying to help. And Grandma's expectations are the most compelling reasons to put my writing on hold and tackle this mess. Her faith he will come home gives me the courage to begin.

Roger Wood is apologetic. He announces he has been promoted to detective. I ask if we can just call him Roger and he agrees. I don't want a constant reminder I'm working with a cop. It's not going to be easy, mister. Your looks can't influence me.

I relish the surprised look on his face when we enter my office, a converted bedroom behind the kitchen. Small, bright, with a window framing the large cedars and firs in the backyard, the office contains the latest in office machines. Law books and investigation manuals fill the bookshelves on two walls.

I wait, enjoy his facial expression when he notices my name on the spines of several investigation texts I placed together so he wouldn't miss them. He turns toward me and accidentally knocks over a pile of magazines. I pretend not to notice, ease onto the desk chair and look intently at the cop, showing my best smile.

"I organize law offices and teach organizational skills to lawyers and investigators. I don't let any of them see my office."

Roger smiles. I think he relaxes a little.

He moves some books off a chair seat and sits down opposite me, shifting to look at me when he says, "You cannot imagine the hassle I'll get from the guys when they hear I've asked a PI, a female PI, for help in sorting out Vivian's allegations."

"Tell me what you have learned since you were last here." I won't ask him what I can do for him. I'm taking charge. No need for him to know my heart is pounding out of my chest.

"Years of interviews, scene visits, reading and re-reading reports, making arrests and I end up with crazy Vivian's stories. Not much in exchange for losing my life, huh?"

The tan lines haven't quite faded where his wedding ring used to be.

"Your wife got tired of sharing the bed with dead people, right?"

He looks shocked.

"Hey, Roger, we've all been there. Doesn't matter if you're a cop or a PI, when we get involved in a case, something must go. Too often it's the people we love the most."

"PIs go through it, too?"

"Oh, yeah. Those important people in our lives can't take it anymore and first thing you know, we're out on our rears and the case is all we have left. Why do you think I live by myself? My old man had no quarrel with my work since it paid the bills while he drank up his meager earnings. He didn't understand mine wasn't an eight to five job or maybe a baby needs a father."

"Sorry, I know what you mean. Not the drinking part. She didn't drink."

"It's difficult, if not impossible, to have a personal life if you're good at your job."

"I haven't had a personal life for so long I forget what it was like. My brothers gripe because I never have time for them."

"Hey, if we find a solution to the problem, we'll be rich, Roger."

"An old detective I met in Portland a long time ago told me, 'It's a disease, son. A virus. It gets in your gut, in your brain and you become what it needs you to be. You do what must be done. It can drive you crazy, cost you your family, your health, your sanity. Be careful or it will own you.' I was too young to understand. Too full of myself."

He stares out the window, then turns to me.

"You're not making me feel any better."

"Not my job."

"What is your job?"

"That's up to you. You are the one asking for help."

"I want to figure out if Vivian's suspicions about Hank are true or if Vivian is as crazy as she seems. I can't let it go. If he's done this, he should be arrested. It's also important for Chance to know the truth, one way or another."

"Chance doesn't know much about this yet."

"OK. Works for me. Everywhere I turn, I get the same thing; either people won't talk to me at all, or they say, 'Have you talked to Ellie?' I've never had this much trouble getting information. Never seen a town where people are so tightlipped and suspicious of outsiders as they are on this reservation."

"This isn't a reservation. You must understand our history, at least this much of it. This was a reservation. Established in the 1850s. A hundred years later, the government terminated us. Declared we weren't Indians anymore and this wasn't a reservation."

I notice his puzzled expression and continue, "Makes a lot of sense doesn't it? Sign a paper and obliterate the whole race. Some of our leaders did sign those papers. We've only recently sought restoration as a tribe and now we're fighting to get some of our land back. There is no reservation. …yet."

He continues to stare at me.

"They tried to exterminate our ancestors in what they called the "Indian Wars" down near the California border. Soldiers rode into our camps and shot as many people as they could, especially the women and children, as they slept or when they ran. Those soldiers liked running targets."

"Do we have to talk about this, Ellie? I know the old Injuns had it rough. Let's stick to the investigation."

Ignoring his protests and disrespectful slang, I continue, "Shoot 'em in the back, in the face, in bellies swollen with new life, get them off the face of the earth. Those they didn't kill were marched over the hills or sent up the coast by barge to this valley, the new concentration camp. The soldiers and government-appointed agents prevented escape. Called it a reservation."

"Ellie, please. …"

"I don't care if your patience is thin. If you want my help, you will hear this."

He frowns, but nods.

"Took away all their weapons and hunting equipment. Wouldn't allow the men to hunt for deer, or to fish for salmon. My people, my ancestors, were hunters and gatherers. The government's plan was to turn them into farmers. They were told to plant potatoes. Don't think about leaving this room, Roger, if you want my help."

He turns at the door. "Why is this so important for you to say, Ellie?"

"It's not important for me to say. It is important for you to hear so you can understand the people you want to interview and ask for their help."

His steel blue eyes lock in battle with this brown-eyed earth woman. I see his mind settle, watch him return to the chair. I detect a bit of playacting on the detective's part. He knows more about our people and customs than he wants me to realize.

Roger nods again and I continue.

"No one taught them what to do with the potatoes. Records show hundreds died the first winters. They ate the flesh of their dead and rotting horses. While the potatoes decayed in the ground, fish swam the rivers and deer roamed the forest, our people were not allowed to hunt or fish. Most people here are descendants of those few who managed to survive starvation."

I pause to let this sink in.

He asks, "So, if this isn't a reservation, what is it?"

"Recently, a small group of people, Indians and white friends, formed a committee to explore restoration of the tribe. Congress will soon approve our restoration to federal recognition--only the second one in the nation."

"I thought you told me it isn't a reservation anymore."

"The tribe is almost restored. Soon we will be recognized as Indians again. We're still fighting to get some of our land base returned to us. We hope to build a casino on the coast and some tribal buildings here in Siletz. The city returned Government Hill to us. We don't trust outsiders who have racist attitudes like yours, Detective"

"I'm not racist, Ellie, but I don't buy the poor Injun stories."

"You are being ignorant and racist. We'll have to deal with that if you want my help." I stand with my hands on my hips, determined to show him how serious the issue is to me—to our possible collaboration. His silence betrays his desperation.

"Many outsiders who come here are up to no good. They hurt someone eventually, one way or another. Because of the discrimination and harsh treatment over the years, we do not like or trust cops. Especially FBI. A whole 'nother story. Might have something to do with this situation. We'll know soon enough."

"What the hell would the FBI have to do with this?"

"Like I mentioned, we'll wait and see. I'm taking a big chance talking to you. You've been in town so many times people wonder why you haven't arrested someone. Story's going 'round you're not a real cop."

"What?"

"People wonder who you really are. We must make something happen or I will be under suspicion. By the time the story gets around once, you will be FBI. Doesn't take much to be fit with a snitch jacket. I have some leeway because I'm related to so many folks. They knew me. Grew up with me. I left so there will be some who are suspicious, especially if you don't help me with the murder investigation, which of course, also includes the grave robbing problem."

"I come here, ask a few questions and suddenly I'm FBI and have to help you solve all your problems? How the hell did this happen?"

"You have our conversation a little skewed. You have information Chance's adoptive father may have bought him and may be selling babies. Chance believes his birth mother was Jean, the woman whose murder we are investigating. You say Vivian believes it, too. Seems to me we can safely assume all this might be connected. Maybe, if Hank Andrews is Chance's birth father, he killed Jean Kline, which would help us prove Mark Thom's innocence."

Roger growls out an unintelligible remark when I suggest he plan to be at my office early tomorrow.

"I'll have Chance come over. He doesn't have to work at the tribe's office on Saturdays unless there is a meeting, which there isn't this week. We can do a complete review of everything we're facing. Of course, we'll have to tell him about Vivian's suspicions. I doubt he'll like it.

"What time is early?"

"About ten, Indian time."

Before the front door slams, I hear, "About ten. Indian time. Whatever that means."

14

THE LEATHERY NEW CAR SMELL OF CHANCE'S JEEP WAGONEER fills my nose, leaving me anxious for fresh, clean air. I need the cool breeze that filters through the trees and wafts into my little house by the Siletz River.

I could open a window, though the rushing wind might make Chance irritable if it tangles his long, black hair flowing in a straight line from the top of his head to his mid back. He's kind of touchy about his appearance. Quite vain, in fact.

Seated in the luxurious front passenger seat, I listen to him explain this popular new category of vehicles called SUVs. But my mind wanders back to the previous evening spent sorting through the collection of transcripts, photos and newspaper articles regarding Jean's death and Mark's arrest and conviction.

"I am nervous about this trip, Chance. I've never visited Mark in prison. I was nine when he went away. Too young. Then, I wasn't an Indian anymore because the tribe was terminated by the government. I ran off with a guitar player who wandered through Siletz. Married him in Montana and had Logan. Even after Russ left and I made enough money in Chicago to travel home, I didn't visit Mark."

"You think he understands, Ellie?"

"Maybe. I've worked some of the biggest criminal defense cases in the nation. I'm usually in demand when Indian defendants need investigative assistance. I write about wrongful convictions, speak to countless groups. How did I manage to neglect my own cousin's plight?"

"Ellie, enough already. You're borrowing trouble. If he doesn't understand, you'll know why; right now, you're rambling. Marge told me the wailing of the elder women continued for days after my mother's body was discovered up on Dewey Creek."

"I know. Mama told me years later Grandpa Thom found Marge's battered body lying in his woodshed a few weeks after Mark's arrest. He grabbed his .30.30 and went looking for the man who attacked her but didn't find him."

"She didn't tell me. No wonder she started drinking. Wait, did she get pregnant? Do you think I am her son?"

"I honestly don't know, Chance. The thought has crossed my mind."

I have wondered if Chance was conceived in the rape. Is he Marge's son and not Jean's? Perhaps he should never find the truth. Knowing he was the child of a brutal rapist might not set well with him. I look at him driving his fancy new Jeep and marvel again at the physical similarities between him and the cousin who never returned to his family, the guy we are on our way to visit at the state pen in Salem.

"Ellie? You still here?"

"Sorry. I was thinking of how I simply accepted Mark was gone. Why didn't I question his guilt when I became an adult? Or when I began defense investigations and concentrating on wrongful convictions? Why didn't I visit him?"

"Here we go again. The way I see it. ..." Chance's ability to find humor in the situation evokes a pang of loneliness. So much like my dear lost son. Logan's death has been a little easier to bear in recent months. Late at night I feel guilty, struggle to determine if my heart substitutes Chance for Logan. Perhaps I am once again throwing myself into a case to escape my personal world. Chance brings me back to the moment.

"You were a little girl in puppy love with an older cousin. Your heart got broken."

"Enit! How would you know about such things?"

Chance continues, a smile playing across his face, "I think later you didn't want to seem really old."

"Old? I'm not old, you pipsqueak."

"Pipsqueak? The word dates you to prehistoric times."

I swat Chance's shoulder and laugh as I reach into the back seat and pull papers from my briefcase.

"We need to review this timeline before we get there."

"I'm surprised it's only a few pages."

"There isn't much substance in those transcripts."

"Still missing a lot of information, aren't we?"

"Yes, particularly all the investigation reports from the sheriff's office about Jean's murder," I remind him.

"How will we ever get them? No one at the sheriff's office will talk to us."

"We don't have a certified copy of her autopsy report or an Oregon birth record for you. It's interesting your adoptive mother has an original birth certificate that shows you were born in Portland, though the state has no record. We're almost to the prison. This will be a very difficult day, Chance. We will be different people when we return to the car."

He steers the car down the lane to the first available spot in the visitor's parking lot and shuts off the engine.

"Before we go in, Chance, remember there is a lot of nervousness in police communities since the South Dakota incident last year where the FBI attacked the Indians on the Pine Ridge Reservation. Don't push your luck with smart-aleck comments."

"Yeah, I know."

I hurry toward the main prison building. Dry maple leaves crunch under my feet. The musty, acrid, old building odor mingles with the crisp autumn air and burns my nostrils. I see the silhouette of a guard in the tower, rifle ready, and wonder if he is this alert for all visitors, or only ones with long black hair and brown skin.

I move, watched but unhindered, up the crumbling concrete stairway, through the front door to where two officers stand on either side of the inner door, waiting to direct visitors through the metal detector. I knew to leave my jewelry at home and to not wear shoes with metal in the soles. It took only one session of submitting to a full body search when a metal detector in an ancient New York state prison picked up the underwires in my bra to convince me to let gravity win. Today, I'm wearing my prison bra with no support stays or underwires to set off these machines.

This is Chance's first visit to any kind of jail. He will never make it through without setting off alarms. He will remove jewelry, his belt, and shoes before he gets past these guards. I tried to warn him.

A tall, thin man, with close-cropped graying hair and the requisite potbelly introduces himself after we sign in, then instructs me to follow him. I take only a couple of steps before another voice shouts from behind me, "Not you, young man. You're not going anywhere."

I glance back and see a young officer step between Chance and me. His left hand points toward the waiting area, the other hand ready to whip his pistol from its holster on his right hip. The guard stands ready, eager, to take Chance down. The gun is his only hope of accomplishing it.

"Wait there, Chance," I shout and hope he recognizes the futility of arguing; for once, he will think before he acts. Any argument from him will get both of us thrown from the building, with no opportunity to meet with Mark.

Anger flashes across the young Indian's face as he realizes that here he is nobody. His tribal position, the charm and finely chiseled good looks can command instant attention mean nothing to these men assigned to keep control within the prison walls. This is their territory and the guard, eager to make Chance understand, has a sarcastic tone as he explains. "You're not going anywhere, Chief. Take a seat over there."

I continue walking behind the sergeant and hope Chance won't react to the insulting stereotypical slur. I follow, tense and aware, ready to call for help at the slightest misstep by this guard leading me to an area that is not for visitors. After a few turns down narrow hallways, he opens a door and leads the way into a freshly painted, nicely furnished room where he motions for me sit.

"I'll be back with Mark. He asked to see you first," he says as he pulls the door shut.

The lock falls into place and I experience the familiar moment of panic. Besides my usual discomfort at being in a prison, there is the unfamiliarity of this room, this whole section of the facility. This is nowhere near the inmates' visiting rooms. It certainly isn't one of the usual attorney rooms used to interview defendants. I can think of no logical reason why we are in this part of the building. I've been in enough old prisons to know the difference between the regular visiting rooms and this one. They probably have this room wired for sound and maybe even cameras. The newly-painted walls, the fine oak conference table and chairs, and the matching bookcases lined with legal books indicate press conference. The scent of paint and lacquer blunt the unpleasant odor of mildew and mold, but there is nothing to identify the room, or its significance.

Suddenly, I realize my hand is gripping my purse. No one inspected it or ordered me to leave it in a locker; a definite violation of prison rules anywhere. Why would the sergeant let me keep it? Why didn't he search it?

With a click of the key in the lock, the sergeant steps back into the room.

"Here you go. Warden ordered the best room in the house because you had important business to tend to. So, here you are right next to the warden's office. He uses this for his official conference room when the media comes calling. I'll be right outside, Ms. Carlisle, if you need to escape from this big, ugly guy."

His laughter is cut off as the door clicks shut. He answered my concerns about the room, but I still have my purse.

I cannot speak or rise from the chair. Before me stands the cousin I have not seen in two decades. Now, through woman's eyes, he is not as tall as I remember, probably five feet ten at most. His long, black braids are touched with gray, his face older and creased with the wrinkles of a fiftyish man who has done hard time, his skin several shades lighter than those men at home who go outside at will.

The hands outstretched to me are not the supple young ones of the boy who braided my hair. Not the hands that taught me to hold a fishing pole, to peel bark from chittum trees and to stack fern fronds clipped from the shaded hillsides of our little valley. It doesn't matter. I would know him anywhere. I am nine again.

"Did you miss me?"

His question, so unexpected, yet so typical, releases long denied tears falling unhindered, down my cheeks. I take Mark's hand and lead him to a chair at the table, then walk around the table to face him. Groping in my purse for a tissue, I struggle to find words, any words.

Trembling, I answer, "Of course, I missed you. I couldn't understand what happened to you or why the sheriff took you away. I grew up and ran away to marry Russ. My life was a mess for a very long time. When my son and I began to build a good life far away from the rez, everything I hated about Siletz also came true in our new world. Only recently have I been able to miss you again, to understand I must find the answers to so many questions for our people. Like who raped Marge? Oh, I didn't mean to tell, Mark."

Why do I always talk too much? Grandma says it's 'cause I have too much white blood.

"Is that where young Chance Andrews came from? Why he is using the Thom name?

"No. It doesn't seem to be."

"Seems like a world-famous investigator could find an answer to those two simple questions."

Mark teases as he used to. I don't ask how he knew I am a PI. The prison grapevine. Nothing escapes the inmates' attention. Information is as valuable inside the walls as the drugs some manage to sneak through security. I remember when I called the warden to schedule this visit, he mentioned Mark read the newspaper feature about Chance.

"Speaking of Chance. …they wouldn't let him come in with me. He's extra mad by now, I'm sure."

"He'll be OK. He can come in later. I wanted some time alone with you. It's been a couple of days, you know."

I cringe with guilt.

"Yes, for sure. A couple of days. I'm so sorry, Mark."

He accepts my apology with a smile. "It's important you find who killed Jean. If you don't, nothing else will work in your investigation. The truth will never come out. The grave robbing will get worse. You have to prepare yourself and think this through."

"Do you know who killed her?"

I hate myself for asking. Not something I should have done. Tradition demands I be patient and wait for answers. It seems an impossible lesson for me to master. I can't determine what is behind Mark's steady gaze. His composure unnerves me. It is not the action of a guilty person, yet he provides no clue to the truth.

"If you're going to tell me you were guilty after all, I will not accept it. I know there's something rotten about this situation. I knew you were with Ruthie. I didn't know you lied until I read the transcript."

I hope the depth of my belief and the look in my eyes as I stare back at him strengthens my words. I am an investigator. I do the interviews, the interrogations, know how to find and analyze clues, get the confessions--not this time. I am not in control of this conversation. This is new to me. With any luck, he won't notice the beads of sweat on my forehead.

A smile plays briefly in the corners of Mark's mouth as he leans back in his chair, locks his hands behind his head. "I remember the little girl who always asked too many questions. You didn't buy my story, huh? When you were a little girl, or the grown-up investigator woman?"

"I told you, I didn't know what you did in the trial until a couple of weeks ago when a woman gave me a transcript. I knew the sheriff took you away. I was mad at you for leaving me. You broke my heart. I wanted to run away from Siletz. My husband, Russ, couldn't understand my continuing sorrow, my mistrust of men who always vanished out of my life. Like Tommy."

"Tommy. A name from the past. Good guy. Wonder what happened to him?"

"I don't know, and I don't care. He broke Mama's heart--and mine."

"It wasn't his choice."

"I know now. Mama explained before she died."

"So, what's the reason for Chance's comments in the article about the grave robbing?"

"More graves are robbed every week, Mark. We ask questions."

"Getting any answers?"

"No, but I have some suspicions."

I am not ready to talk about the graves yet. I must know if he under-stands my years of neglecting him, so I say, "When I realized I investigated wrongful convictions across the country, but never thought to look at your case, it wasn't an easy time for me,"

"You had to grow up to understand. You used your work to escape your life. Now you're back in your own skin again."

I gasp at his understanding. This man, my beloved cousin, hasn't seen me in decades, never as an adult, yet he understands me. A level of empathy I have only felt from Grandma Kline.

"So, have you decided who killed her? Jean, I mean," Mark asks.

The conversation has changed now. We are discussing what I know as an investigator. Questions will be allowed--perhaps even answered.

"I don't know. He's still around and getting nervous."

Mark leans across the table and grabs my hand with such force it sends my pen flying. "Nervous? What do you mean? Has he threat-ened you?"

I don't have to answer. My silence, my twitching about in the chair, my shaking hands, tell him all he needs to know.

"Only a phone call."

My tiny voice sounds much like little Ellie who hid behind things to watch life on the reservation. I worry as Mark walks to the door, knocks twice and steps back so the guard can enter.

"It's time to bring the young man in. Better take Ellie with you so he doesn't get an attitude."

The guard waves me to the door. I carry my purse, careful not to give the guard a reason to accuse me of smuggling something in for Mark. As we enter the unadorned reception area, with its peeling pale green paint and asbestos tile ceiling, I see Chance sitting on a metal folding chair, facing the entrance door where two hefty guards lean against the metal detector. To his left, windows overlook the parking lot. To his right is the cluttered sign-in desk manned by the obnoxious, pimple-faced guard with eager hand ready to show his gun.

Chance doesn't hear me when I say his name. I walk closer and he looks up to see me and the sergeant standing on either side of him.

"Chance. Come on. It's time to meet Mark." I rest my hand on his left shoulder.

"Maybe I don't want to meet him. I guess the two of you have every-thing figured out. No need for me to talk to him."

He looks to the door, starts to stand, but I press hard on his shoulder hoping to discourage any thought of leaving the building. He calms, stands and we move down the hall. The sergeant opens the door and I re-enter the room. Chance hesitates a moment. With a quick tuck of his shirt, a shoul-der shrug to readjust his jacket, he flips his hair back, smiles down at me, and strides into the room.

My frustration melts as I watch the two men move slowly, silently, toward one another. Years fade as I watch Chance, with his youthful good looks and eager stride so like the Mark I lost to the sheriff's truck. Life fast forwards when I turn toward Mark, still handsome and confident, older, weathered by prison life. They embrace, don't speak.

We choose chairs. I sit at one end of the long table. Chance and Mark sit facing one another, midway to the other end. Unable to bear the silence, I spit out, "Chance, this is Mark."

The men's laughter clatters around the room.

"Ah, little one. You can't stand the quiet, can you?"

The last time I heard those words from Mark we were in a fern patch up Dewey Creek. My tiny, nine-year-old hands were pressed against my mouth to stifle giggles as we watched a fawn slowly pick his way into the clearing. I lost the battle, as usual. The giggles burst through my tightly pressed fingers, sending the little deer scampering back into the protective underbrush of the coastal forest. Now, I grow silent, leaving it to Mark, my elder, who deserves the respect and honor I give Grandma Kline, to move the conversation.

"So, young man, I hear you thundered onto the rez in your fancy red pony, ready to tackle the bad guys." He smiles at the questioning look from Chance. "I hear things, you know. The 'rez holds no secrets from me."

Ha. You sure didn't know about Chance all these years.

"There are things. ..." Chance begins.

"Yes, 'things' to be taken care of," Mark interrupts. "Things you have no idea about." His voice rises, stern now, commanding.

Chance leans back in his chair, surprised by the man's intensity. I lean forward, anxious to observe the expected confrontation between youthful arrogance and maturity. Mark's next words, and his demeanor, are a surprise.

"You are both in so much danger." He looks at Chance and commands, "You must listen to me, boy. Think carefully about what I tell you. If you can't handle it, go away from our tribe. Find a new life. Forget us before you get killed."

I'm astonished to see tears flow down Mark's cheeks as he touches Chance's arms. I see shock on Chance's face. Now he will listen.

"I will tell you a story from long ago. When I finish, you must leave," Mark begins.

"Won't we talk about it?"

"No, this is a story to be told to you and Ellie. It is not a story to be discussed with anyone else. You will go away to decide what to do. If you decide to continue, Ellie will know what to do next. If you decide to leave

Siletz, to leave our people, you must do it respectfully and with no mention of my story."

"I'm not going. ..."

"Don't make decisions before you have facts. That is the way of the young and you were chosen for an elder's path, chosen early because our people are suffering. The ancestors have given you this path. It is a big responsibility. Because you are young, you can walk away."

Chance sits with his jaw set, eyes blazing. Mark has met his match.

I ask, "What if Chance decides to walk? Then what?"

"You have the same choice."

"Right! I can pack up and walk from our people. Leave them with the molested graves of our relatives, Grandma's broken heart and the fear of more murders in our family? You think I'm about to do that? You can't be serious. How could I walk away?"

"You did it once."

"I was young." Mark's retort hurts. I hate my hot tears and manage to glare at him, adult to adult.

"Yes, you were. You learned you needed your people. You came home again. Chance is young, Ellie. Remember, he only became an Indian yesterday. How can he understand what's at stake here?"

"Yesterday?" Chance stands and leans across the table. "Why would you say that? It's not like I'm a wannabe." His hands rest inches from Mark. Their eyes lock. "I am your relative. Same blood. Doesn't it make me an Indian?"

"Yes, by blood. Being an Indian must also come from the heart. It will come from understanding our ways and our people. You have much to learn, Beginning with listening."

Chastised, Chance folds back into his chair, crosses his arms and waits.

"We don't have much time. The warden assured me I could take my time since I never have visitors. He could change his mind."

My heart hurts at the words. I hope my guilt at not ever visiting doesn't show on my face like it feels inside me.

"I will tell the story without interruption," Mark says and looks at Chance for emphasis. Then he rises, walks behind my chair and places his hands on my shoulders.

"A long time ago, when I was a young man, this one was a nuisance girl, always tagging along wherever I went. We picked fern. I tried to teach her to catch salmon in the river and dig clams in the sand by the bay. She wasn't very good at it but made me smile. She thought she knew all my secrets. There was one she didn't know. There was one place I never took her."

Mark pauses, brushes his hand across my hair and walks over to his own chair. We wait while Mark looks into Chance's eyes for what seems an eternity.

"I went to the ocean a lot. First, I walked through the hills, usually on Saturday. Needed a whole day to get there and back," he begins. "When I learned to drive Grandpa Thom's old black pickup truck, I went more often. On one of those trips I met the most beautiful girl. Tall, with long red hair blowing in the ocean wind as she walked along the tide's edge. Bright blue eyes and a tinkling laugh. Exactly the kind of girl a skinny Indian kid couldn't touch. They used to have laws against it. Earlier, not then. White parents didn't allow it. Our people encouraged us to date Indian girls."

Now he pulls out a chair and sits down, never taking his eyes off Chance.

"But, we managed."

He chuckles and leaves out the parts I want to know. I imagine Chance is eager to hear this part of the story, too. When Mark continues, he skips a lot.

"Eventually she met Marge at a ballgame. Then it became easier for us because she could come to visit my sister. We spent hours together planning, loving, talking. We were going to be married as soon as she graduated--when her parents no longer could control her life. We were young. It sounded simple."

He drinks from the glass of water the guard placed on the table. "She occasionally dated other guys in her town. Didn't want her parents to find out about me. She spent a lot of time with one of her guy cousins, too. Most of her friends, and everyone in Siletz, knew. The difference was many of her friends thought she was rebelling against her parents by spending time with me. My family saw our love. Grandma Kline called us spirit souls-- what some people say are soul mates.

"There was one guy who wanted her bad. Friend of her cousin Hank. She dated him when he was home from training. Another cover to keep her parents happy. He told her she would marry him as soon as she realized what she was giving up being with me. He spent a lot of time up Dewey Creek hunting or fishing, maybe just nosing around. My cousins often saw him there. He worked at the Toledo Mill through the summer, then went away for training. Funny thing, I never ran into him."

I feel Mark's eyes on me and remember the look. His way of keeping me from asking questions.

"Right before Ruthie graduated from high school, we had more problems with vandals in the cemeteries. Then, an uncle found one of the graves opened. Bone fragments and beads were scattered across the ground. He called the sheriff and a deputy came out. Harrington, I think. Yeah, Dan Harrington. Same guy who started the investigation into Jean's death. Happened several weeks later, of course. Harrington died before he solved anything. After, the sheriff wouldn't send anyone when graves were opened, uncle told me."

"What happened to Harrington?"

Hm. Apparently, it is permissible for Chance to ask questions.

"Died in a car wreck right after Jean was found. Strange. He wrecked on a straight part of the old highway in the middle of the night. No other cars around. I saw one newspaper article about it.

"When Jean was found," Mark continues, "Grandma Kline told me, 'I told her he was a bad man. I told her.' Grandma didn't know who Jean was seeing, or maybe she was too scared to tell. I heard Grandma quit speaking to anyone when the sheriff took me away. Just sat in her chair and stared. Some of the aunties went there every day to fix food. Went at night to put her to bed and returned in the morning to put her back into the chair."

I remember going many times to help Mama take care of Grandma. I sat beside her stroking her hands, willing her to speak. Gradually, Grandma returned to us. She never mentioned Jean's name, or Mark's, in all these years until Chance came. In a house filled with photos of her large family, there is not one of Jean or Mark, as if neither ever existed. I wonder if he knows.

"It was obvious I couldn't win in a white man's court," Mark says. "I told Marge to send Ruthie away. I would be in prison for a long time, but the real killer would still be out there. Ruthie would fight to get the conviction overturned. She and my family would be harassed and scared. I told her to go away. She left, moved to Alaska with her relatives and later married a fisherman."

Glancing at me, Mark says, "Marge kept me informed when she wasn't too drunk to write."

He moves from his chair, paces back and forth. I wonder why he hesitates. When he finally sits down, he says, "I did not kill Jean. You must believe it. I will tell you who I think did. You can decide if you will stay to help our people."

The name rocks Chance back in his chair. He sits, mouth slack, eyes wide.

I suspected someone in the legal system, perhaps a cop. The name Mark threw at us will take the investigation on a different path. Chance's stunned look doesn't reveal his decision.

15

THE WIND WHISTLES OUTSIDE, BRUSHING THE LIMBS OF THE old cedars across the edge of my porch roof. Today the summer storm sounds, usually comforting in their familiarity, add to my nervousness.

I expected the two-hour drive home to be uncomfortable. The silence was a surprise. I exit the truck, purse and briefcase in hand, fumble with my keys and enter the living room without so much as a word or signal from Chance. My thoughts race, nearly obscuring the sound of his tires crunching gravel as he heads back to the street.

I make a sandwich of leftover elk roast and spicy mustard between two slices of bread from the loaf I baked in the early morning hours before we left for Salem, then settle onto the couch, wrapped in the Pendleton blanket, too tired to build a fire. I lose track of time, know I should sleep, but can't accept the information Mark presented.

He insisted we must accept his words to save our own lives and those of many others inside the tribe and out. I can't, or perhaps won't. How will Chance make the leap?

My hand brushes against remnants of the half-eaten sandwich and knocks the plate to the floor. As I reach for it, I see the glimmer of the silver band on my finger. The ring! With all the shock and commotion from what I will remember as 'the meeting,' I forgot about the beautiful gift from Mark.

He has learned silversmithing in prison. The ring he created especially for me is a wide band of silver, beautifully engraved with symbols of our childhood. There is the river, the fern he taught me to pick, the eels that used to race up the creeks in the spring, a deer and a tiny little pick-up truck, a reminder of Grandpa Thom. It is such a delicate, artistic piece. I marvel not only at the artistry and the symbolism, but it fits so perfectly. How did he know what size to make it? Mark didn't answer when I asked.

It is so cold in this room the tips of my fingers are numb. Time to be a responsible human again. I'll build a fire and then I'll think.

The blanket drops onto the couch when I stand to push my feet into furry slippers. I trudge out of the living room, through the kitchen and out to the back porch for kindling and stove wood. My arms will be full, so I leave the back door open despite the wind and rain pounding the porch. The wood gathered, I step back through the door and freeze. Someone is in the house.

No one passed me on the porch. There isn't room for someone to slip by unnoticed even in my present state of confusion. Only a sliver of a ghost could have squeezed by in the space left when I leaned over to get wood. The front door is locked. I'm sure. I never forget to lock my doors. There *is* someone in the house. I am still, waiting, wondering what to do, wishing I had not left my gun in the bedroom.

"Ellie, it's me, Chance. Are you going to leave the door open all night?"

The wood crashes to the floor as I stagger to one of the straight-backed oak kitchen chairs, my heart racing.

"What the hell, Chance? Why would you do that? Couldn't you knock?"

"I did. When you didn't answer, I thought you were asleep, so I came in."

"Good thing for you I wasn't asleep. If I'd been in the bedroom, I might have shot you."

His instant smile is calming. I begin to gather the spilled wood.

"Get over here and help me."

I snicker at how quickly he obeys. I also notice he closes and locks the back door. He's nervous, too.

Laying out the paper and kindling to start the fire, I realize I should have heard Chance's Jeep approach before I went to the back porch. How long had he been sitting out there? Was this what caused me to stir from my nap and knock the plate onto the floor?

"I didn't bring the Jeep. I went for a walk to try to clear my mind and make sense of everything and here I am."

"A walk! You live at least three miles from here. Are you telling me you have been out in this storm all this time? Are you crazy? Look at you. You have only soggy pants and a thin, wet tee shirt on. Let's get those wet clothes off. Bring them to the bathroom and I'll put them into the washer."

"And how is the washer going to make my pants and shirt dry?" Chance teases.

"And you're barefooted. Good lord. I don't know what you were thinking."

I grab his boots from near the front door and start toward the stove.

"Probably the same thing you were thinking sitting in front of a cold stove. People would have felt sorry for me if I'd been killed by a falling tree in this windstorm. Who would feel sorry for a woman who sits and watches herself freeze?" He ducks as one of his boots sails past him and lands with a slosh on the kitchen floor.

I look at him for a long moment, then walk into the spare bedroom and close the door. I haven't been in this room much since moving into the house. I stored all Logan's belongings here for later decisions. There are clothes that will fit Chance. Clothes Logan wore before he died. He liked Chance.

I gather underwear, heavy wool socks, a bright red tee shirt with "Warrior Power" emblazoned on the front, a lightweight gray sweatshirt and matching pants, then open the door and step back into the living room.

"Here. Take these to the bathroom. Take a quick shower to warm yourself. We don't have time for you to get sick."

He takes the clothing without comment, closes the bathroom door behind himself and hollers, "I hope you have the icebox of a room warmed up when I get out there. Some breakfast would be nice, too."

I smile, build a fire and head for the kitchen.

"Where do we start?"

Chance's words are expected, though I feel a twinge of resentment when he speaks them. I don't want to start. Don't want to think. I want it all to go away. The table is littered with breakfast remains. He ate everything offered, as I knew he would. Sourdough pancakes, fried venison steaks, scrambled eggs. His plate is slicked clean. Like Logan. Maybe it's the clothes.

As the early morning light filters through the steamed windows, I say, "I simply do not know where to start. This is not like any case I've worked. There are so many twists and tangles. Too many personal ties, for sure."

I've told him about Logan's attempt to fight against the grave robbers. He seemed genuinely astonished, but I am not in a generous mood. Everyone is on my suspect list.

"Come on, we have to start somewhere. Say the word and I'll start looking."

He's trying to lighten the heavy burden of knowing things we wish were not true. Trying to help, but I'm not used to working with a partner.

I prefer to do my own thinking and planning. The ringing phone makes me jump.

"Who could call at this early hour?" I blurt as I reach for the phone.

"You didn't take my advice and get out! Listen, bitch, this is your last warning!"

I hold the phone away from my ear to let Chance hear.

"Stay away from this. Stay away from Mark Thom. Don't go to the prison again or you won't make it home next time. And keep your fancy Injun away, too."

As I put the receiver down to disconnect the call, Chance asks who it was.

"I don't know. The same voice again."

I feel fear almost as overwhelming as when a shank was held to my throat by an unhappy client in an old Illinois prison.

"I think it's time to talk to the sheriff again, Ellie. There must be something he can do."

"Previous attempts to get the sheriff involved in the investigation of Jean's murder and the grave robbing have met with insults and disinterest. The sheriff has been in the department for years, Chance. He was a deputy when Jean was murdered. Nothing was done then, except to convict the wrong man. Now he's sheriff, he doesn't care anymore than he did then."

"I know! Your boyfriend, the city cop from River City, has tried to get them involved, too. Have you heard anything from him lately?"

"Detective Wood? He'll be here. He's still kind of a jerk, though."

"True, but we have to get information out of the sheriff's office on the old case, don't we, Ellie?"

"Yes, we do. We may have to get most of the details from the people who were around then. Doesn't look like the sheriff will ever release the file-- if it exists."

I sit on the couch, frustrated, twisting my hair around my fingers, summoning the professional perspective I usually bring to a case.

In the bathroom, I check on the laundry, pull the wet clothes from the washer, put them into the dryer and turn it on. Reluctant to return to the dreaded conversation, I gather an armload of white items, stuff them into the washer and add detergent. As I turn the knob to the 'on' position, I try to think of other tasks to delay my return to the living room.

"Hey, El. Come on out of there. I don't want to do this, either, but we seem to be stuck with it."

Think! I must think. This cold case and the grave robbing must be handled in straightforward, carefully planned steps. I search my mind for the right words, search my heart for the right feelings.

Chance takes his usual seat in the chair near the window. Logan's chair. He didn't live in this house, of course, but it is the chair he liked in Chicago.

I glance at Chance staring through the rain-soaked window and notice the trees swaying to the will of the storm. I suppose he's waiting for the professional Ellie to quit swaying and return to the conversation. When peace comes, followed by the instinct that allows me to find the proper place to start an investigation, I speak with intent.

"I think we must talk about our feelings. Discuss what Mark told us."

Chance swings his chair to face me as I continue, "Then we will try to piece it all together with what we already know about Jean's murder."

"Shouldn't we. …?"

I ignore the interruption. I don't want Chance to speak before I get the question out. The question must be answered before we can continue our investigation. I reach for his hand, look into his troubled eyes.

"Chance, how did you feel when Mark whispered he believes Hank Andrews is your biological father and murdered Jean because she was pregnant?"

16

CHANCE HAS NO ANSWER FOR MY QUESTION. NOT WHEN I asked it last night. Not now. He must decide whether he can accept it before he can decide if he'll stay with our tribe and help solve these mysteries.

We are driving deep into the forest this morning in search of solitude, somewhere away from people and distractions, somewhere to sort through our feelings. Chance has never been up Dewey Creek to where Jean's body was found, so we head there, spend some time and move on. He parks in a clearing off the side of a gravel logging road and we hike to the creek to the tune of cawing jays who announce our arrival.

Chance sits on a flat rock and rests his back against the massive roots of an ancient cedar tree. I stand opposite him, leaning against a tree trunk, staring at the water. Thoughts swirl in my mind, smash against one another, echoing the intensity of the water crashing against boulders. Did Hank kill Jean, as Mark believes? Mark thinks he killed her because she was pregnant. If it's true, why did he keep the baby? And how did Hank get the baby?

"Ellie, as much as I dislike my Dad, I still felt an instant loyalty to him when Mark made his accusation. I wanted to defend him, but I couldn't." He pauses, then continues. "Mark's statement sounded so logical when he told us Hank killed Jean because she was pregnant. Like he said, Hank was married and fooling around. Jean probably refused to have an abortion. Remember Mark said he thought Hank killed Jean and convinced his deputy friend, Kramer, to put it on me? Mark also said, 'Hank knew I was seeing Ruthie. She's his cousin.'"

I push my hair back, take a deep breath before saying, "I took it he really knew all about it. Maybe Mark's guessing like the rest of us, Chance."

"Yeah, if Dad is Ruthie's cousin, why haven't I ever heard of her? He has never mentioned a cousin in Alaska."

The midmorning sun shines on us as Chance tosses tiny gray rocks into the creek. The welcome warmth is relaxing and helps ease the tension and confusion. Chance reaches into the pack on the ground near his left leg, draws out a canteen of water and lifts it to his lips. As he tips his head back to drink, the jays caw again.

Warned, I step forward, my .38 Special already drawn from its hidden holster and pointed directly at Sheriff Kramer as he lumbers down the hillside. Chance sees me, turns and immediately slides his right hand down to his holster as he stands. Now his .357 is also pointed at the sheriff.

"Hey, Ellie, It's me, Sheriff Kramer. You, too, kid! What are you doing out here?"

"What are you doing here, Sheriff? Are you following me again?"

"Put it down, boy, before I arrest you. You can't pull a gun on a sheriff."

"I sure as hell can when the idiot sneaks up on me for no reason."

Chance lowers his gun, slowly lets the hammer down and pushes the safety into place. He doesn't move from the spot where he first whirled to face the intruder. Neither has the sheriff moved since being confronted by my gun. Short, maybe five feet six, with a definite potbelly and an 'it's about time to retire' look about him, the sheriff doesn't appear dangerous, but why is he here? I lock eyes with Kramer and wait for an explanation.

Out stared, the sheriff speaks. "I was out here driving around this morning and saw the truck. Didn't know it was yours. Thought I'd see who was lurking about."

Liar.

Chance stays put, remains silent. He has reason to know the sheriff is lying. One of the deputies tailed him again last Friday. They know the old black Ford truck is Chance's beater. It is battered, with blue paint here and there. Much better to drive on the back roads than his Jeep. The sheriff and his lackeys have no problem switching a tail from one vehicle to another. Wherever he goes these days, a deputy is close behind. He's mentioned he remembers Grandma Kline's comments about the sheriff being happy to arrest him. "What did I do, other than be an Indian?" he asked me this morning.

"Can we sit? My back hurts when I stand on a side hill like this," Kramer asks.

"Sure. Come on down. You can be comfortable while you explain what you're doing sneaking around the reservation."

I watch the sheriff slump heavily onto one of the cedar stumps and kick his heavy combat boot at a rotten log, releasing a parade of tiny ants.

"I've been coming out here a lot lately. Hoping the newspaper article about Chance would attract the murderer back here. When I saw your truck, I thought I'd caught him." He shifts to one side and looks behind himself.

"So, you refuse to come when we call you. You won't sit down with us to talk about our investigation of Jean's murder, or help us stop the grave robbers, but you'll sneak around, alone, in Indian Country. Why?" Chance asks as he puts his gun away.

I keep mine at my side.

"Listen, boy. ..." Again, Kramer looks around and changes positions.

"Why are you so nervous, Sheriff?" Chance says. "My gun's put away."

There are other men above us, for sure. I wish I could warn Chance.

"Look, I want this killer as much as you do. I was a deputy when this happened. We didn't get the killer, but I thought this was over. Now it seems like there's more work to do."

They didn't get the killer? Mark will be glad to hear this. I don't dare look at Chance. The stupid sheriff doesn't realize what he has admitted.

Chance chokes back his anger enough to say, "If you're so interested, why don't you do more investigation? What about Ellie? Why won't you give her a copy of your files?"

"Ellie? This little squaw?"

Jerked to his feet in one swift motion, the sheriff can only stare into the smoldering eyes of the angry young Indian. Chance draws his right hand back, squeezes it into a fist as he holds the squat, trembling man against the cedar tree with his left hand.

I see victory in the pale, watery eyes of the sheriff. Not fear, victory.

"Chance, stop! He wants you to hit him. He'll arrest you. Stop!"

"You son-of-a-bitch." Chance steps back from the tree, releases his hold, and Kramer falls to the ground.

The continued cawing of jays nearly covers the softer sound of boots breaking tiny twigs as two deputies move out of the shadows toward us, guns drawn. My heart thumps as I realize what could have happened to Chance if he had been here alone. Arrested--or killed.

"It's okay, boys. Me and the Injuns were coming to an understanding."

The sheriff stands, brushes bark chunks and ants from his uniform, a thin smile spread across his puffed, sallow face. He motions the deputies to retreat up the hill, then throws a last hate-filled look at Chance.

"Watch your step, kid. Ellie Carlisle, you best remember who you are!"

We watch until the three men are up the hill out of sight, listen for crunching of heavy footsteps on the old gravel road. Minutes later I hear the faint whir of an engine. When the sound fades, my nerves settle some.

Chance gathers his pack, pulls his pistol from the holster, and heads up the hill to the old Ford. He checks the truck's perimeter and under-carriage carefully, then we climb in, make a U-turn and head home. I can finally put my gun away.

"We didn't get the real killer. Can you believe he said that? The crazy loon sheriff doesn't know what he admitted, Chance."

We are silent for a long time, struggling with the realization the investigation has taken a new and more sinister turn. Finally, I say, "We have wanted the sheriff's file on Jean's murder. Now it is vital. We have to find a way to get it."

"He's denied the file exists, Ellie."

"Maybe it doesn't. We can't take his word for it. I think he has reasons for it to have disappeared. We need a cop who can get close enough to the sheriff to win his trust."

"What can we do? We can't be this close to proving Mark's innocence and let it go. The bastard knows who killed Jean. He probably also knows who digs in our graves. Now I understand why my people don't trust him."

"I'll pray Roger changes his mind. Meanwhile, you be careful, Chance. We've made the sheriff look foolish in front of his deputies. He'll be looking for his chance to arrest you. Or shoot you."

"I know."

17

TODAY I'M VISITING GRANDMA KLINE IN HER LITTLE HOME ON the Hill. Investigating by committee has not been productive. At least not as productive or as quick as I am used to. It is time to get some input from an elder and Grandma is the one I trust.

As Grandma opens her door her bedraggled cat bursts past me and runs for the forest. I'm glad but wonder why she dislikes me. Grandma says it's because I talk too much. "Cat used to peace and quiet."

Inside, I notice the house is very warm on this cool Fall day. But I know Grandma thinks it is just perfect, so I shed my sweater without comment and join her in the kitchen.

"I need to go to Upper Farm today, Ellie."

"Sure, Grandma. I need your opinion on some situations. We can discuss those while we drive up there. Who are we seeing?"

"No people. Burial grounds calling me. Something wrong with relatives there."

"Oh, I hope not, Grandma. We have had reports of possible loot-ers approaching some of the family plots, but I'm told they have all been chased away. It is difficult to monitor all the burial grounds, though. I'm sorry if you feel someone violated a relative's grave." There are no phones in a burial ground, of course. The call Grandma feels is not manmade.

"Talk about your questions now, Ellie," she says as she gets settled in the passenger seat.

We meet a car or two as we leave the Hill. Heads turn when they see Grandma in the car with me. Soon the phone lines will buzz with the news we were last seen heading east on Logsden Road. Someone will drive by after we arrive at the site, so they can hurry to the Logsden Store to call to someone in Siletz. It's the way of our people.

"I hate to ask this question, Grandma, but how do I contact Russ?"

"Hmmm. Russell? The man you hate and never want to speak to again in your whole life? I think I don't know where he is."

No lazy talk today, I see. To get to Russ, I'll have to pass a test with this wise woman. She's no different than the rest of us who want to stay ahead of the latest news. If Russ and I talk, it will be big news in this little valley. But I must.

"I have information Logan had an important discussion with his father just before the wreck. Russ reportedly knew Logan planned to put a stop to the grave robbing. He tried to warn Logan of the danger, but Logan got an attitude about Russ trying to be his dad."

"You want to holler at Russell?"

"No. I want to find out whether my son died in a wreck caused by teenagers drinking, or if he was murdered by grave robbers because I didn't warn him, Grandma."

"You're hollering at me and you like me."

I see the small crinkle of a smile and know I must lighten up a bit.

"Yes, and I am sorry. But I really don't plan to badger Russ about times gone past. Ellie the investigator has to get answers and she suspects he has some."

"Phone number at my house. What else you need to know?"

"I think you know who Chance's real parents are, or maybe just his mother. Why did you say, 'Boy not know the truth?' Was Jean his mother? Or maybe Marge? It is so important to him, Grandma, and I think it is a key to who killed Jean."

"No, not them. Not Jean. Not Marge."

"Truth, Grandma? Neither of them? Then who? Do you know? Of course, you do. Who? Please." I have trouble keeping my mind on the road.

"Yes. Truth. But I cannot tell. I promised never to tell, only to confirm if he found mother."

"You promised? Who? His mother?"

"Yes."

"And do you know who his father is?"

"Yes. Can't tell."

"And you aren't the only one in this tribe who knows, are you? Everyone knows the secret just like everyone knew who my father was."

Silence.

But before I move to the next question, I see the burial grounds in the distance. As we approach a family cemetery in this part of the old reservation, it is obvious which graves were hit. By the time I park the car and open my door, Grandma's wails smash against the mountain and echo across the valley.

"I will check to see whose grave is right there, Grandma," I said, not expecting my words to penetrate her agony.

"Baby! It is baby niece. She drowned in '35." Grandma says as she exits the car and heads toward the grave, her chest heaving with painful sobs.

Oh my God. Her baby niece. *Finger bones.* The realization shocks me. But not as much as seeing my 92-year-old grandmother go down to her knees and begin to scoop handfuls of dirt into the gaping holes of her little niece's grave. Thank god nothing is visible. No casket, no bones. Just holes. Not deep enough to have reached the baby.

"Grandma. No. Here let me help you up. We will have some of your grandsons come do this. We'll have the drum group and singers come, too. We'll fix it for you." In the car, I use tissues to wipe her tears and brush some of the dirt from her hands, knowing replacing the dirt will not fix the hole in Grandma's heart.

"Now you know, Ellie? Really know?"

Holding my beautiful grandmother in my arms, I say through sobs, "I see it is real, Grandma. People are digging in our graves. I know now why you are so frightened and angry. I thought I knew, but oh god, I didn't."

Later, when we had calmed ourselves and I could drive home, I said, 'Grandma, it's wrong on so many levels, but our county DA won't do anything about it because he thinks the law is only for dead white bodies, for *humans.* No one cares in the outside world. Not in this nation full of politicians descended from families whose leaders vowed extermination in their westward push for land and gold. Full of people who attempt to teach children our Native culture by digging for arrowheads and making fake tomahawks."

Grandma sits patiently while I rant. Over the years this burial ground has been hit the hardest. Diggers took beads, rifles, whatever they could steal for their collections. Now, with the chance to make money from leftover items and maybe some bones, the plots have been hit again, perhaps by a new generation.

I knew all this. I made a nice speech in the tribal meeting, but today I know in a different way. I feel the burden of responsibility in a new way. I ache with pain for the elders who have suffered for far too many decades. I think I'm becoming Ellie the Indian woman, finding my way back to our ways.

18

———

Back at Grandma's house, we find she has several "just wanting to say 'Hi'" messages. Some from folks she hasn't heard from in months. Curiosity rules the town. Someone wanted to be first to talk to her after we returned from our trip to the burial grounds.

While she settles into her chair, I put on a pot of coffee and make some peanut butter and blackberry jam sandwiches. Grandma's favorite. I hesitate to ask more questions after our emotional discovery.

She takes the sandwich plate and coffee cup and places them on the little table beside her chair and motions for me to draw a chair near to the other side of the table. She looks ready to talk, but still I hesitate.

"I have some information, Ellie. I had a call last week from a friend in California. You remember? From the Yurok tribe. She told me there is a new group called Northwest Indian Cemetery Protection Association. NICPA. First one in the country. They have worked for so many years to stop the looters of their gravesites, especially by the universities and museums down there. Always digging. Always stealing. In 1970 she and the men made a real group. The sheriff is beginning to listen to them."

"Wonderful!" I say, keeping my comments sparse so Grandma can talk.

"She sent names and phone numbers you can get from the top drawer in my bedroom. Someone might be able to help you."

"I will call, Grandma. As you know better than I do, grave robbing has been a national problem since the white man first landed, it seems. One U.S. president looted hundreds, maybe thousands, of Indian graves in his scientific studies. Some Army doctors specialized in collecting the brains of Indian leaders and warriors in their attempts to determine if we were the same race as the white soldiers."

"Just few years ago bad people arrested in Oregon for digging in Indian graves. Someday, you write big book. Tell all about atrocities. You hear?"

"Yes, Grandma, I hear you. Can't think about a book right now."

19

My hand fumbles across the nightstand in search of the button to silence the irritating alarm, then I burrow into my nest of blankets to avoid the shock of early morning in the frostbitten house. I love wood heat, but it's a shivery time between feet hitting the cold floor and feeling warmth from a new fire. I can't snuggle in my cozy bed for long. Roger and Chance will be here at ten for what may be an all-day session.

Up now, wrapped in an old light blue terrycloth robe, I plod toward the stove, my feet warm again in fuzzy red slippers after a very brief touch on the icy floor. I'm not a clothes person or a shopper. There are better things to spend my money on, like books and magazines, but the recent nippy days and a substantial royalty check from my second investigation manual, prompted a shopping spree. I came home with a good supply of warm apparel, including four new sweaters, some flannel shirts, lots of socks, several pairs of pants, these warm slippers, one nice skirt in case I have a reason to appear professional, and Vincent Bugliosi's new book, "Till Death Do Us Part, a True Murder Mystery."

I'm happy to have prepared kindling last night so there is no need to open the back door to the cold. The fire laid and lit, I move to the window and carefully draw open the drapes hoping against a repeat of last week's disaster when the whole assembly fell to the floor.

Snow fell silently in the night. Now, a soft, white blanket covers the ground. Across the fields, the firs and cedars lining the river bank look like frosted holiday cookies. Ice crystals shine on the landscape as if a troop of elves had spent the night spreading glitter. Snow days, so rare here, remind me of favorite scenes from the movie, 'Dr. Zhivago,' and of Montana winters on the ranch near Phillipsburg with Russ and baby Logan. I don't want to think about Russ or Montana. The sadness of the movie can't compete with my painful personal memories.

I glance at the clock. Surprised to realize how long I've stood at the window, I hurry across the room to punch the bread left to rise overnight, shape the dough into biscuits and cover them to rise once again.

There's nothing like a warm fire and the fragrance of baking bread to help make folks comfortable. I do want Roger to be comfortable. The fire's burning, but why didn't I open the bathroom door to let some heat in there? I start the shower to let the steam warm the air while I choose my outfit for the day.

Chance and Roger are at the door. I hear them stomping the snow from their boots and hope they leave them on the covered porch before they step into the warm living room. Inside, Roger bends to put on a pair of loafers, but Chance, in his stocking feet, stares at me, an eyebrow raised. An all-knowing smile cracks his face.

Looking beyond him to what I believe is admiration in the eyes of the man I may have erroneously labeled stupid cop, I see his expression and know my closet didn't fail me, New, cobalt blue cashmere turtleneck sweater with black pants and black, low top, heeled boots. Could have chosen to wear my cowboy boots, but they would be too obvious since Roger always wears his fancy, handcrafted boots from Central Oregon's famous brand. My dangling earrings of iridescent white and cobalt blue beads are the perfect touch. Not my usual sweatshirt and jeans look, but a quick glance in the bathroom mirror assures me there are still some curves in this 39-year-old body worth emphasizing. No time this morning to braid my long, salt and pepper hair, so it flows of its own slightly curly accord.

"Hey, Wood. Do you think you could shut the door before we all freeze?"

Chance smirks at me as he grouches at the cop.

"Oh, yeah, right. Don't know what I was thinking."

"I do."

Chance laughs as I hurry past him and disappear into the guest room in search of slippers, shoes, something for Chance's feet. It doesn't matter--any excuse to escape the uncomfortable situation I created for myself. What was I thinking? But, I'm in these clothes and Roger noticed.

"Here, Chance. Try these moccasins. I think they'll fit if you take off those heavy socks. I'll get lighter ones from the dresser," I mumble as I escape into the bedroom again.

"Yes, please. And maybe you could bring me a coat and tie, too. Didn't realize we were having a formal meeting today."

He ducks to avoid the rolled-up socks flying toward him.

"Can't a woman wear something to keep warm without a smart aleck kid making comments?"

"You look great. ...I mean *warm*, Ellie," Roger stammers.

"Yes, you do, Ellie. Your face is red enough to keep us all warm." Chance can't control his tongue.

"Enough, already. Come have something to drink. I'll have fresh biscuits soon. Chance, here's your cup. Roger, would you like coffee or tea?" I babble.

Chance brushes past me, pauses to whisper, "Hot pants and hot bread. I don't think he'll survive."

I elbow Chance's ribs and turn to hear Roger reply, "Coffee is fine."

"I couldn't believe my eyes when I looked out this morning, the snow was so beautiful."

"Yeah, the weatherman sure missed this one, Ellie. It was supposed to warm up and rain last night," Roger says. "Why don't we make a list of the topics we have to cover today?"

"I started a list in the office." I leave, hoping the new focus of conversation will detour Chance.

Returning with copies of my list, some legal pads, pens, and the file box filled with case-related documents, I am greeted by Chance's more mature, "Let's get to work" attitude. Placing everything on the table, I mention the first item on the list is the matter of confidentiality. Roger, stiffens.

"With all due respect, Ms. Carlisle, I don't need a lecture on confidentiality after all these years."

Chance jumps in, "Don't get touchy, man, or it'll be a hell of a long day. We're in a much different situation here than any of us are used to. We have to be sure we're all on the same page."

"I don't want any special rules telling me how to do my investigations." Roger pushes his chair back, folds his arms across his chest and glares at me.

"Roger, please understand there are significant differences between this investigation and our usual lives. Each of our lives will depend on what the rest do. One slip to the wrong person could mean death to one or all of us."

Roger stands, stares at me for a long moment, then sits back down, settles back in the chair and again crosses his arms over his chest.

"Confidentiality," I continue, "is different for each of us in our regular jobs and lives."

I pull out a chair, push aside the file box, and sit.

"Chance has to. …go ahead. Chance, you explain it."

"In my job, as economic director for the tribe, I'm constantly aware of the confidential nature of things. Personal information about my staff is confidential. Statistical reports I prepare are confidential until they are presented to the tribal council. Development plans and preliminary negotiations are, too. I have to be careful in dealing with the feds 'cause some stuff is none of their business. It gets complicated."

"Yeah, but none of. …" Roger says as he spreads blackberry jam on a biscuit.

"Hold on, we're getting there."

"Ellie, your work is a lot like mine, so your situation shouldn't have to be explained."

I forget Chance's earlier amusement and reach across to pat Roger's hand. "Thank you. I guess we've come a long way since our first meeting."

Roger turns red. I hope it's because he remembers his own foul disposition and nasty comments.

"I'm still here folks," Chance says.

The heat rises in my cheeks as I jerk my hand back. I jump up and ask, "More coffee, anyone?" What is wrong with me?

Both men hold their cups toward me. The look of confusion on the cop's face saddens me. Taking a deep breath, I swipe my hand under my hair to lift it away from my burning face. "As I was explaining," I begin as I once again pull a chair away from the table and sit. "I am in a particularly precarious situation here as far as confidentiality is concerned. I'm not only a member of the tribe and a niece of the murdered woman, these are the bones of my people. My relatives will want to know what's going on, what we're finding out."

"Maybe if we tell them some of it, they'll help us."

"No, Roger. There are so many things you don't understand. Believe me, our lives are in danger here and someone in my own tribe may be responsible. This isn't necessarily an outside job."

Chance jerks to attention.

"This is all so convoluted I barely know where to start. I'm telling both of you, right now, right here, if you don't swear on your lives you will never, and I mean never, breathe a word of anything I tell you, or what we find, without first discussing it with the rest of us, I will not include either of you in this investigation."

Turning first to Chance, then to Roger, I look intently at each, then lower my gaze to await their replies.

Chance, of course, is the first to speak.

"I'll follow your lead, Ellie, though I don't understand your comment about someone from our own tribe being involved."

"I will explain when I have assurances from each of you this basic rule will be honored."

"Hey, I'm in," Roger says, his blue eyes steeled with determination. "But, I need a lot more information about why you two keep tying the murder and the grave robbing together. I don't see the connection. I don't see why we should spend precious time worrying about old bones."

I must ignore his comment until I figure out how to make him feel the pain Indians feel when loved ones are dug up from their final resting place. He must feel the violation and understand what happens if their journeys are interrupted. He must think of them as *humans*, rather than 'old bones.'

Roger shifts in his chair. "What about you, Ellie?"

"In this case, Roger, I answer to no one. The tribe is my client, but they have agreed in writing I won't report to them until we have finished investigating the robbing of graves or if I need their assistance on a major issue. I will not get paid, or reimbursed for expenses, until the issue is resolved."

"Doesn't seem fair," Chance says.

"It works for this case. Otherwise, my phone would constantly ring from people wanting to be the first to know every little detail. If a tribal member is involved, we can't take a chance on reporting to anyone."

"So, have we agreed to speak only with one another?"

Both say "Yes." The cop sounds reluctant. Chance has some answering to do when I get him alone.

"OK. Let's move to the living room. We'll have lunch in there. It's storytelling time."

The rest of the meeting drags on far too long as the two men hassle over their conclusions to questions no one asked. I am not happy with this "investigation by committee" situation.

I grab a plate of ham sandwiches from the refrigerator. Chance has the basket of chocolate chip cookies. Roger picks up the stack of paper plates and napkins I point out to him. Everything is placed on the cedar chest. I transfer the coffee into an old granite pot on the woodstove. Chance refills the stove, brings a bag of chips from the counter, then nestles into the chair near the window as I sink onto the couch and wave Roger toward the over-stuffed chair.

No one speaks as we munch. I use the time to gather my thoughts, to be able to present my explanations, suspicions and a plan to these two independent, headstrong men. Keeping it all on track, and everyone safe, will be an overwhelming task.

"Now about the tribal person involved in robbing of graves," I begin.

"I thought you meant someone was involved in the murder. I don't want to hear about grave. ..."

"Excuse me. You must hear this. You can ask questions when I've finished telling."

A deep scowl disfigures Roger's handsome face as he settles back.

"A lot of investigation is based on 'gut feelings,' on instinctual reactions to tidbits of information. Roger, I think you'll agree with me."

He nods.

"Some of what I hear piques my interest and leads me to an initial conclusion someone in the tribe, someone with knowledge of gravesites and schedules, is either feeding information to the grave robbers or is actually involved in the digging. Either scenario makes me sick to my stomach."

"Why, Ellie? Why would a tribal member do this?" Chance is out of his chair, pacing.

"Money, probably. Remember, our tribe struggles to stay connected to our beliefs, our culture. The government was very thorough in their assimilation project here. They beat the beliefs and languages right out of our relatives in the old days."

"I don't understand. Where is there money involved in digging up Grandma and Grandpa Thom? No one buries rifles or beadwork with the deceased anymore. What could they be selling?"

I smile to myself at his questions. He knows the answers but is quick to realize this is lesson time for Roger.

"*Bones.* There's an international market for Indian bones. Native American bones. Some people here in the states will also pay big money for them. Part of the interest is they need a way to launder drug money. Some medical schools still buy skeletons without asking where they come from, and there are plenty of collectors and museums who don't mind buying grave items.

"What do they do with the bones?" Roger seems interested now.

"The international market is mainly for satanic uses. Children's finger bones bring a high price. As do skulls. They're highly-prized because Indian bones are thought to have more power than others. Plus, there is still a market at some museums. It's illegal to sell human bones in the United States, though it still happens. I saw a human skull advertised for $1,250. A skeleton sells for at least $4,500. There was a human leg bone advertised to dog trainers. 'Fresh from Mexico, originally buried.' These lucrative markets encourage people to chance robbing a grave."

"I don't believe anyone in our tribe would be involved in this," Chance says. "The graves are those of our relatives--our ancestors. How could they dig them up, let alone sell them? Aren't they afraid of disturbing the person's final journey? Or of getting caught and arrested?"

"The punishment is so minor. In this state, it's only a misdemeanor to disturb a grave and I can't find anyone has ever been arrested, let alone convicted. No one will be arrested in Lincoln County for digging up an Indian grave because the DA thinks the law is only for human graves."

"What about the state police or some other agency?"

"Not much interest from any of them over the years, except the FBI and they weren't here to look for grave robbers."

This doesn't seem like the best time to mention a phone call from a state police lieutenant yesterday. He insisted I tell no one.

Roger leans forward to look at Chance. "I don't understand. How do you know so much about this grave robbing stuff? What makes you feel the pain as they say? You didn't grow up here. Vivian and Hank didn't teach you all this."

"I may not know much about our tribal history or our ceremonies, but I love my people and I can't imagine anyone digging up another human to sell their bones. My feelings are not easily explained. Doesn't seem like they have to be."

"They are always referred to as Indian bones or Native bones. Most people don't hear or read this as human bones, Chance. Across the world, museums display bones, skulls and personal items dug from Indian graves. Those items are used to teach what we are supposed to believe about Indians of the past. They might be dog bones or deer bones. Some non-natives don't understand these are people. OUR people."

I struggle to hold my tears. Chance stands and pulls me from the couch for a hug while Roger remains rooted to his chair. Then we pull apart and return to our chairs.

"Roger, for the time being, take our word for it, we must investigate the murder and the grave robbers. We will find a way to show you how this gruesome activity affects our people. Can you be patient on this issue, so we can move forward?"

Looking at those blue eyes this time, I think only of the importance of his answer.

"I think so. Yeah, I can if it will help me find the answers to my questions about Hank."

"Not good enough. We must have absolute certainty in every decision, in every action. People could be killed by our mistakes. If you don't take everything seriously. If you don't have absolute trust in each of us, we can't work with you. We can't trust you."

Roger stares. We wait. He stands, looks at each of us and says, "Yes, I will trust both of you though I don't like rules. I respect commitment and trust are important to you. For now, it will be enough."

He walks toward Chance, hand outstretched.

Chance grabs his hand, pulls him forward into a huge bear hug. Screeching with laughter, I join them in the hug. Finally, breathless, we return to our chairs.

"You people are crazy," Roger wheezes between snorts.

"Ah, lesson number one." Pointing my red-tipped index finger at him, my eyes automatically narrow to a slit, I tell him, "Do not refer to us as you people. Not ever."

"Sorry, I didn't mean to offend you."

"Hey, it's OK, El. We squeezed the piss out of him. Can't expect him to have a brain left," Chance says.

I am relieved to feel the tension evaporate from the room. Now I can begin.

"In May 1949, Jean Kline was murdered up Dewey Creek."

The men grow quiet.

"Marge says Jean was seeing a man from the mill in Toledo where she answered office phones. First girl from our tribe hired there. Right out of high school. Everyone was proud of her. But, despite warnings against it, she dated a white guy. Grandma warned her about the man. Marge says Grandma didn't like when he wouldn't come to the reservation in daylight to see Jean. Also, Marge heard the aunties say sometimes Jean came home crying or with bruises on her face and arms.

"One day, Grandma heard Jean being sick in the outhouse. She realized Jean was pregnant when she noticed her paleness and too tight clothes. Soon, Jean was fired from her job. She stayed home with Grandma. One day, she told Grandma she needed a break and walked off down the hill toward the grocery store. Grandma never saw her again."

"What. ..." Roger begins, stops.

"When an uncle came the next morning to tell Grandma Jean was found up Dewey Creek, a deputy came right behind him. Said Jean and her baby had died in a Portland hospital. Grandma insisted uncle take her to the grocery store. She went into the store, talked to Willie and never spoke of Jean again. She refused to attend Jean's funeral."

"Whoa. Poor Grandma."

"Grandma told me the other day, 'It's time for the deaths to end.' She said Willie let Jean use the phone at the store and overheard her telling someone..."

"Grandma told you? I thought she doesn't talk about Jean."

"Finally, she has, Chance. Anyway, Willie overheard Jean crying and saying on the phone, 'I have to see you. Please come talk to me before the baby is born.' When she hung up, she said she would go down to the bridge to wait for a friend."

"Who is Willie. ...oh, sorry, later," Chance apologized.

"Willie is gone now, Chance. So, it seems no one saw Jean on the bridge. One uncle told me he remembers seeing Jean walking near the bridge, and Old Joe Logsden says he saw Jean headed toward the bridge. That's it. No one saw her get into a car. No one seems to know how Jean got to the area where they found her up Dewey Creek."

I look to Chance to continue the story.

"So, a fisherman found her. Said he noticed a smoldering bonfire and thought someone had beaten him to his favorite fishing hole. Then he saw Jean lying there bloody and beaten, with only a breath of life in her. He drove back to town to the phone booth on Egbert Street, near Nocl's Market, to call an ambulance. Probably took at least two hours from when he found her until the ambulance got to the site. She was sent to the hospital in Toledo, then to the Multnomah County Hospital in Portland where Indian patients were treated then. We've heard rumors a nurse rode in the ambulance with her to Portland."

"Grandma gave me the nurse's name. Cynthia Tompkins. We will find her. I hope she's still alive," I add.

"What? How did Mrs. Kline know the nurse's name?" Roger asks.

"When the nurse came to see Grandma to talk to her about Jean and the baby, Grandma sent her away. She got into her car but came back to knock on the door again. When Grandma answered, the nurse handed her a note with her name and phone number. Yesterday, Grandma gave me the note. Grandma thought the baby died. Later, Marge told her he was adopted by white people. The aunties put him on the tribal roll. Grandma doesn't know how they got the name, but Marge was involved. We wonder how the baby could be adopted out. Jean was dead. Who signed the papers?"

"Ellie, are you saying my name has been on the tribal roll all this time?"

"Maybe, if the story is true that you are the baby, Chance".

I hope my comment sparks some thought. His special story is hogwash.

"I'll look at the records. It's about time Hank and Vivian come clean with the details of my adoption. Perhaps they have more papers, too."

"As we know," I continue, "the sheriff immediately focused on Mark Thom as the killer. Mark was Jean's cousin. Sum total of their evidence. At trial the prosecutor theorized Mark took it upon himself to kill her to save the family the embarrassment of an illegitimate child."

"Seems odd," Roger says. "I've met several adoptees who were illegitimate kids of Indian women and white guys."

"True. Lots of our babies have been given away over the years, beginning with those fathered by the agents and soldiers stationed here in the early days of the reservation. No one should have believed the reasons the authorities gave for the murder. Children are treasured by our people, no matter the circumstances of their birth. Mark had no alibi. At least not one he would share, so the cops were happy to arrest him."

"Where is the sheriff now?" Roger asks.

"We think he's dead. We have to check," Chance answers.

"Now," I tell them, for Roger's enlightenment, "The big secret Mark kept, the whole reservation kept, was he was in love with a young, high school girl. A white girl from Newport. She was with him on the day and evening Jean disappeared. Alone with Mark and Grandpa Thom in their little house here in Siletz. Her parents thought she was visiting Mark's sister, Marge. He wouldn't tell. He knew they would convict him no matter what and he didn't want to leave his girl to deal with her parents. His cousin was dead, and Mark was presumed guilty."

I turn to see Roger's reaction to what Chance would now share.

"Ellie and I visited Mark at the prison recently and he believes my adoptive father, Hank Andrews, your friend, killed Jean. He thinks Hank had an affair with Jean and panicked when he learned she was pregnant."

"Your mother thinks so, too. This is weird shit," Roger says under his breath.

"No, it's rez talk."

The day disappears as we struggle with the issues. I am certain Roger will never fully understand the significance of the grave robbings, so I've developed a plan and am eager to share it with Chance. If Chance agrees, it will take several days and some careful planning to implement. If it works, there is an emotional realization in store for Detective Wood. For the time being, I keep it a secret.

As evening shadows settle across the valley, Chance stokes the fire and announces, "We'd better finish planning. Roger is going home to River City tonight, a long drive."

"Let's agree on the basic responsibilities for each of us."

"Yeah. You and I have already done a lot in a few weeks," Chance agrees.

I find a clean sheet on my legal pad and turn to Roger. "We need the police reports from Jean's death. We've tried to get them, but we're told they don't exist. Can you take care of this and bring them to our next meeting?"

"If they don't exist, how am I supposed to get them?"

Good. Now he understands the difficulty.

"We don't believe the records don't exist. The sheriff hasn't cleaned his office in years. Either he can't find the records or there is something in them he doesn't want us to know. You're a cop. They might find them for you."

I stress the word 'cop'.

Chance says, "Roger, the current sheriff was the deputy in charge of Jean's murder investigation all those years ago."

"What? I thought the deputy on the case was named Harrington."

"He died unexpectedly in a car crash and Kramer took over."

"Kramer. The one who threatened you the other day, up by some creek?"

"Yeah. He's the one, Roger," Chance says.

"When I sent Rose to request the files, Kramer denied he had them. Said he should know since it was his case. She told me Kramer was totally obnoxious."

"It seems you two have a problem with authority," Roger says. "All these complaints about the sheriff. Won't come when you call. Doesn't do investigations. But when he does investigate, he won't give you the reports."

"And why is that untrue?" I ask.

"It just seems you're always having trouble with cops."

"Like I said, 'Welcome to Indian Country,'" Chance responds. "You'll see soon enough. Get those records before their surveillance guy reports you're hanging out with Ellie."

"You might want to get a room at the coast tonight," I add. "Go by the sheriff's office after about eleven. He's never around late at night. Some young recruit will be at the front desk. Make the kid think you must get back to River City tonight. You've been so busy this was your first chance to check on a report. Really insignificant in the case, but since you're here you thought you'd stop by and get it. Low key stuff, you know. Don't mention us."

Roger bristles and mutters, "OK."

"So, Roger, you'll get the police reports. I'll organize and copy everything we've gathered in recent weeks and have them ready for our next meeting," I say, making notes as I speak.

"When is the next meeting?" Roger asks.

"I don't know yet. I have some things to work out. I'll let you know by this weekend. Should be soon. Chance talk to uncle again at the nursing home in Newport. Maybe take him for a stroll in his wheelchair. See if he remembers anything else about the murder or the grave robbers. He's old and struggling, but he remembers stuff from back in the day."

Roger rises to leave. Chance brings his jacket from the bedroom where I placed it earlier.

"I'll let you know what I find out tonight, Ellie. How late will you be up?"

"At least until midnight. Call me whenever. Let me know if you get the file."

I'm standing near the stove and Roger is across the room opening the door to leave when I feel a hand on my shoulder. I brace for Chance's comment.

"Wouldn't it be easier to be in the motel room waiting for him?" he whispers into my hair.

When Roger's truck is out of sight, Chance searches the kitchen for a snack and settles on more chips, salsa and water. He has a meeting with the sawmill manager at seven. I am eager to share my plan.

"Roger doesn't understand the pain and anguish caused by the molestation of the graves of our loved ones."

"What do you have in mind, Ellie?"

"Here's my plan. We take Roger over the mountain to visit Delvin Jones. He and his tribe have made amazing progress in bringing the message to non-native people. They work with anthropologists and archaeologists on a national level. They're planning a reburial ceremony soon for ancestor bones returned by a university in Washington state. If attending this ceremony can't get through to him, nothing will."

"Isn't there someone in our own tribe who can talk to him?"

"Not yet. Delvin is one of our cousins. It's only through his work some in our tribe realized we should do reburial ceremonies. Always before, the guys just closed the graves. We never expected to bury our loved ones twice. No reburial ceremonies were handed down to us."

"Are you sure this will work? Roger doesn't want to hear it."

"It will work, Chance, believe me. If he can get through a ceremony with Delvin and not have a compassionate understanding at the end, we don't want to be involved with him. I'll call Delvin tonight and make the arrangements. Keep your calendar open."

Chance heads for the door. He stops when I ask, "Why are you writing reports on our meetings?"

"Ray asked for them. Wants to keep track of what. ...oh, damn! I didn't think anything about it. It's not unusual for him to request information on committee activities."

"No, I'm sure you didn't think, but you also didn't mention it when you pledged confidentiality. You cannot discuss this investigation with anyone, no matter what they tell you."

"Sorry. I really screwed up."

"It's OK. I asked Ray to help me check on you. There were hints you weren't ready for this responsibility."

I pull his report from a file folder and shake it at him.

"I hope you've learned a lesson. Now get to your meeting."

As Chance hurries out the door, I give thanks for the friendship formed so many years ago here on the rez with Ray, the quiet boy who spoke up for me when I addressed the council. He just helped test to see if Chance cooperates too easily.

20

―――――――

"ELLIE? ELLIE, WAKE UP."

The voice filters through the fog of sleep. Oh. "What? Roger is that you?"

"I'm sorry, Ellie. It's late. Probably after two. I need to talk to you right away. I'm driving out there. Call Chance to meet me at your house."

He hangs up without further explanation. I reach down to retrieve a blanket from the floor, pull it tight around my shoulders and glance around trying to remember why I am in the cold living room. I remember staying on the couch after Chance left, thinking about the day's events. I must have fallen asleep right here. Roger asked for Chance to meet him here. Dialing the number, I realize Roger must have found something at the sheriff's office. Chance answers, sounding fully awake and alert.

"Ellie, what's wrong?"

"Nothing. I mean, I don't know, Roger is coming back and wants you to meet him here."

"Good! He must have got the file. Be right there. but, Ellie, we are coming to my house. No one will think anything of your lights being on at this hour, probably wouldn't think anything of my car in your driveway. Roger's car will draw attention."

"You stay home. I'll ride with Roger."

"You can't be seen riding around at two o'clock in the morning with a cop."

I hang up, walk to the kitchen. Chance is right. Way too easy to be fitted with a snitch jacket here. Riding around with a cop in the middle of the night would be interpreted badly by those with things to hide, and there are plenty of them, especially since the new highway made it easier for creeps to wander into town.

I change my clothes, freshen up a bit and grab my briefcase before Roger's truck comes down the driveway. I turn off the lamp and walk to the front door. Roger is driving more sanely than his earlier bouncing over potholes, throwing mud. As I reach the front door, I notice lights of another vehicle appear behind Roger. Must be Chance.

When Roger opens his car door, I flick on the porch light and step onto the porch.

"Get in the house," he yells.

Instinct guides my hand to the light switch as I back into the house. In the darkness, a blaze of light flashes behind Roger's car. At the sound of a bullet smashing metal, I fall to the floor. Feeling inside the briefcase for my .38 Special, I hear three more quick shots followed by two louder, closer ones, then a motor racing and tires throwing gravel. Sounds of confusion elicit terror. I wait breathlessly, glued to the living room floor, wondering, waiting until a muffled sound of shoes on the front porch catches my attention. I roll over and point the gun at the opening front door.

"Ellie, it's me. Roger. Don't shoot."

I don't move, don't lower the gun. The door closes, while I remain motionless training the gun on the shadow inside my house. He is right at my feet. I pray he can't see me.

"Ellie, I'm in the house. We're safe. I'm turning the light on. Don't shoot me. When you see me, put down the gun."

It sounds like Roger. I want it to be Roger. My mind is confused by the unexpected gunfire. With my body so tense I am not sure my muscles will answer a command to pull the trigger, I keep the gun trained on the shadow as its hand moves upward to the light switch.

He turns the porch light on by mistake. Roger's face is illuminated by the light coming through the small glass pane in the door. I lower my gun. As the rest of my pent-up breath leaves my body, I sprawl on the old fir flooring, weak and relieved. Now I see his fancy boots.

Roger fumbles for the switch again, but the room is flooded by the headlights of another car coming up the driveway. He drops to his knees beside me, whispers to me to get to the bedroom. I don't move.

Standing he says, "Go! Crawl to the bedroom and lock the door. Now!"

I begin to crawl. When I reach the bedroom door, I recognize the sound of Chance's Jeep.

"Roger. It's Chance."

Roger turns off the porch light and waits.

"Hey! Turn the light on. How am I supposed to see?"

I jump up, brush myself off. Roger stands to turn the porch light on and opens the door for Chance as I carefully place my gun back into the briefcase.

Chance comes through the door shouting, "You two. Can't leave you alone for two minutes or you're up to some sort of nonsense. What were you doing in the dark?"

I feel the blood of anger rush up my neck, over my face and onto the top of my head. I hope the men don't notice. Chance does and misinterprets it.

"You should blush, Miss Ellie. I'm surprised at your behavior," he teases.

He laughs, stops, when he sees Roger's look is anything but friendly and backed by the .357 still in his hand.

"Listen, smartass Indian punk. We were shot at. My truck is full of bullet holes. You're lucky Ellie is still here for you to torment. I'm lucky she didn't shoot me."

"I wasn't going to shoot you. But I wasn't sure it was you."

"What are you two blubbering about? There isn't anyone out there. I didn't see a single car on the street."

"This is not a joke. A car followed Roger into the driveway. I thought it was you, so I went outside. They shot at Roger."

"Shit."

"When I got back into the house, I grabbed my gun and kept it pointed at the front door because I didn't know who would come in, Roger or the other guys."

"How did they miss you, Roger? It's like a football arena on game night out there when the porch light is on," Chance says.

"Lucky for me, Ellie hit the light switch before she hit the floor. Saved me. They flew out the driveway, shots just missed the open door right above where I was on the ground."

"Did you see who it was? Do you know the car?" Chance asks me.

"I didn't see anything except headlights. I don't remember the sound of the car. Mostly gravel crunching, the roar of the engine and those shots. About ten shots, and a couple of them were real loud."

"Those were mine," Roger says. "I shot twice. Hit the car both times, I think."

"How did you know I had a gun, Roger?"

He knew when he came through the door and he couldn't have seen me or the gun from the porch.

"I didn't know for sure. Assumed you wouldn't be living here without one. Don't all PIs carry guns?"

Chance, seated now, and quiet, stares at Roger for several seconds, then asks, "Now what? My plan was to go to my house, so people wouldn't notice your truck here."

I shake my head and sink onto the couch. Chance grins. Roger looks annoyed as he struggles to understand our amusement. Native humor isn't easy for him.

"Ellie could have been killed, you idiot. She was standing on the porch in full view of those maniacs when they started shooting."

"I'm sorry. It is amusing. Ellie and I carefully planned so no one would notice us meeting in the middle of the night and I arrive to find a war raging."

"Forget whoever tried to kill us. What did you find, Roger?"

"First, shouldn't we call the sheriff?"

We stare at him, mouths agape.

"What?"

"You can't be serious! We send you to the sheriff's office to get files he says don't exist, then someone tries to kill you and you want us to call the sheriff?" Chance is irritated again.

"No. I guess not. What about your tribal police?"

"We don't have tribal cops yet," Chance explains. "Wait. Tell me how the car ended up in Ellie's driveway. How did you drive all the way from Newport to Ellie's without noticing a car following you?"

"There wasn't anyone following me when I left the sheriff's office. No one followed me to the motel room. I called Ellie and left. There was no one outside. No one followed me from Newport."

"They didn't fall out of the sky."

"I didn't see a car on either side of the road for the entire trip. As I came over the bridge into town, I noticed a car start to move in the parking lot at the apartment building farther up Gaither Street. I didn't see any headlights until they were turned on as I got out of the truck."

"I didn't think about it at the time, Chance but I didn't see any headlights coming up the driveway behind Roger. They came on as Roger stopped his truck. The shooting started right when his door opened."

We grow quiet again. I drift toward the kitchen to make more coffee. The water heated, I pile chocolate chip cookies on a large white stoneware plate, one of Grandma's treasures from the old Indian Shaker Church building on Swan Avenue. These old remnants of her family's, her tribe's, history always give me comfort in times of stress. The men will enjoy the cookies without a clue to the origin of the plate. Something to tell Chance later.

My hand trembles when I give a cup to Chance. He cradles the steaming cup in his cold hands, looks up at me and asks, "You OK?" Then he suggests we go to his house. "You know, where it's warm and cozy all the time because I have electric heat."

I nod and give a cup to Roger. "He's too lazy to cut wood."

"I don't care where we talk. We must talk about what the kid at the jail gave me. I think we finally have the information we need to get started," Roger says.

Before we can respond, I hear a light thud outside and hit the floor for the second time.

Roger yells, "I left the file in the truck." He moves his gun from its holster in one swift motion and runs for the front door.

Chance close behind, stops only long enough to reach into my brief-case to grab the .38.

"Chance! Chance!"

I hear the cry when Roger flicks the light switch to bathe the house in darkness again. He is at the front door with gun in hand.

"Roger, it's Rose." My voice mixes with Chance's as I leap from the floor and head for the window. What is Rose doing out there at four o'clock in the morning?

Jerking the drapes aside, I forget their precarious position on the flimsy rod but step backward in time to avoid the tumbling mass of fabric, rod and hooks. The rush of cold air sweeps around me as the two men hurry out the front door and down the steps. Rose struggles to carry her boy who appears to be fast asleep despite his mother's screams. I drop the edge of the drape still crumpled in my hand, step over the mess and hurry to Rose.

Chance passes me at the door as he hurries to get the boy out of the morning dampness and cold. Roger helps an exhausted and tearful Rose to the porch, carefully places his arm around her waist and supports her as she steps inside.

"What is going on? What are you doing here in the middle of the night? Where is your car? How did you walk all this way carrying your boy? Why didn't you call? The questions pour out of me, but Rose doesn't respond. Is there no end to the crises and mysteries tonight?

I grab Rose's purse, hold the door for her and note Roger's gentleness and concern. Note, too, his gun is still firmly ensconced in his right hand, ready for whatever may come.

He takes Rose through the kitchen to the far side of the living room to avoid the pile of drapes blocking the near side and helps her settle onto the couch where she pulls my blanket around herself.

As I return from the back porch where I got kindling to start the fire, Chance comes out of the bedroom.

"He's all tucked into bed. Sure is a sound sleeper. What the hell did you do to the drapes, Ellie?"

"They fell down, again, when I looked out to see what was wrong with Rose. Can you get them back up there, please?" I watch as he lifts the whole thing—drapes, hooks and rod—back onto the flimsy brackets and pulls the fabric together, covering the window.

"Thanks."

"Yeah. We'll have to get them fixed before you knock yourself out."

"Okay, little miss, what is going on?" he asks as he sits beside Rose, pulls her to him and strokes her hair. "Why are you walking around in the night?"

This is uncomfortable to watch. These two are so close and I'm not sure if it's a good thing. What if he is Marge's son? Is this a sister-brother connection they have or is it developing into something else?

My heart pounds as I wait for Rose to reply, knowing there is only one answer to Chance's question. Rose and her child must have been escaping her man. I dread Chance's reaction. He doesn't like Lee and loudly voiced disapproval when Rose let Lee move into her apartment.

"I had to get away. I didn't know where else to go. Chance, I called. You didn't answer."

"Let's start at the beginning," Roger interrupts.

Chance shows his annoyance as Roger explains, "This is my kind of work. You and Ellie are family, so it is better if I ask the questions."

His explanation irritates me. I'll let Roger have his way—this time. He waits for Chance's approval and receives it after a few tense seconds.

"Rose, what happened? Start at the beginning. Take it slow and. ..." Roger begins.

"He, Lee, left when I went to bed. Said he was going over to Harvey's to drink some beer. When I woke up, the lights were on all over the house and there was a bunch of guys going in and out of the bathroom."

"What guys?" Chance asks. Roger's stern look would stop anyone cold, even a young hothead.

"Lee came into the bedroom and told me to stay in there. Said there was a shoot-out and some guys got hurt."

Roger and Chance turn to stare at me when I gasp. I'm glad Roger is in charge of this interrogation. I'm used to other people's problems, to interviewing victims, the accused, and some obviously guilty murderers. Those were not my relatives and certainly not people who might have been shooting at Roger in my own front yard less than an hour ago.

"Did he tell you about the shoot-out?"

"Yes, Roger. They got a call someone was digging in the graveyard on the Hill, so he and Harvey went up in Lee's car. The grave robbers shot at them. He backed up and got out of there."

"So, who was hurt?"

"When he left the bedroom, I heard Lee go into the bathroom, so I got up and saw him washing up. He had blood all over his hands and one arm. When I tried to help him, he said it was nothing, just a cut from window glass. He told me the car was parked out back with the front window shot out."

I open the stove door to add wood, then check to make sure the front and back doors are locked. I can keep quiet but sitting still is impossible with all these questions bubbling in my mind. Every answer Roger elicits from Rose leads to more questions.

Chance moves his arm and turns to stare at his sister. I mean at Rose.

"Did he say who else was hurt?" Roger continues.

"No. I heard them talking and recognized Harvey's voice saying, 'We have to get him to the hospital before he bleeds to death' but I don't know who he meant."

"Did you recognize any other voices?"

"No, only Harvey, you know the guy from Klamath. There were a couple of other guys. One white guy, I think."

"You saw him?"

"No. I told you, Roger, I didn't see any of them except Lee."

"How do you know he was a white guy, Rose?"

I stifle a giggle behind my hand and see a slight smile on Rose's face.

"You guys talk funny. Don't sound like us."

"Okay. Whatever. You're sure you didn't see any of them? How do you know they were going in and out of the bathroom?"

"My place isn't very big. If someone is in the bathroom, you can hear everything. They weren't using the toilet. They kept running water in the sink, over and over. It was a mess. After they left, I went in there. There is blood all over my front room carpet. Blood in the bathroom sink. On the floor. On the doors. It's awful. I'll never get it clean."

Rose brushes away tears with the back of her hand as she looks up at Roger, waiting for the next question. I've never seen her so calm and obedient. What a strange night.

"Rose, why did you walk here instead of driving your car?"

"They took my car. Lee came in to get the key, so Harvey could drive my car. I reminded him Harvey doesn't have a license, but he growled at me, "Give me the keys, bitch. Now!"

She flinches when Chance jumps from the couch, forgetting his place in the unfolding scenario. "I told you to stay away from. …"

"Settle down, man. You're not helping." Roger puts his hand firmly on Chance's arm and waits until Chance sits down.

"Then what did Lee do?"

"Grabbed my purse and dumped it on the bed. When he found the keys, he started out of the bedroom. I tried to grab them away. He told me to stop. I didn't, and he threatened to take care of me when he comes back because I was a bitch and embarrassed him in front of his friends. He smelled awful like he'd been drinking a lot. I'm sorry, Chance. I thought he was different. I was so scared."

Chance pulls her to him again. He doesn't speak. Looks at Roger for the next question. I hope those guys don't show up while Chance is this angry.

"They planned to tow his car to a garage to work on it while Harvey took the guy to the hospital in my car. Oh, god. They'll get blood all over my car," Rose says.

"So, they left towing the car. Who towed it?"

"I didn't recognize the truck. I saw it when I came home from work. A big green Ford. Probably belongs to the white guy."

"The white guy. The one who talks funny, right?" Roger smiles, then asks, "So why are you here? Why didn't you wait for Lee to come home?"

"Hey man. Are you crazy? She told you Lee was coming back for her." Chance is up again, in Roger's face.

"Sit down. If you don't quit interrupting, you can leave until I am finished here."

And Chance returns to Rose's side. Wow.

"Now, Rose. ..."

"Yeah, I was scared. Chance wasn't home, so I called here. The phone was busy. I grabbed the baby and started to walk. I couldn't wait there. Didn't know when they would be back.

"They? Do you expect someone to come back with Lee?"

Rose looks at her hands, doesn't answer right away.

"When they went outside, I opened the bathroom window a crack. Heard someone say, 'I'm coming back with you, man. It's time you get her under control. I told you to take care of the situation. Now I'm going to do it for you.'"

Something about her answers, or at least the tone of her answers doesn't seem right. Why am I doubting her story? Too much detail, perhaps?

"Did Lee answer?"

"I didn't hear him say anything. He does whatever Harvey tells him most of the time. But Harvey hates me because sometimes Lee listens to me."

"What time did you wake up?"

"About two something, I think. Yeah 2:20. It was 2:20 when they came through the front door. I remember wondering why he was bringing people so late at night."

Roger was quiet for a while.

"How do you know it was 2:20?"

"The clock by the bed glows in the dark. I looked at it when I heard them."

"What time did they leave?"

"About three. I started walking as soon as I was dressed. Oh, and I had to put my purse back together. Called here again. The phone was still busy."

Busy. She's mentioned it twice.

I'm standing behind the couch, so I pick up the phone, listen and replace the receiver. I notice Roger turn slightly my way. I shake my head, so he will know there's nothing wrong with my phone. There was no one using it when Rose said it was busy.

21

THE STRONG ODOR OF FRESH COFFEE WAFTING THROUGH MY bedroom causes me to sit straight up in bed. Who is in my house? Who is making coffee?

I throw my robe around my shoulders and reach out to jerk open the door. The sudden realization of who might be in the kitchen stops me with a bone rattling abruptness. Roger! Whoa. Can't go out there like this.

Falling back onto the bed, I silently curse the freedom of being single allows me to leave all my toiletries in the bathroom down the hall. How will I get to the bathroom without him seeing me in all my morning glory? There isn't even a mirror in this room. There was no other choice except to let everyone crash at my house after all the drama last night. Makes it difficult to function this morning. There's a slight tap on the door.

"Hey, Ellie. I'm going to the store to get some pastries for breakfast. Roger's going with me. Just checking to be sure you're awake."

"Okay, I'll be right out. After you leave."

"Be sure the doors stay locked. Don't open them to anyone while we're gone. No one."

"Chance, thanks!"

"You're welcome, he whispers before moving toward the front door. "Let's go, man. I don't want to leave the ladies here by themselves very long."

"Shouldn't I stay here?" Roger asks.

"Nope. Nice try."

Chance's laughter is cut short by the slamming door.

I grab the .38 off the nightstand, drop it in my bathrobe pocket, and head for the bathroom.

22

AFTER MY SHOWER, I PULL ON JEANS, AND A BLACK, SHORT sleeved V-neck sweater, put my hair in a French braid, fasten it with a clip of red and black beads and head for the kitchen. Midway through peeling potatoes for the hash browns Chance will appreciate, I wash my hands and hurry to the bedroom feeling naked without any jewelry. What to wear? Something subtle so Chance won't think I wore it to impress Roger. What if Roger doesn't notice? Ah. The little turquoise squash blossom necklace Logan gave me. Perfect. Hurry. Get back to those potatoes before the guys come through the door.

Chance and Roger are back from the grocery store, all hyped up as they carry food into my house. As I unlock the door for them, Roger says, "So, this is reservation life. I'm beginning to believe I do come from a different world as you said before Ellie. In all my years on the police force I've never been shot at. At least not like last night when someone targeted me."

"It was quiet here before you showed up, Roger. Murders took place in the quiet of the night. Didn't disturb anyone's sleep. Normal stuff. Nothing a cop would worry about. At least not our sheriff," Chance responds.

"So, you've said. Why me? I can't get answers, so my questions shouldn't bother anyone."

"You invaded their territory last night, remember?"

"Their terri. ...Oh! The file. They wouldn't know. Besides, what does Jean's death have to do with someone shooting at me?"

"What's got you two in a dither?" I ask as they place more groceries on the kitchen counter.

"There were several women in the back near the end of the meat counter when we went into Noels Grocery, Ellie," Chance explains. "The yellowish, wrinkled woman who works at the checkout had on the same ragged jeans and torn, red T-shirt as the last time I saw her. Rog, you couldn't see them, but she always wears grungy, deerskin moccasins. Missing most of their beads.

"Uh huh."

"Anyway, this woman asked me if you are okay. Said she heard shots near the river last night. Someone came in the store earlier and said it was at Ellie's house."

"When I said, 'Far as I know, Ellie's okay,' she said, 'Ah, c'mon. Everybody's saying a car got shot to shit last night. Blaming it on the city cop."

"Yeah, she said she didn't recognize me in my regular clothes. I sure was uncomfortable with those sad, watery eyes sliding over me. Wished I had a jacket, or maybe a long raincoat," Roger adds.

Chance ignores Roger's grouching and continues. "I asked what else people are saying. Anybody give a reason for a shootout? Anybody killed? Maybe a dead body in your cooler?'"

She responded with another question, 'What happened down there? People are saying a lot of crazy stuff.' Then she turned toward Roger to say, 'Frankly, I'm not happy having him in this store.'"

"She stabbed her long, bony finger at me." Roger says, clearly angry at something other than the finger pointing.

"Anyway," Chance says, "apparently someone told her Lee came home and found the city cop with Rose, so he chased him over here. Then the cop shot Lee's car up. The usual."

Roger glares at Chance and then looks toward me. "I tried to defend myself, but Chance's elbow bashed my ribs. Then he sent me to the car."

"Quit whining. Now let me tell Ellie what else happened."

Roger sits on a kitchen chair and listens while Chance continues.

"The clerk jerked her head toward the back of the store, so I guess it was one of the women near the meat counter in back who is spreading the story. I also found out the guy from Klamath hangs out at Sandy Wilford's. Guess she's finally got a man to help with all those kids."

"Same old same old. So, Lee was the one who shot at Roger? What were you doing at Rose's apartment in the middle of the night, Roger?" I ask.

"Why the hell would I go there? I was headed here, remember?"

Yeah, I remember but rez rumors usually start with a fragment of truth. This one seems to be Roger was at Rose's apartment last night. Did he call me from there when he told me he was at the motel?

"So, Chance," I say to steer the conversation in another direction. "Why did you mention the guy from Klamath?"

"I suspect he and his group are behind this current rash of grave robbing. I don't understand why they are being so brazen. They dig in broad daylight near the tribal office. Seem to have an inside track on everyone's whereabouts, too, since they never get caught," Chance says.

"I think this might be where Lee fits in," I remind the guys. "The Klamath guy is his friend. Lee works for our tribe and brings strangers to town. Looks suspicious to me."

"They definitely need a good look. I hear Ellie assigned the looting investigation to you, Chance," Roger says as he looks toward me.

"No. She assigned some vital tasks to me to develop specific information she needs. This is her baby. I got a major task because I opened my big yap to a reporter. Hey, the woman at the store also told me she cashed a $500 check for Harvey, the Klamath guy, last week."

"From Canada?"

"No, a company called Bones, Inc. in Wenatchee, Washington."

Maybe a clue I should follow, but right now I'm concentrating on why Roger's hands are shaking so much he had to put them under the table.

23

BREAKFAST IS OVER. CHANCE IS LEAVING FOR WORK. HE'LL drop Rose off at Margie's.

Roger closes and locks my front door after watching Chance walk to the Jeep. Then he comes to the couch, sits beside me and asks, "Now, we have some uninterrupted time, shall we start with the file, or shall we talk about us?"

Us. Definitely. Though I say, "I should get busy with this file."

Roger chuckles softly. "I thought you'd say that. Okay. One of these days we need to talk, Baby."

This is impossible. I wish Chance was here. How did this happen? I can't be alone with this man. Can't trust myself. He's already sensed the attraction, but 'Baby'? I don't trust men who use that word. Makes my skin crawl.

"How could she let you go?" Ohhhh, Noo! I didn't mean to say that. I want to sink into the couch until only my shoes are visible. Nothing in my head or coming out of my mouth makes sense today.

"My first thought when she told me to leave."

Roger pulls me toward him. His warmth draws me in. His lips beckon. Instead, acting like the professional lady PI I strive to be, I dive across the arm of the couch to answer the jangling phone.

"I guess the damsel has been rescued."

"I'm not sure she wanted to be rescued," I murmur before saying a little too loudly into the phone, "Hello."

"Hah. I didn't know you had a phone by your bed. Sorry if I disturbed you."

"Go to hell. What do you want, anyway?"

"Might have known it was Chance," Roger grumbles.

"Let me talk to Roger. You get back to whatever you were doing. If Roger can talk while you're doing it."

"I hate you, you little punk. I'm reading the file. Here's Roger."

I hand the phone to Roger, step around the end of the couch and dash to the kitchen. Tea. I must have a cup of tea. I'm sure Roger wants tea.

I hear him say, "I know," and "I sure will." I don't want to know, though as soon as the receiver clicks into place I ask, "What did he want? What was so important?"

"What was so important he had to interrupt our first time alone, you mean?"

"No, not what I meant."

I keep busy cleaning the kitchen counters, rearranging things. It's been several days since I've done this. Perhaps I should remove everything and give the counter a thorough cleaning. Anything to avoid sitting on the couch with him.

"I'm making tea. Do you want a cup?"

"Tea wasn't exactly what I had in mind."

"What did he want? Chance?"

"He's stopping by the cafe to buy 'burgers so you can read and not worry about cooking."

"Oh. Good. Tea?"

I'm not sure I trust these two. Chance could have told me he was bringing dinner.

"I'll have a cup. Can I come over there or will it cause you to run into another room?"

"Roger, we have so much work to do. Let's not complicate it with feelings."

Aren't I the tough one? Miss Take Charge. Maybe I should go into the bedroom with him. Explore his amazing body until we're both too worn out to think about guns and bullets and...oh, thank goodness Chance is returning soon.

"My thoughts exactly. Let's not complicate things. Besides Chance would bring the 'burgers right into the bedroom."

Now he's reading my mind. As he approaches, I set his cup on the counter and back away.

"The bedroom? A big leap. I thought you only wanted to talk, Roger."

Am I good or what? He has no idea what I'm thinking.

"Ellie, we both know where we'd be if Chance wasn't coming to rescue you from the big, bad cop. Or from yourself. You're right. We should concentrate on this hellacious investigation first."

I bite back my words, scrunch my face into what I hope serves as a reproach and sit at the table to begin the file review. The egotistical cop can fend for himself until Chance returns. His boots thud across the old fir flooring as he walks toward Chance's chair. I sneak a quick peek at his backside. Some things are too good to ignore.

Within seconds, I realize the pages of the file are a jumble. I'll spend several hours putting them in chronological order before I can analyze them. First, I check to see if there is any logic to the way the pages were placed in the folder.

Chance returns, places my food on the table near my right hand. "More tea?" he asks.

"Yes, thanks. This file is a mess. After I eat, I'll take it into the bedroom and put it in order before I get some sleep. First thing in the morning, I'll start reading."

"Okay. I'm going to take the first shift tonight. I'll wake Roger around midnight."

24

WE ARE GATHERED AT THE KITCHEN TABLE WHEN I NOTICE Chance's face is uncharacteristically somber.

Feeling my stare, he states, "I'm worried about Rose."

"Why?" I ask, though I have my own worries about her.

"Something is not right. Can't figure it out yet. Maybe she's being used to obtain information and doesn't realize it. Rog, did you mention what motel you stayed at in Newport?"

"No, I don't think so. Did I, Ellie?"

"I don't know where you were. You only said you got a motel room as far as I remember."

"What I remember, too," Chance continues. "Over at Rose's, Lee and I talked about the shots fired at Roger. Rose interrupted and said somebody must have known Roger was coming back to Ellie's because he called Ellie from the Tides Motel and then came right out."

"Was that where. ..." I began. The look on Roger's face stopped me.

"Maybe one of us mentioned it and in all the uproar we've forgotten."

"No, wait. The Tides! It's the tiny, secluded place right near the beach. Right Roger?" I ask.

"Yes. I thought my truck would be less noticeable there in case someone came looking for me after I visited the sheriff's office."

"Remember the woman Harvey is hanging out with now?" I ask. "She works at the motel sometimes. I thought she worked days cleaning rooms, but she might be working the desk. They're not particular about who they hire. Or Harvey might have another connection there through her. A friend, maybe?"

"Alright. Good. Doesn't explain how Rose knew where Roger was, Chance says.

"Anything else?"

"Roger! Isn't this enough?"

"Sorry, man. I only meant do you have anything else to say? We should keep Rose somewhat involved so we can figure out how she plays into all of this. Probably too early to decide," Roger says.

"Uh, that's not all I had to tell you," Chance says. "Rose told her boy she had to work at the store in the morning"

"And?" I have no patience for long stories right now.

"The little guy said, 'Mommy, you don't have to work. You have lots of money.' She told him she didn't, but he argued, 'Yes, you do. You have a suitcase full of money under my bed. I saw it!'"

I gasp. Roger stares. We wait for Chance to continue.

"She denied it, of course. I knew by the look on her face it is true. She rushed the kid off to bed and I left. Couldn't trust myself to talk to her right then."

"Where was Lee?" Roger asks.

"He was up at Grandma Kline's. Rose asked him to take some groceries up there."

"I don't like all these strangers going up to Grandma's."

"Me neither, Ellie. I was surprised the crew had cleaned Rose's apartment and left before we arrived. Archie saw me at the café and gave me the keys. Said there wasn't much to clean. Some blood in the sink, a few drops on the carpet, and a broken bottle in the trash with a little blood on it," Chance says.

As I expected. Rose can stretch a story. Roger doesn't seem surprised, either.

We sit in silence for several moments before Roger says, "Look, this hurts both of you a lot. I'll stop by and talk to Rose some more, maybe catch Lee, too. By tomorrow we'll know who is lying to us. No decisions, today."

Chance and I nod in agreement, but I doubt it will be easy.

25

I READ THROUGH THE SHERIFF'S FILE AND AM STARTLED WHEN
Roger calls out breakfast is ready. Anticipation draws me toward the kitchen
where I will join Roger and Chance at the table to attack ham and cheese
omelets, hash browns and piles of toast made from the loaf of bread I froze
on the last baking day. Good thing I always pre-slice the loaves.

"It looks like you didn't get much sleep last night, Miss Investigator."
Chance pulls a chair out and gives a plate to me.

"No sleep at all. I'm afraid I may nod off while I'm eating."

"Tell us something about the file before you sleep. We've been patient.
All good things end. Your time's up," Roger says as he slides a plate of toast
across the table. "Hand me your cup and I'll pour your tea."

Amazing! He cooks and pours tea.

"For one, we have lots of work to do."

"I figured," Chance says.

I continue, "Everything in there is from the Sheriff's office, except
reports from the CI."

"The what?" Chance asks.

"Sorry. Confidential informant. We call them CIs, like the cops do. It appears he fingered Mark right away. There are several references to the CI. About Jean's murder, and about the grave robbing."

"They have an informer on grave robbers?" Roger asks. "Weird. Wonder how they got him."

"The strange thing is the early reports on Jean's murder were all written by Deputy Dan Harrington. Another deputy took over the case with no explanation of what happened to Harrington. Odd. Usually you stick with a case until it's solved. Maybe he quit the department. Something's not right. Especially since it was Deputy Kramer who took over."

"The sheriff? So, he was telling the truth when he told Rose he was the primary investigator on the case, and when he told me they didn't get the real killer the first time?" Chance asks.

"Yes! We'll have a tough time working through all this. At least now we know why he's concentrating on following us instead of solving the murder. It took me all night to read through the file. I made some notes. The next step is to make a more complete timeline. When we have it, we'll be able to find the holes, the inconsistencies," I explain.

"How long will it take?"

Roger seems impatient today. But he should know every successful investigation relies on a solid understanding of what occurred. Someone must thoroughly understand the case, especially when it involves a case about a wrongfully convicted person sentenced to life in prison. Like Mark.

"A timeline is never complete, never finished. It will take at least a full day to do a preliminary timeline. Perhaps with help from one of you, it will go a little faster."

"I can help, Ellie," Roger offers. "Chance has to go to his office this morning. Let's get the timeline worked up so we can discuss the case on our way over the mountain on Friday."

"Friday? I thought we were going on Saturday."

"Ellie, Roger and I talked about the trip this morning," Chance says. "We decided to change it to Friday because it is better for Delvin. "I called him. Friday is better for him. His son has a ball game on Saturday. Their reburial ceremony has been scheduled for Friday afternoon and evening."

"We'll leave here about 5:30. Will give us time to stop and copy the file somewhere," Roger says.

"5:30 a.m.? Ohhh." I groan and hold my head.

"Hey, stay up all night and you'll be ready to go." Chance is always so helpful.

"Let's get back to the file, shall we? There's some important stuff in there you need to hear about."

"Like what?" Roger asks.

"The informant was not Indian."

"That was in the reports?" Chance asks.

"No, it didn't say so."

"How do you know then?" Chance is confused. So young and innocent.

"The informant communicates by pay phone. Few of the Indians living here on the rez at the time would have used a pay phone to call the sheriff to snitch on someone. There were only two pay phones. Too public."

"What if the informant was one of our people being paid by the sheriff?" Chance asks. "You told us this was a possibility. We had to be careful of who we trust."

"Yes, I did. Now. I'm talking about when Jean was murdered. It is very unlikely there was a paid Indian informant in those years because someone would have known. He or she would have been killed in an accident if discovered. Nothing happened here the aunties didn't know about."

"It's not impossible, Ellie, and we have to assume it could have happened. Since we now know there was an informant, we must keep all options open," Roger says.

I stare at him, struggling to believe anyone in our community had offered the information I'd read in the file. My professional brain soon gained control but remembering what I'd seen years ago and the ultimatum I received from a grave robber, anything is possible.

"You're right, Roger. We'll keep our options open."

"I need to get ready for work. What else, Ellie?" Chance asks.

"Let me run through my list. We can save the discussion 'til later. For Jean's murder," I continue, "in addition to the informant, and the mystery of the disappearing deputy, there was suspicion Mark acted on behalf of another person. Perhaps the father of Jean's child."

"I'll talk to Grandma Kline. I mean I'll make a note one of us should, probably you, Ellie."

He's learning.

"Yes, thanks. Then the deputy interviewed a co-worker of Jean's, supposedly a close friend who remembered Jean talking suicide."

"Right Tried to strangle herself and stabs herself in the chest? Who kills themselves that way?" Roger interrupts.

I choke back a gasp. How does he know about the stabbing?

"And, there is a follow-up report by a completely different deputy saying Jean gave birth to a boy at the county hospital in Portland."

"No one came to tell my family?" Chance pounds his fist on the table, rattling the dishes.

"According to the report, a deputy did tell Grandma. Or tried to. He drove to her house to tell her. When he got to the open door, Grandma held a shotgun and told him to get back into his truck. She told him whatever he had come to say, she already knew and didn't want to hear it from a white cop."

"He didn't tell her?"

"No. That's one report in the file I don't question. Exactly the way Grandma would handle the situation now, so I can imagine she was scary then. She doesn't miss with her shotgun. I will carefully compare the sheriff's reports with the transcripts of Mark's trial. I didn't see anything in those reports they could have used to convict him."

"Any witness interviews?"

"None, Roger. There isn't even an interview with the fisherman who found Jean's body. He is mentioned, but no report of an interview."

"Let's be sure we find him," Roger tells Chance. "Be sure he's on the list."

"Chance, you need to get to work on time. I'll sleep for a few hours and then Roger and I can work on the timeline."

"I'm going. I should be able to wrap it up by two o'clock, maybe three. What are your plans, Roger?" Chance asks as he heads to the door.

"As soon as I get the dishes done. ..." He grins and pauses until our laughter ceases. "I'll read the reports about the murder scene. When Ellie wakes, I can help her with that part of the timeline."

Chance puts on his jacket and quietly asks, "So you plan to let her sleep?"

"Get out of here," I shout.

Chance closes the door as the pillow hits it. I retrieve the pillow and place it back on the couch while Roger clears the table and carries the dishes to the sink.

"Roger, I'm convinced Chance should concentrate on the grave robbing while you and I investigate the murder."

"I don't have time to do that, Ellie. I want to know if Chance was stolen and sold to Hank Andrews. And, also, whether Hank is, or was, selling Indian babies. Not interested in an old murder case or thieves."

Not the response I expected. We're right back where we started with Detective Roger Wood, except he did get the sheriff's file. I am waiting for his explanation. So far, he's avoided telling me.

26

THE SUN IS RISING OVER THE EASTERN HILLS WHEN I LOCK MY house door and climb into Chance's Jeep. The sun shines on the barren hillsides raped by the greedy timber corporations whose payrolls are a major source of income for my people.

We travel the ribbon of two-lane highway through the corridor of majestic evergreens, leafy alders and vine maples, basking in nature's beauty, though I know just out of sight the land lays barren all the way to the Pacific on the west, and towards the fertile fields of the Willamette to the east.

It's sad. Chance has no memories of the huge second growth trees covering the hills in a glorious green forest. No memories of the one-log loads of magnificent old growth trees headed to the mills to be cut into lumber to build the nation's houses. The forests he sees are only tree farms planted in compliance with government rules after the corporations sweep the hillsides clean. He's new to the area.

After being away for so many years, with only my dreams of days spent beneath the cedars watching Mark pick fern, or along the river bank, sitting in the shade of an old spruce, waiting for a nibble on my fishing line, I was shocked nearly speechless at the first sight of the hills covered with tiny seedlings.

Chance turns east onto Highway 20. I recognize the green Ford pickup pulling out from the first side road. It drops in behind us. I didn't see the driver, didn't dare turn to look. The truck belongs to one of the sheriff's deputies, the one who usually works as a jailer on day shift. He left the courthouse parking lot when I was there a few weeks ago to change my voter registration. Now I reach into my bag to ensure the sheriff's file is tucked away.

Though the road which connects coastal Oregon with the Willamette Valley is somewhat improved from when I lived here before, it still takes nearly an hour to reach Corvallis, home of the Beavers of Oregon State University. One of my relatives showed the state what an Indian athlete from a tiny reservation could accomplish on a college football field.

"Why so quiet this morning, Ellie? Is my driving making you nervous?"

"Oh, no. Looking at the hillsides and feeling sad. I don't much like traveling this road."

"You were wringing your hands together. Does the logging bother you so much?"

I look down at my hands and see they are turning white.

"Nostalgia, I guess. There's no way to explain what it used to look like. It's so sad."

Plus, it is irritating you haven't noticed someone is following us.

"I've seen the pictures in the museum. Huge old trees. The men standing on the saws look like ants."

"I played on some of the stumps of those old trees. You could climb up the side of one, sit there and pretend it was your house it was so big.

Even when I left here, there were some very large trees in the woods. The trucks coming through town carried two, sometimes three, logs.

As we pass by the store called Burnt Woods, I notice a gray Chevy sedan, older, in good shape, backed into a space near the east end of the lone store. It looks ready for a quick exit. I catch a brief glimpse of the driver, a 60ish guy, looking west. I watch in the side mirror as the pickup turns off and parks in front of the store. The Chevy pulls onto the highway after letting another car pass. I sigh and wonder why these incompetent fools are following Chance, again.

"The trucks now have so many logs you can't count them all before they're out of sight," Chance continues.

He is oblivious to the activity behind us, but I say only, "I know. Most of the trees will be chipped. Mostly alder."

"Your connection to this area, what it used to be, reminds me of a conversation I had with Old Joe Logsden the other day, Ellie."

"Oh, I'm glad you've heard Old Joe's stories. I used to sit beside him in front of Bensell's Store and listen for hours when I was a little girl."

"He told me his people missed their Rogue River homes so much that many were punished for running away from the reservation toward their old homes. He was curious about what the homeland was like so one day he just started running. Ran all the way to Agness, a historic community near the Rogue River. Camped by the river for a couple weeks and ran all the way home again in time to help bring in the hay from his Dad's fields at Upper Farm. Where is Upper Farm, Ellie?"

"Logsden area. Out east of Siletz. All the beautiful land up there was part of the original reservation, of course. There was Upper Farm, Lower Farm down towards Kernville, and Agency Farm in Siletz. Those government agents were determined to make farmers out of our hunters and gatherers."

"Old Joe said it took him about a week to get to the Rogue," Chance continues. "Said the sadness he felt at Port Orford where our people were kept in cages until they could be put on ships for the trip to the Columbia brought tears to his eyes, and to mine, as he described it. As he ran alone at night carrying his Eagle staff and hearing the ocean pound, he felt as if the elders were running with him. The anticipation of the last mile brought unbelievable joy with connection to the land."

"His stories are so beautiful and moving. I've heard some of the old women walked all the way to the Rogue, too. They all wanted so desperately to return to their homeland and their old ways, back to honor the land and the graves of their ancestors."

"So much sadness in our history, Ellie. Maybe someday the tribe will take the children on a run to the Rogue. Maybe everybody will want to go."

"Got any good suggestions for breakfast? We're almost to Corvallis and I am ready to stop."

"The best place to eat is Burton's. Best breakfast in the area. Turn here. It'll take us right there."

Chance steps inside the restaurant door and watches a man leave the sedan and head for Burton's. Maybe he was aware of the tag game the deputies played as they followed us, after all. From the stern look on his face, I think I misjudged his observation skills.

"Ignore him, Chance. He's too stupid to pull off his masquerade."

"Son of a. …" Chance sputters.

I squeeze his arm and whisper, "Don't."

Inside, Chance chooses a booth. The deputy takes a seat across from us.

A little too loud, I ask, "Chance, are you ready to place some bets on the ball games? I think the White Sox are headed for the World Series this year." I pull a pen and notepad from my bag.

Chance looks at me, momentarily stunned by my sudden interest in baseball. He recovers and says, "Are you nuts? The Cubs have it all the way this year. White Sox? Where did you get such a screwy idea?" He picks up the pen and writes, "Where is the file?"

"In my bag," I scribble.

"May I take your order?" The waitress is young, probably an Oregon State student. She chews the eraser on her pencil and flips her stringy, auburn hair as she stares at Chance.

"Good morning Miss," Chance begins. "This is my first time in your restaurant. I'm told the food is excellent."

When she doesn't respond, he continues, "We want the best breakfast you have. What do you recommend?"

His charm works, as usual, but why now? Why not just order?

The girl seems mesmerized. She removes the eraser from her pouty mouth to answer, "Our breakfast special is pancakes, hash browns, two eggs cooked any way you wish."

And anything else you wish at this moment, sir. Chance's effect on women is so predictable. Like Logan did, he knows how to use the power that comes with his looks.

"Ok. I'll have the special. Eggs over easy, rye toast, sausage links. And coffee."

She writes his order. When she looks toward me, Chance says, "Oh, Melanie, could you please move us to the very back of the room? We have business to discuss and it's a little crowded up here,"

"Of course, sir. Follow me." She touches his shoulder, and her chubby fingers brush, just a little, through the tips of the shiny, black hair spread across his shoulders. "Show me where you'd like to sit."

Clever. Now if the guy moves, he'll expose himself. Blow his cover. Of course, Melanie's forgotten I haven't ordered. I smile as I follow her exaggerated hip swing knowing she thinks Chance is directly behind her.

We pass the far end of the line of booths when I hear Chance say, "Sorry man, we decided to move farther back. Microphones and tape recorders ruin my appetite, if you know what I mean."

I turn to see Chance shaking hands with the astonished deputy. Not a smart move Chance but I enjoy the look on the guy's face.

Later, as we're leaving, Chance sees a pay phone near the door, dials a number and I hear, "Hey, man. Got your girlfriend here with me. Be careful what you say. We're leaving Corvallis. Had an escort all the way from Toledo. They changed tails a couple times. Not too smart, those deputies."

Now I'm ashamed to have doubted him.

"What time? Okay, good. If you get to Hood River first, look around for a quiet print shop where we can make copies." He listens, then says, "I'll tell her. OK. See ya." He hangs up the phone and begins to whistle as we walk to his Jeep.

When I could no longer stand the suspense, I demand, "Quit whistling and tell me what Roger said."

"Roger? Why do you think it was Roger?" He grins and ducks, probably expecting to feel my purse connect with his head.

"Reminded me to tell you we won't be going home until tomorrow."

"Tomorrow? Why?"

"Delvin believes the ceremony will go into the night and Roger should attend. He insists Roger and I both need to experience this. We have to stay over."

"Great. I don't suppose you could have told me before we left home? What am I supposed to do about clothes? Where are we staying?"

"Yesterday while you were totally engrossed in reading the file, we packed a change of clothes for you. I even remembered your traditional regalia for the ceremony. Then last night when I went up to check on my place, I bought some personal items like a toothbrush and a hairbrush for you and put them in your bag."

His grin is so huge I'm not certain I want to hear any more.

"Why? Wouldn't it have been easier to tell me to pack?"

"I thought so. Roger was afraid you'd refuse to go if you knew about it."

"What is the big deal about staying overnight somewhere? You're obviously leaving something out. . .where are we staying?"

"I wasn't supposed to tell you. Guess I screwed up."

"Where? Tell me. What can be so awful I would refuse to go?"

"We've been invited to spend the night with Roger's mother. Now don't give me a look. Roger will be insulted if we don't show up,"

"A look is not what you deserve. How could you do this to me? Roger's mother's house? My god."

"It'll be fine. You'll see."

I slap his hand away as he tries to reassure me. I could do without his silly grin. This is impossible. What if Roger's mother suspects how I feel about her son? She probably loves his ex and wants them back together. I glare at the road for several miles, then turn to shout at Chance, "You think you're pretty clever, don't you? How can I make a presentable appearance before his mother? God knows what you packed for me."

"It will be fine. You'll look beautiful, as always. Roger picked out your clothes for you. The outer clothes, anyway. I made him stay out of your underwear drawer."

He laughs more. After a moment of stony silence, I begin to laugh, too, until the tears flow. It has been a long time since anyone has tricked me this well. No one has dared since Logan died.

27

WE MEET ROGER AT THE POLICE STATION IN RIVER CITY, THEN travel through the Columbia Gorge, where I point out important historical landmarks to Chance.

"I had no idea this area was so amazing," Chance says as we pass Multnomah Falls.

"Too bad we have to get to Delvin's office this afternoon or we could stop for a while," I comment as Chance slows for an extended view.

"It would take some time. I'd want to hike up there to the bridge. See where people are crossing over the falls?"

"It's a beautiful view from there. You can go all the way to the top. My first trip here when I left Siletz with Russ, the cool mist of the falls brushed my face as we climbed higher and higher on the narrow trail."

Past the falls area, we ride in silence, taking in the panoramic vistas. Tug boats plying the Columbia River pull barges and log rafts. Someone is on a board with a sail gliding across the choppy water like an unchoreographed ballet for a giant butterfly. Rock bluffs give way to rolling hills.

Across the river on the Washington side of the Gorge, I see vineyards and the Maryhill Museum, former home of the late financier, Sam Hill, where ancient Indian baskets, Paris fashions and Rodin art share display space.

"I've always wanted to take the sternwheeler trip on the Columbia River," I say to no one in particular.

"That would be fun. What are you writing in your notebook?" Chance asks.

Roger doesn't answer. Before he closes the little cop book, I see 'Take Ellie on Columbia trip.' I look away, hope he didn't see me snooping. I'm glad Chance lets the incident drop without further comment.

We stop at a restaurant in Hood River. While we wait for our lunch orders, I decide to continue a prior conversation. Being careful to keep my voice just louder than a whisper, I say, "I found some more interesting information in the sheriff's file."

"Tell us," Chance says.

"For one thing, the deputy who wrote most of the early reports is not the same deputy who testified at trial. I double-checked the transcript."

"You mean they let someone else testify he did the initial investigation?" Roger leans closer.

"Yes, it seems so. Of course, we don't have the exhibits to go with the transcript, but the deputy testified the reports were his even though the reports in the sheriff's file were signed by Harrington."

"Strange."

"Either the defense attorney was stupid, or someone doctored the discovery before it was turned over to him."

"Wow. Can it be used to prove Mark's innocence?" Chance leans forward, straining to hear my words.

"It won't walk him out, though it might help get a new trial."

"We don't have time to worry about Mark. We have to solve the stuff about your Dad, remember?" Roger fixes his frustrated gaze on Chance.

"We can do it all, Roger. It takes more work, especially on my part." I hope to divert his intense concentration on Chance, but it doesn't work.

"How so?" he asks and keeps his eyes on Chance.

"As I review each document and make comparisons and timelines, I watch for information that might be helpful to Mark. I keep good notes."

"And then what?" More interested now, Roger looks away from Chance and stares at me, waiting for more convincing answers.

"When we have all we can find, we present it to a good criminal defense attorney. One who isn't afraid to fight for justice."

"Like we're going to find one who can convince the government an Indian was wrongfully convicted," Chance sneers.

"Oh, that's the easy part. We have the attorney. We have to bring the information to him and find funds to pay him."

"You know someone who could, would, do it?"

"Yes, I do. It's way too early to call him. No use to waste his time."

"So back to the fake deputy, the fake reports. What happened to the first guy?" Roger asks.

"There wasn't anything in the sheriff's file. Nothing in the trial transcript about him at all. He vanished."

Roger pulls out his notebook again, flips it open to a clean page and asks, "What's his name, again? Sounds like it should be my assignment. Find this guy."

"Nah. A few local questions, some smoke signals, will turn him up. His name is Daniel Harrington. Badge number LC-569. We heard he died in a wreck on the Siletz Highway."

"If he didn't, he's probably retired by now," Chance guesses. "Or a sheriff in another county."

"Be careful if either of you mention him to anyone. Don't mention why we are looking for him. We don't want to stir up anything and have him disappear completely," I caution.

"If he's still alive," Roger says.

"If he isn't, it makes the investigation even more important. We want to know where, when, why, and how he died," I say.

Roger makes a few more notes, then looks at me.

"What's the name of the deputy who testified?"

"Jim Lofton. I made a copy of the timeline for each of you. I want you to read it, make notes on questions that come to mind. As soon as you've finished, we will discuss them."

I pull two thirty-page documents from my bag and hand one to Roger, one to Chance.

"Holy. … This is huge. How long did it take to finish? There were only ten pages when I left for River City on Wednesday."

Roger's approval ignites a familiar glow. I push it away, intent on forgetting Roger until the investigation is completed.

"All I've done since we got the file. Reading and typing. I do all these reports, timeline, people lists, notes for special topics, as I read through the second time. Saves some time. Of course, I have to read the whole thing again."

"Again? Why?" Chance asks, a puzzled look on his face.

I can't determine what Roger's gaze holds.

"I'm sorry, Chance. I forget how new all this is to you. Nothing is ever considered complete because every tiny piece of new evidence or rumor we turn up has to be evaluated against what we thought we knew before."

"Sounds like a lot of work."

"It is a lot of work. This mess will be even more work than usual. In addition to the tribe's grave robbing travesty, we have a cold murder case--always terribly difficult re-investigations--a wrongful conviction and allegations your Dad sells Indian babies. This is beyond a lot of work."

Saying it aloud, reminds me of the enormity of what we have taken on. I'm thankful the men are silent as they eat. Grateful for the hand that squeezes mine. Compared to the difficulty in identifying and stopping grave robbers, solving the murder seems like an easy assignment. The pressure of Chance's hand tells me his heart feels the same agony and apprehension. Roger is another story. I dare not look into his eyes. Not now. Not until later when I hope he'll finally understand.

Chance turns to the left, makes two quick turns. Roger recognizes the area and asks, "Where you going? This isn't right. You want me to drive?"

"Nope. There's a cemetery out here we wanted to check out. Lots of old graves. Some pioneer graves. Should be interesting," Chance explains.

I watch my hands pale as I twist them together. I don't trust myself to speak.

"I know there's a cemetery here. My grandparents, one set, are buried here. You didn't have time to stop at Multnomah Falls, so why visit a cemetery?"

Chance parks inside the cemetery gate, turns off the engine. He opens his door and hits the release button to open the trunk.

"Hurry, Ellie. It doesn't look like anyone's around. Grab one of those shovels."

Already out the door. I grope in the open trunk, grab a shovel and push past Roger who is standing at the front passenger door, bewilderment on his handsome face. I feel a terrible surge of guilt for what we are about to do to him.

"C'mon. Hurry! We don't have much time before the watchman comes back. He's probably on a break," Chance shouts back at Roger as he runs past me straight for the row of graves we identified in a phone call with a relative last night.

Chance pushes the edge of a shovel into the grass before I reach the grave, out of breath. *Elizabeth J. Wood*, I read to myself and smile.

I turn to see Roger running hard and hear him shout, "Hey, hey. Quit, dammit."

He skids to a stop, grabs the shovel from Chance and throws it three graves eastward.

"What the hell are you doing, Chance? This is my grandmother's grave."

"Yep, sure is."

"Roger, this is important. Delvin's tribe has this wonderful museum." I grab his arm, stare up into his face, praying for the strength to carry this out. "There's a section for the white pioneers, lots of children's skeletons. Even some miscellaneous bones for visitors to handle," I explain.

Roger jerks away from me.

"What? They can't have such displays."

"Why not?"

"It's not right. There are laws. What're you doing? Stop!"

Roger struggles to push the shovel aside when Chance puts it in his hand. Chance keeps his hand firmly over Roger's to maintain control of the shovel.

"Dig, man. They need a woman's skull for the front entrance to the museum. A white woman's skull," Chance emphasizes. He forces Roger's hand down so the shovel slides into the slit in the sod.

"Think how proud you'll be when all those tourists stare at her skull and try to decide if it was big enough to hold a good working brain or if she was an animal," I exclaim with faked excitement, clapping my hands, feigning happiness. This is so sick. I sure hope it works.

I hear a vehicle approaching at a rapid speed and turn as a white truck rounds a corner and skids to a stop.

"Uh, oh," I say and back away, leaving Chance and Roger to face the stern Indian man who jumps out of the truck.

"Hey, what's going on here? What are you doing with a shovel?" The man approaches Roger, who since Chance has backed away, stands holding the shovel embedded in the soil at the edge of his own grandmother's grave. He shakes, and his normally tanned face is a sickly yellow.

"It's okay, sir. We need a white woman's skull for the museum over across the mountain and this man has volunteered his grandmother," I begin as I step forward to shake the guard's hand.

"No! I did not. I'm a cop. These people are crazy. Help me." Roger sounds like he is begging for his life while standing there with the shovel stuck in the ground. I feel so guilty and take a couple of steps toward him, then back away again when I see the warning scowl on Chance's face.

"Help you what? Dig up your grandmother? No, I don't want to ruin your donation. You must do it," the guard says as he walks back to his truck.

"No. I am not digging up this grave. They're making me do it."

"I think it's great you want to help us Indians. Usually your people are over in our cemeteries digging up our grandmothers."

Roger looks again at the guard and appears surprised to be talking to an Indian. As his knees begin to buckle, Chance grabs him from behind in a bear hug, and gently says, "Relax man. Now you know a little of what it feels like." He sets Roger on the ground and kneels beside him as Roger loses his lunch all over his grandmother's grave.

I hurry over to hug the guard. "Thanks, Arnold."

"Any time, Ellie."

He bends down to touch Roger's shoulder. "Sorry man. I'll see you tonight at the ceremony."

Roger remains motionless, staring straight ahead as the pickup moves slowly back down the lane. There is bewilderment, and something else, on his tortured face. Chance has helped him to a clean, grassy spot where I join them. Roger buries his face in his hands. When I try to touch him, he jerks away.

"You had to know, Man. We couldn't make you understand about the pain digging up our people causes us, so we thought we'd show you just a little. You have been given the gift of understanding," Chance explains.

"Gift!" Roger's head shoots straight up in unison with his arms flying out on each side. The force of his movement knocks me backward and knocks Chance off balance and onto the grass. "Gift! What the hell kind of gift was that? Digging up my grandmother is your idea of a gift?"

He glares at me sprawled in the grass, stands up and shakes violently to rid himself of clippings from the freshly mowed grass. He so resembles a wet dog shaking himself I quickly clamp my hand over my mouth, look up at him, wait for his reaction.

Roger stares back at me. His tan has returned. His eyes are cold and unfriendly. I stay seated, even though the cold grass urges me to pee.

Chance is still sprawled behind Roger. His head is turned away from me. His heaving shoulders the only outward sign of his laughter.

Finally, Roger looks down at me, then turns to look at Chance. "Are you two lamebrains going to sit around laughing all day or are you going to help me restore this sod?"

Is there a twinkle in those blue eyes? Lord, I hope so.

I roll to one side to push myself up. Suddenly, strong arms lift me, and I am nose to nose with the blue-eyed face. Now my knees shake. He holds me there for several seconds before he whispers, "You're going to pay for this little trick, miss." His lips brush against my cheek before he drops his arms and turns toward Chance who is staring at us.

"And you, mister. Is this one of the 'Old Indian tricks' you've mentioned?" He slaps Chance's shoulder and walks back to the gravesite.

Chance follows, picks up a shovel and repairs the sod while I retrieve the other shovel, carry it to the car, then walk back to the men.

"Let's say prayers for your grandmother, Roger. We owe her an explanation."

"You sure as hell do!" he replies, then asks, "What do we do?"

"Whatever makes peace in your heart," Chance says.

"I'll go first with our apology," I offer. "We did prayers last night for blessings to protect us from what it might appear we were doing."

"And to make sure you didn't have a heart attack while we were gifting you," Chance adds.

Roger's snort is a comment I can't decipher.

28

ROGER'S BEHIND THE WHEEL AS WE POUND EASTWARD ON I-84. I'm in the back seat again with the police reports, not reading. Lost in thought, wondering what Delvin will say tonight, what the ceremony will be like. The bones to be reburied are from the Smithsonian, not from a university in Washington. Messed-up smoke signal, I guess.

"So, Ellie," Roger says. "Tell us more about the file. What else is in there?"

"Regarding the actual scene of Jean's death, I only found information about where she was discovered, a list of the physical evidence, a list of the photos, no actual photos," I begin.

"Does it say exactly where she was found? Anything you could use to locate the spot?" Roger asks.

"No, there's a crude map, but it doesn't show identifiers. It's a drawing of where she was lying, where the car was, and where the bonfire with the bones. . . .. Good lord, Roger! What are you doing?" I scream and grab at a door handle to support myself in the wildly weaving vehicle.

"Sorry. What you said about bones. Forgot I was driving. You okay?"

I shout at him as he looks at me in the rearview mirror, "Yes. Keep your eyes on the road."

Chance has his right hand braced on the dashboard as he turns to glare at Roger. "Me, too. Not that you asked. Is this how cops drive?"

"I was so surprised. ..."

"Oh no."

"What? What's wrong, Ellie?" Chance asks.

"The cops left the bones in the fire."

"Damn!"

"That's not good," Roger agreed. "If they were still in the sheriff's evidence room, we could try to determine if they were animal bones."

"Doesn't look like they are there."

"Maybe if they put the fire out somebody from the tribe picked up the bones," Chance suggests.

"Oh, no way!" I didn't mean to respond so loudly, but the thought horrifies me. "No one would touch those bones, Chance."

"Not even someone like the old guy who helps with the reburial for Delvin's tribe when the museums return bones?"

"Not then. Now he probably would. He would know the ceremonies. He was over the mountain at the other rez. No one would have known to ask him to come here. Remember our tribe is researching and learning our traditions. We never had ceremonies to rebury people. They were supposed to stay buried."

"If there weren't any ceremonies, how are you learning them now?" Roger asks.

"It's been a long process. Some of the elders have helped create ceremonies and some younger tribal members have been in touch with related tribes on the southern coast who have retained their customs and traditions. There weren't any for reburials."

"I've been invited to participate in a couple of the giftings of old dances since I came home," Chance comments. "It was an emotional experience knowing we were learning what our ancestors knew."

"I'll bet," Roger says. "Anyway, back to the file. There's always the possibility someone from the sheriff's office picked up the bones as evidence and didn't put it in the report."

"So, it isn't out of the realm of possibility one of the deputies, or even the sheriff, might have taken a bone or two?" I ask.

"No, not at all. Check to see if anyone reported returning to the scene later. He would be the most likely person. Fire would be cold. Bones would be cold. No one around to notice."

"Here! In Ellie's timeline," Chance shouts. "It says Harrington went back out to the scene the next day to take more photos. Looks like he went by himself. Do you remember, Ellie?"

"He signed the report and mentioned he was there. No other officers listed, or it would be on my timeline."

"When we find his widow, we must ask about those bones. He might have stashed them away somewhere or talked about them," Chance said.

"Maybe. Getting anyone to talk about bones will be difficult. There is a law against stealing human bones from a grave," I remind them.

"If they were human. We've assumed so, I guess."

"Chance, you're right. We have always assumed it, but there's nothing anywhere that tells us they were human bones."

"I checked on a phone call Hank made one night. Found out it was the number for a company up in Washington state. They sells bones," Roger offers. "That same one you mentioned a check was from."

"Good god, Roger. And you've been telling us grave robbing has nothing to do with your investigation of my adoptive father? Why didn't you mention this when I told you about the check?" Chance hits the dashboard for emphasis.

"I don't know, Chance. It didn't click before. Sorry. I know you tried to tell me. All this Indian stuff is new to me. For me the idea of people digging up graves, taking the bones home with them, is unreal. It didn't compute until now."

"Ever hear of archaeologists?" I ask.

Chance groans. "Don't confuse him with facts, Ellie."

"You lost me again. What do archaeologists have to do with this?" Roger glances in the mirror again as he seeks my answer.

"Never mind. It's an ongoing dispute over whether archaeologists are scientists who serve a useful purpose or are grave robbers with university degrees," Chance explains. "Nothing to do with this case."

"As far as we know," I mutter, not willing to give up my prejudice against the professional diggers.

"I had an old uncle, great uncle, who called himself an amateur archaeologist," Roger says. "He was a doctor in Wenatchee. People came over from London to buy pieces from his collection."

"I'm warning you, don't get her started."

"He did a lot of scientific. ..."

"Stop it," I snap. "I don't want to hear another word. Someday we'll discuss this uncle of yours. Not today. I don't want to think about him or the other Wenatchee amateur archaeologists right now."

"Okay, already. Sorry."

I regret my bluntness, sort of.

We will meet Delvin at his office on the reservation. Before we get there, I must calm down and do some explaining to the cop.

29

THE TRIBAL CEMETERY ON THE EASTERN OREGON RESERVA-
tion is smaller than ours. Standing with the crowd, I notice the wind-
swept land, the lack of evergreen trees and underbrush so familiar on
our coastal land. Here the cemetery is surrounded by yellow wheat fields.
Rows of tombstones carry the names of local families. Some gravesites are
mounded with dirt and decorated with honor gifts just as we have in our
Paul Washington Cemetery.

In front of me an open gravesite waits for conclusion of the ceremony to return stolen bones to the earth; bones tossed into a storeroom at
the Smithsonian decades ago.

Tiny whirlwinds gather dust, swirl it up and into my nose. It covers
my long, traditional beaded buckskin dress with a gritty, brown powder
and settles on my braids. I sneeze, swat at my dress, and shake my braids a
bit, trying not to be too obvious. Will my hosts think it rude to brush away
the dust of their land as I fight to stifle another sneeze? I look around, don't
recognize anyone close by. No one seems to notice me.

A hush falls over the crowd as Delvin Jones makes his way to the gravesite. I marvel at the strength and power of this Indian man. Though he has chosen to live among his mother's clan, he more closely resembles his paternal cousins on the Siletz, where our men are short, stocky, powerful and handsome in their youth. The difficult task of growing up Indian can leave them broken in their later years. Facing defeat and the early death of their dreams, many succumb before their prime to alcohol, diabetes, tragic accidents, or the cancers caused by poisons sprayed on our forests by timber companies. Few reach their sixties. Delvin is different. In his late forties, he looks young and physically fit. He might make it to become a real elder.

He is my cousin. Second cousin. He's become a leader in his tribe. Despite a difficult childhood, and more than his share of tragedies and sorrow, his bronzed face still holds the glow of youth. His hair, caught and tied at the nape of his neck with a strip of elk hide, flows down the center of his back. Rather than regalia seen in public events like the popular Pow Wows, he wears boots, jeans and a blue Ribbon Shirt.

I recall a quote from a recent newspaper article as I admire the uncommon gentleness in his face and manner. "Delvin Jones is a survivor, a fighter destined to lead the people of many tribes, Indian and white alike, to a new place of understanding and cohesive peace."

His fight is on paper, in quiet, forceful presentations in board rooms and legislative offices against the prejudice and misconceptions fostered by politicians and businessmen. His way of educating the white man in Indian ways has been quite successful.

This was my dream for Logan when I realized his strong connection to our culture. That dream died with him in an instant of crushed and tangled metal. As I struggle against tears which still come without warning from deep within. I feel a large, warm hand cradle mine. I don't look up as I squeeze my eyelids shut to stem the flow of tears but am thankful for Chance's thoughtfulness.

As Delvin's strong voice penetrates my sorrow, a calmness fills me. But a sideways glance brings a shocking revelation. It is Roger's hand I so desperately clutch in my grief. The burning rush of warmth floods my face and elicits a sympathetic smile from the cop.

Here I am at the most sacred of Native ceremonies, acting like a love-starved divorcee holding hands with a white cop. I'm going to hear about this from the aunties.

"We don't choose to speak for our ancestors," I hear Delvin say. "We are chosen by them. They come to us in many ways and it is left to us to recognize our path. We must come to know they are reaching out to us."

Upwards of a hundred brown faces look toward him.

"They reach out to us now, telling us they didn't make it to the other side," the strong voice continues. "Their journey to the next world was interrupted. Someone violated their resting places. Someone stole their bones. Someone may have used these bones for evil purposes."

I look up at Roger and wonder if he understands the words, if he feels the pain after what he experienced at his grandmother's grave. He doesn't seem to notice my glance. His eyes are fixed on Delvin's face, his attention on the words.

"We must be ever mindful of the old ways. We must practice them and teach our children to respect the ancestors, to have respect for the natural world. We have a purpose beyond making money and owning big houses," Delvin says. He paces in front of the crowd, locking eyes with the people.

"These stolen bones of our ancestors have been returned to us because we recognized our responsibility and worked with the authorities to retrieve them. This has not always been the way of our people. We haven't cooperated with police and government agencies in the past. We knew we couldn't trust them."

Did I imagine he looked right at Roger?

Roger's hand tightens around mine as I realize how difficult this must be for him. A white cop standing among people conditioned to mistrust and hate him. He might be holding my hand to gather strength from me. Imagine! Roger needing my strength and comfort. It is a new concept, for sure. I reach to pat his hand. A tiny pat. Nothing to give him the wrong impression.

The crowd grows silent. The young people no longer fidget. The elders sit straight and attentive in their chairs under the arbor erected to shield them from the sun and wind.

"More of our people need to hear the call of the ancestors. You, young people, must wake up and realize the ancestors call for you to remember who you are."

The young teens ahead of me who jostled one another and complained to their mothers earlier, now neither speak nor move, their eyes locked on Delvin's face.

He takes time to focus his gaze on one group of young people, then on another, finally coming to rest on a taller Indian man near the front. He points an eagle feather at him and says, "There are those chosen to lead the fight. *Chosen*, you understand. It is not your choice."

I watch the tall man's head turn and I gasp as I realize it is Chance. As he searches the crowd for someone, I see a flicker of acknowledgment, a slight bow of his head to someone near me. Roger? I look up and see tears in the cop's eyes. The Creator is working in mysterious ways today.

"Those who have been here before are crying out for justice. They are reaching out to me, to you," and again Delvin looks at Chance. "To bring them home again. To bring peace to our people."

Moving toward the open gravesite, Delvin continues. "We are sad today because we don't know where these bones of our ancestors have been or how they were treated before they arrived at the museum. We don't know what has been done to them. When they are returned to us, we don't know if we are receiving our grandmother or a mixture of bones of several relatives. So disrespectful. So disturbing."

Tears flow down his chiseled cheekbones; some fall onto his shirt, others dry in mid-air.

"We cannot return these ancestors to their original burial spot because we don't know where it is. We don't know who is in this bundle. Out of respect, we give them a new burial site and prayers to help them find the peace they sought before the ghouls came to violate them. We rejoice they are back home. We pray their journey will now continue and be completed."

Delvin begins the reburial prayers as he lowers the sacred bundle into the hole.

My heart aches. The gentle breeze turns into a fierce wind to carry the agonized wails of sorrow across the reservation.

30

It is already nine-thirty when I wake up in a hotel room. I jerk the covers back and swing my legs off the bed to let my feet snuggle into the cozy warmth of my slippers. Instead, I feel the rough texture of carpet and remember my slippers are at home in Siletz.

Like Chance would have thought to pack my slippers. A quick peek out the window reveals a dreary, cloudy day. It fits my lousy mood.

The ceremony yesterday was emotionally draining. I'm exhausted despite a night of sleep. It went so late that Chance called to apologize to Roger's mother and reserved rooms here at the hotel. Just remembering my escape from meeting Roger's mother and staying at her home puts me in a lighter mood.

In the shower, I think about yesterday's events. The sadness was tempered a bit by Delvin's healing ceremony. I wonder if the museum staff who hurried away after placing the bones in Delvin's care, knew the danger they were in prior to his blessing. The spirits of disturbed graves are powerful. Delvin's prayers now protect those people.

Roger's warm hug last evening, the changes in the cop, seem remarkable. I am so relieved. I hope the gentleness and compassion I saw in him resulted from some understanding of the agony of our people. Some gift we gave him. Maybe he'll be a better detective now.

After a hot shower, I order an omelet from room service, then dial Chance's room phone to leave a brief message. Roger calls to check on me and says Chance was called to a meeting with Delvin.

I draw open the drapes and settle into a comfortable brown wingback chair near the window to read the newspaper delivered outside my door.

Two hours later, prepared to check out of my room, I answer the phone to hear Chance say, "El. Bad news. Marge called. She found Grandma Kline wandering in the cemetery this morning."

"Is she alright?" I yell.

"They took her to the hospital. Marge will keep her there until you get home. She won't talk to anyone, except you."

"I'll meet you at the front desk."

31

CHANCE PARKS NEAR THE FRONT DOOR OF THE RIVER CITY
police station so Roger can retrieve the truck he left here for safekeeping. I
walk to a pay phone to call Marge at the hospital in Newport.

"Hey. How is Grandma doing?"

"She seems fine. Won't tell us anything. When I told her you would
be here tonight, she smiled and decided to eat her breakfast."

"Good. I wonder what's bothering her?"

I realize I'm twisting one of my braids with my right hand as we
talk. I know the signs. Grandma isn't sick. At least not the kind of sick
which means going to the hospital or even seeing a doctor. Something else
is wrong. She will only tell someone she trusts.

"I can't figure it out, Ellie."

"We're in River City now. Roger's heading home. Chance and I
should be there around eight or nine, I think."

"Don't rush. Grandma's fine. Nothing was wrong with her. She
decided to find you and forgot she was too old to walk to town."

"We'll find out what's going on with Grandma when I get there. Are you going to stay with her until then?"

"Of course."

Chance wants the phone, so I add, "Chance will talk to you. Be careful, Marge."

"Hey. Do they have security at the hospital? Anybody standing around there with a badge?" Chance says into the phone without taking it from me.

I hear Marge say, "No. They call the sheriff if they have a problem, or the city cops, I guess. Why?"

"Just wondering. You be careful. People are being strange these days." Chance has no idea his relative is sitting in a public hospital with a .38 revolver in her pocket.

As I hang up, Chance asks, "Why would Marge say, 'Don't worry about me, I'm prepared.' What do you think she meant, Ellie?" His face shows his concern.

"You know Marge. Could be anything." I hate lying to him, but it doesn't seem right to betray Marge's secret. She's carried her .38 for as long as I can remember. If it isn't in her apron pocket, it's in her purse. She even admitted once she puts it under her pillow at night. She refuses to discuss her reasons.

"I guess." Chance pats his right hand up and down on the steering wheel as he watches for Roger.

"We're two paranoid Indians, Ellie."

Roger walks out of the police station, waves, dangles his keys at us, then turns toward his truck.

Chance begins to back out of the lot as he asks, "Speaking of paranoid. What's up with Roger? He had a difficult time sitting still this morning. Seemed worried about something."

"He called me right after I woke up. Apologized for waking me. Said he had to make sure I was okay. Didn't he tell you when you returned from your meeting?"

"No, he didn't. How did you know I had a meeting?"

"Roger told me you were called to a meeting with Delvin."

"I guess I'll have to keep a closer watch on him next time. I told him to let you sleep. He was in a little better mood when I returned. Wonder how he knew about the meeting? Sneaky." Chance laughs and turns on the radio.

He pulls his hand back when I say, "Don't Chance. I want to talk to you. We must get past your problem with admitting Hank Andrews is your natural father as Mark explained when we saw him at the prison. Why are you fighting it?"

"I don't want. ..."

"I know and I'm sorry. You must deal with it before we can continue with this investigation. Much as I hate to say this, Chance, if you don't deal with it, you'll have to back away. You won't be any good to us if you're refusing to acknowledge the possibility."

"What will my accepting or rejecting him as my real father have to do with Jean's murder? Doesn't make sense to me."

"I don't know yet. Mark believes Hank is your father. He also believes Hank killed Jean, remember?"

"Yeah." Stiff behind the wheel, he stares straight ahead.

This won't be easy. What if he's right and Mark's theory is messed up? Is Grandma right when she says neither Jean nor Marge were his mother? Now I'm questioning Grandma's word?

"How will you deal with those issues or find out how this all fits together, if you haven't dealt with the father question?"

"It shouldn't matter." His face is set, chin jutting forward.

I can't see his eyes as he stares at the highway. I've seen this look often enough to know those eyes are glaring in indignation. Proceeding without making him angrier will be difficult.

"Chance think about it. You already have a love/hate relationship with the man."

"No, I don't. Just hate him. No love for him at all."

"Maybe we should start there. Have you ever thought about why you hate him so much? Let's talk and see where it takes us."

"Let's not." He turns to me with a slight grin. "Okay. What do you want to know?"

"Whatever you need to say to figure out why you hate him."

"From as far back as I can remember he's called me a little savage. As I got older it was damn savage."

"Maybe it was a term of endearment."

"Sure, Ellie. Everybody calls their kid a savage. How you talked about your son? Oh, hell. I'm sorry. I shouldn't have said that." He reaches across the seat and grabs my hand.

"No, I didn't, but I believe you."

"Hank always referred to me that way. Once I heard him explain to a fisherman at the docks they adopted me because his wife needed a project. Doesn't sound like a real father, does it?"

"No, I guess not! No wonder you have such bad feelings."

"I think I could have thought of him as my father even with the name calling. The beatings took care of those thoughts."

"He beat you? Why?"

"Didn't always know the reason. If I was late getting home, Mother would be upset and afraid. Never did understand what she was afraid of. It was enough to make the old man furious and his belt would come off."

"Oh."

"One time he wound up in jail. Roger arrested him. They let him out the next morning after he cooled down."

"I understand now why you hate him, Chance. I also understand why you wouldn't want him to be your natural father."

"The fact remains he might be. I have to consider it, right?"

This time I reach for his hand. "Yes, dear boy, it's tough. But look what you've been through already."

"He doesn't deserve to be my father, you know? He doesn't." Chance jerks his hand back and slams it against the steering wheel.

"You're right. And you're proving what you can do on your own, Chance. We don't get to choose our fathers or our sperm donors. It gets done for us. You must clear your mind of confusion, of hate, before you get any deeper into this investigation."

"I see what you mean but I don't know if I can get there."

"When we get home, maybe you should ask for a sweat. Spending time in the sweat lodge might help you get past this blockage." I see his quizzical look and add, "I don't mean disrespect to you. The hurts and anger of childhood experiences must be put aside to allow us to function as responsible adults. That's all I meant. The sweat lodge ceremony might be the best place."

"Sounds good to me. I have only been in one sweat. Right after I arrived here. Marge insisted it was necessary. I didn't know why or even what I was doing. Felt like a new person afterward. You're avoiding my question. Why does Mark think Andrews is my father?"

"Unfortunately, he didn't say. He threw out his opinion and expected us to understand his reasoning."

"So, all of this is speculation?"

"No. You have to know Mark. He wouldn't say it if he didn't believe it to be true. I need to go back to the prison for another visit. Maybe this time we can focus on one issue at a time.

"But something Grandma said seems likely to be a fact. She denies Jean was your mother. She also denies Marge is your mother. She knows, but says she promised not to tell the name of your biological mother or your father."

"Promised who?"

"Your mother. See what I mean about the rez secrets? Nobody knows but everybody knows. That never changes."

"Start with this fact then. I want this settled one way or another, and soon. It would simplify things if Marge would tell me who she thinks my father is. I've asked but she ignores the question. She's like Grandma Kline, always knows the answers."

"Maybe it's her secret to keep, Chance."

32

GRANDMA LOOKS UP WHEN I WALK INTO THE HOSPITAL ROOM. I feel a cold ache in my heart. There is no sign of recognition in the old woman's eyes. I glance back at Chance and Rose, then move to the bedside and lay my bag on the floor beside the night table.

"Gram, it's me. Ellie."

Still not a muscle twitches in the wrinkled brown skin although now I see the familiar twinkle in Grandma's eyes. I know better than to let on about Gram's game.

"Grandma," I say as I place my hands on the old woman's shoulders to draw her near. "See, I'm here. And Chance, too."

"Yeah, Gram. We're all here." Chance's voice sounds far away though he is only at the door.

Grandma Kline sits straight up and shouts, "Take her to the canyon!"

Startled, I drop my hands and step back. Chance brushes past me and strides quickly to the bed.

"Who, Grandma? Who should I take to the canyon?" he asks, cradling her tiny, gnarled brown hands in his own strong ones.

. "Her!" she says, pointing to Rose. "Take her away." Then exhausted by the effort, she falls back onto the bed.

Rose runs toward the door. Marge blocks it, her arms folded across her chest.

"See, I told you your man was no good."

Rose bursts into tears and would have collapsed to the floor if Chance had not come up behind her and wrapped her in his arms.

I turn back to Grandma, lean over the bed to tuck the covers around her, pat her on the head and bend down to kiss her cheek. Her voice is so quiet I am not certain I heard it.

"Get them out of here so I can tell you what happened," she whispers.

I sink into the chair recently vacated by Rose, reach for Grandma's hand and caress it. "Maybe we should take turns staying with Grandma. I'll take the first shift and you guys can figure out the rest."

When I didn't hear an answer, I turned to find an empty room.

There is no sign of them in the hall, when I look. I do hear muffled sounds of Rose's sobbing. Pretty certain I would not want to be in Rose's shoes right now. Answering to either Chance or Marge would be difficult. Being questioned by both at the same time would be unbearable. I am anxious to hear what they find out but must return to Grandma. Take her to the canyon! What kind of nonsense is this? It sure cleared the room. Grandma always knows everything. I learned that at a very young age.

I close the door and return to where Grandma sits dangling her wrinkled legs over the edge of the bed.

"What's going on you old trickster?"

"Take me home, please."

"I'm not taking you anywhere until I talk to the doctor, and not until you tell me why you did all this! What's going on Grandma? You made Rose cry. What did she do? Didn't she take care of you when you were wandering in the cemetery? Do you even remember why you're in this hospital?"

"Too many questions."

"Start with Rose. What did she do?"

"She in danger. He's going to get her."

"He, who?"

"Him. He called me. Will take another one. I don't want him to get her, Ellie. Stop him. Stop him!"

I am astonished to see Grandma collapse into sobs as she falls back onto her bed and turns to bury her face in the pillow. I can't make sense of Grandma's rambling. She never cries unless someone dies. The soft moans soon become wails.

"What's going on in here," a voice demands as a flurry of white pushes past me.

One of the nurses comes back to grab my arm.

"What happened? Why is she screaming?"

"I wish I knew."

When I hear the other nurse standing over Grandma say, "We'll give her a sedative to calm her down," I swing back into action.

"No! Let her wail. When she's finished, she'll be fine."

Anger transfixes their faces. There they stand, mouths agape, eyes wide, staring at me.

"She'll be fine if you give her some time. Wailing is a part of our culture. It releases the agony. Honors the dead,"

"I don't care what it does. She has to stop. She's disturbing the other patients," the older nurse says.

"There's no way to make her stop until she's finished."

"When will it be?" the nurse asks as she pulls the blankets off Grandma.

When I see the dark-haired nurse pull a package from her pocket, I have to stop them. A sedative might put the old woman to sleep until sometime tomorrow. Rose may be in terrible danger and only Grandma knows why. This is not the time for a sedative.

I push aside the nearest nurse and scoop up my frail grandmother, hoping the women will be too surprised to act. As we back toward the door, an indignant nurse moves toward us. I scream over Grandma's wails, "Chance! Help! Come help us!"

I back through the doorway. The nurses catch up to us. They push and pull on Grandma trying to wrest her from my arms. Through the wails, I hear the pounding of running feet.

As the nurses ponder what action to take, Chance bursts into the room.

"Ellie, what the hell?" He moves toward me.

"Grandma? Are you alright?"

"Okay ladies. Let's untangle here and get Grandma back to bed. Ellie, what is going on? Why is she yelling? Why are you carrying her around?"

He pushes the nurses away and turns us back toward the bed. He better not take her away from me.

"Stand back!" I shout, hoping my loud voice will scare the nurses.

I lay the old woman back on the bed. The wailing ceases and Grandma once again buries her face in the pillow. A nurse comes forward but backs off when I step between her and Grandma.

Grandma Kline sits up and peers directly into Chance's face as he bends over the bed. She grabs the front of his shirt with her gnarled hands and clutches him to her. "Where's Rose?"

"She's outside with her Mama, Grandma. What's going on? Rose swears she doesn't know why you're mad at her."

Chance looks at me for help. I can only shrug and retreat to a chair.

The nurses move toward Grandma, but Chance raises his hand to stop them. "Let her talk. She isn't sick. She wants to talk. Right, Grandma?"

"Take me home. I want to go home, now."

"Grandma, I told you we have to wait to see what the doctor says." I stand and gently loosen her hands from Chance's shirt. "We'll get everyone out. Then you can tell me what's wrong, Okay?"

"Yes, yes. Go away. I don't need nurses," she says, shooing them away with her hands. "Chance take care of Rose."

Grandma hasn't talked this much in weeks. Something is very important. The nurses leave, and I walk Chance to the door. "She says Rose is in danger, Chance. Some man. She started crying before I could learn who he is. Go talk to Rose," I tell Chance. "Go to my house. Take Rose and Marge with you. Don't let anyone in my office. Pull the door shut and lock it. I have my key."

"Right. Call me when you know something."

When the sound of his footsteps fade, I address the nurses, "My grandmother is scared. She has important information we must get from her, but we keep getting interrupted. She doesn't need a sedative. She needs peace and quiet."

I hope they can see she is sane and honest, though her behavior in the last few minutes has not given them any reason to believe it. They march out the door, still in a huff.

I turn to comfort Grandma and am met by determined black eyes set above the high cheekbones in a face so like my own. I know not to speak. It is Grandma's turn, so I push the door shut and turn the lock.

"Long time ago," Grandma begins, "I told her stay away from him. Bad man. He hurt her lot."

Who is she talking about? Couldn't be Rose. She wouldn't be in one of Grandma's long time ago stories.

"Then I see baby in her belly. She cry. Won't talk." Tears run down through Grandma's face wrinkles, drip off her chin onto the sheets. She continues the story as I wipe her tortured face. When I try to sit beside her, Grandma pushes me away and points to the chair. I had forgotten she needs to see a listener's face when she tells a story.

"He come in truck and take her away lots of nights. After dark so no one see him."

Grandma watches for my reaction. I stare back at her.

"Jean," she whispers. Grandma's tears flow again. Now she motions for the washcloth.

"She love white boy. Thought he would marry her. Take her away to a fancy house in the city. Guess he told her so."

I realize what is happening. She knows more about Jean's death than she has told. This is big.

"I tell her white boy with lots of money don't visit Indian girl in the dark if he want marry her. She don't listen to old mother."

Grandma slides down the side of the bed and walks around the room, oblivious to her gown flapping against her backsides. This is certainly new. I remain seated, afraid to disrupt Grandma's thoughts.

"Belly grow real big and Jean get more sad. Man not come anymore. She not go to work for lot of days. One day she go for walk. Say going to store to call man. I tell her no. I never see her again." Grandma doesn't bother to wipe her tears. The front of her gown is damp, clinging to her chest.

"You get him, Ellie. He goin' to kill my Rosie."

So that's what this is all about. Grandma was thinking about Jean and got scared for Rose. Marge has commented she is surprised how much Rose resembles Jean at the same age. Guiding Grandma to her bed, I help her up and arrange the pillows, so she can lie back. She stays down only long enough to compose herself. By the time I return to my chair, Grandma is sitting up.

"You not listen to me. I say he going to get Rose."

"Yes, yes. I did hear you, Grandma." Leaning forward, I tell her, "Maybe you're thinking about Jean. Why would someone kill Rose?"

"What you not know?"

"Let's do this another way. This time I need to ask questions, okay?"

"Girl not ask questions. Listen to story."

"I know, I know. You didn't tell me the whole story this time, Grandma. I must ask questions, so I can save Rose. That's what you want me to do, isn't it?"

"Ummm. You not try to tell story?"

"No. I won't try to tell the story. I will only ask questions to help Rose." I smile, remembering how irritated Grandma was when interrupted by little Ellie trying to add to her stories. Mark and Marge would put their hands over my mouth, so Grandma could keep talking.

Now, ready to ask questions, I sit on the bed beside her.

"Little girl ask too many questions. Make head hurt," Grandma says, and reaches out to stroke my face.

"We have to do this now."

"Where is Rose?"

"She's with Marge and Chance, remember? Going to my house."

"Chance good boy. Very pretty like his Grandpa." A little snort and her face lights up in a toothless smile. I must remember to ask for more stories about Grandpa Thom on a better day. More secrets?

"Who was the man, Grandma? Jean's man?"

"Jean only say he have lots of money. Take her away to big city. He only come in dark. Say can't let family know. I see him, though."

"You did? Did he come in your house?"

"No. He always honk horn. She run out like bad girl. One time I been in outhouse, walking on trail and hear horn. Hide behind tree. See his head in truck when Jean open door. Big boy, yellow hair."

"Do you remember what the truck looked like?"

"Just truck. Very dark. Black, maybe. Shiny new truck, I think. Like sheriff's truck."

"It looked like the sheriff's truck? Did it have a sign on the door?"

"Uh, huh. Maybe not sheriff sign."

The phone on Grandma's bedside table rings. Chance lets me know they are at my house. They have Rose's boy. Marge went home too irritated to deal with her grandson. They are cooking dinner and will save some for us.

"He call on phone last year," Grandma tells me as I hang up the phone.

"Who?"

"Jean's man. He call."

"Last year? He called you at your house? Why didn't you tell someone?"

"He say he kill another one. He say he get me if I tell. I believe him."

She twists her hands together, and rocks back and forth, her face filled with agony.

"This was a year ago, Grandma?" I try to remain calm, but this is personal and frightening.

"Maybe one year. Nobody die, I think. Then he call again and say he will get another one. Don't know what he's saying."

"When was the call, Grandma?"

She lay back on the crumpled bed as the sobs flee her body in short, spasmodic jerks. I stand over her and stroke her long hair.

"Let's go home, Grandma. We can talk about this after you're safe at my house. While you're getting dressed, tell me why you think he's going to kill Rose."

Thirty minutes later, we are in Chance's truck, headed home. The doctor never came.

Grandma finally answers the question. "He call again. Say going to keep killing my girls until I make them shut up."

"When? When did he call, Grandma?" I struggle to drive to the junction of US Hwy 20 and OR229 while listening to Grandma's story.

"I try to call you. Then I walk to office to tell Chance. Rose find me."

"Yesterday? He called yesterday?"

Grandma stares straight ahead, her hands folded together in her lap.

"We have to remember to go up to feed your dog, too, Gram. Help me remember, OK?" I say to get her to talk.

"Dog dead."

"Nuisance is dead? When did that happen?" I'm shocked Marge didn't mention it. Grandma's little mutt is her constant companion.

"She go outside in night. Not come back. Next day I find her on my porch. Blood all over. Some bad man cut her throat. Then phone ring."

"Oh, Grandma! How awful!"

"That when I call you. Can't find Chance. I talk to your Grandpa."

No wonder Rose found her wandering aimlessly in the cemetery. So frightened and confused, she only knew to go to Grandpa's grave.

"The man called again?" I try to understand the sequence of these terrible events.

"You listen to me, girl? Dog dead. Man call me. Say going to keep killing."

"Yes, yes. I understand. Did he say he would kill Rose? Did he say her name?"

221

"No. Just keep killing my girls. Rose look like Jean, I think."

I feel more confident Rose might not be in as much danger as Grandma thinks. Rose hasn't mentioned any threatening calls. No 'you're next' messages like I've received. I think he meant me and Grandma thinks he means Rose.

"Grandma, let's talk to Rose when we get home. Let's see if she's been threatened by this man."

There is no response, which may mean she agrees. Or it could mean she sees no reason to ask.

33

A WHIFF OF FRIED CHICKEN GREETS US WHEN LEE OPENS MY front door. Grandma steps past him and heads for the couch. She likes to sit right in front of the television, near the warmth of the woodstove. Even when the house is toasty warm, she snuggles in my Pendleton blanket. Rose rushes to get her settled while Chance pushes past Lee to help me with Grandma's suitcase.

"Where's your bag, Ellie?" he whispers as we meet in the doorway.

"On the front seat. Take these and I'll get it," I say, not waiting for an answer. I return to the house through the unguarded front door, lock it and walk to my office. Once inside, my eyes sweep the room as I hurry to put the bag away. Lee is suddenly behind me.

"Why are you keeping everything locked up so tight, Ellie? Have you uncovered some deep, dark secret you don't want Rose to see?"

"What is in my office is none of your business, Lee. Or anyone else's"

He grabs my arm and says, "Look, I don't like the way you treat Rose. And now your grandmother has insulted her. Scared her half to death. What's going on?"

Jerking free, I head to the kitchen as Chance removes the last piece of chicken from the frying pan and places it on the platter.

"Why is he here, Chance?"

Before Chance can answer, Lee grabs my shoulder and turns me around. "I'm talking to you, woman. I want some answers or else. ..."

I am about to slice some bread for dinner, instead I step toward Lee and see his eyes widen at the sight of the large knife in my upraised hand.

"Or else what? What gives you the right to come into my home and make demands?" I take another step toward him, but he doesn't back off.

"You may have the rest of the family intimidated, Ellie. Not me! I think you're all mouth."

Reaching from behind me, Chance grabs the hand holding the knife and at the same time feels to be sure my other hand doesn't hold the .38.

"Whoa. Let's cool down here. Back off, Lee. You don't know what you're doing. C'mon, come sit with Grandma and Rose. Let Ellie have some time to think."

Rose tries to take Lee's arm. He shrugs her away and continues to scowl at me.

"Dinner's ready. Let's eat. Then we can hear why Grandma is so upset," Chance says.

"Not before some questions are answered," I mutter. No way I'm sharing Grandma's information with this guy. I don't care if he's Rose's man. She's probably filled his head with her convoluted stories and suddenly everything is my fault. I retrieve the knife from Chance and begin slicing at the loaf of bread.

"Better go sit down, Lee. I think she's chopping your head."

Chance tries to relieve the tension, but I am too irritated with Lee's arrogance to see the humor in this situation. The loaf of bread is his head. Fortunately for him, my thoughts are always more vicious than my actions.

34

I'M ON MY WAY TO THE STATE POLICE OFFICE IN NEWPORT, BUT
I didn't tell Chance or Roger, or Rose about the call from the lieutenant.
My windshield wipers work overtime as I break over the hill into Newport.
Today, as on most winter days, my vision of the Pacific Ocean is blurred by
the coastal fog and the drizzle tourists call rain.

As I pull into a parking space at the state police headquarters, a
familiar angst envelopes me. I'm used to checking in at these places to
obtain reports. In Chicago, it was less intimidating than here in my own
homeland. My brown face garnered some interest and curiosity there; here,
it may be unwelcome. I was invited or ordered, not certain which, in a
phone call to come to Lt. Thomas Jensen's office.

"Hey, Ellie. Come on back to my office."

So, there he is. Waiting right out front for me. Why?

The lieutenant, a giant compared to my height, takes a seat in a
brown leather chair and points to a matching chair nearby. He rises again
as I remove my coat, takes it to a clothes tree near the door, then waits until
I am seated. I'm thankful he didn't sit behind the desk over there by the

window. The expression of power and control can be unnerving. Resort to it myself sometimes. Certainly, I don't relish being on the hot seat. I hope my stress is not visible to this cop.

"Ellie, do you remember me at all?"

"No. Should I?"

"I wondered if you would. You were very young when I last saw you and a lot has happened in our lives since."

"Are you sure you're talking to the right person, Lieutenant? Why would I have had any contact with you? No offense, but I didn't spend a lot of time with cops when I was a child and teenager on the reservation. I didn't date white guys. Besides, you seem a little too old for me."

Standing now, he chuckles quietly before turning back to look at me. "No, we didn't date. However, you were with me during very wonderful times I considered dates."

I'm interested in where this is going, so I assure him he has mistaken me for some other Ellie Carlisle.

"Don't think so. Can't possibly be two Ellie Carlisles. Not by name or by personality. You are definitely Alice Simpson's daughter. You look so much like her. God rest her soul."

Shocked to hear my mother's name coming from a cop's mouth, I stand to face him. Not exactly facing him, more like staring up into his chin.

Lord, he must be at least six feet five.

"Why would you know anything about my mother?"

Slowly, the face becomes familiar. Someone from the past. I see hands reaching for me, hear my mother laughing.

Oh, my God!

"Tommy?" I ask, almost in my child's voice.

"Yes, welcome home girl. Here sit down."

I collapse into the chair and stare at the man I have not seen since I was six years old. He was often in my mother's house, sometimes in her arms when I peeked from my bedroom door.

He's a state policeman. Was he a policeman then? I don't remember a uniform.

He was Tommy then; a man I loved so much who disappeared from our lives.

"Why now? You left us back then. What do you want from me now?

"Nothing. I had to see you. To talk to you. Did she ever tell you anything about me, us?"

"She? As in my mother? Alice?"

"Yes, Alice."

If this is a game, he's sure good at it. His voice is tender, and he seems almost in tears.

"She never told me why you were suddenly not there anymore. A few days before she died, I asked, "Mama, why did you never marry again after Dad died? You were so young then. There must have been somebody you loved after Dad."

Tommy says, "I'm not sure I want. ..."

"Yes, I think you do. It was your question, remember? She couldn't talk much at that point, so I didn't get the full story. She did say, 'Ellie, there was a man I loved so much. I had to let him go because our lives were completely different. Marrying me would have destroyed his career. I sent him away and I never wanted anyone else."

I watch as the tears run down the cheeks of this man, so strong, so important in his chosen career, so devastated by my answer.

"I asked her if she regretted her decision and she hesitated for a long time, then told me, 'Every day; only that it couldn't be, not that I shouldn't have done it. He has the life that he should have.'"

We sit for a while, each with our own thoughts. I have nothing more to say and he seems too miserable, too lost in the past to communicate. I consider leaving, though it doesn't seem right.

Finally, composed, he resumes some semblance of his former professional attitude and asks if I'd like something to drink. "Water? Soda?"

"A Pepsi would be great," I reply, mostly to make him more comfortable. I am so filled with questions right now I may explode before he returns.

He hands the can to me and asks, "Did she tell you who it was? Mention my name?"

"She knew she didn't have to. I remembered what I saw when I wasn't supposed to be peeking. I remember her crying and crying for days when you didn't come back. She told me I couldn't ask any more questions and I should know Tommy would never be coming to our house again. I hated you for a long time. Then I put you away with other bad dreams."

"I am so sorry, Ellie. You do understand it was your mother's decision for me to leave, not mine?"

"Yes, she said that on her deathbed and seeing you now, a white man, lieutenant of the state police, it all makes more sense. I have a lot of questions."

"I know you do. Let's go somewhere for lunch and I'll answer anything I can for you."

"NO!"

"No?"

"Wow. No wonder my mother sent you away. You are a cop! I am an Indian woman, a PI, trying to solve a murder on the rez the cops messed up and catch grave robbers no one will help stop. If I am seen socializing with you, the story will get back to Siletz before me and it won't be about what we ate for lunch, you can be sure. How in the world did you get to be a lieutenant in the state police?"

Laughing now, he says, "Ha, still as stubborn as when you were little. Your mother would be proud. So much like her. You're right. I still think your mother and I could have married and had children, but she was positive the cultures were too different and my career as a cop would never materialize. So sure she sent me away and messed up both our lives."

"Speaking of children, are you my father?"

"What? No. John Simpson was your. ..."

"Give me a break. I can read tombstones. He died two years before I was born."

"Alice had that tombstone made before I met her. Guess she wasn't thinking."

"Do you know who my father is, or was?

"I don't know for sure. She would never tell me his name. Didn't you ask her?"

"No. Not something I thought a lot about as a kid. I thought it was John Simpson and used to visit his grave. One day, as a teenager, it hit me what those dates meant I'd been reading for years. I never went back. Heard from a cousin a little later Uncle Oscar was my father. I don't know for sure. Mama and I never discussed it. I referred to John as 'Dad,' like she taught me."

"Oscar is exactly who I suspected, mostly because she wouldn't let him in the house when he tried to visit. Didn't want him anywhere near you. I had to step in the last time he came to her door. Let him know he wasn't welcome there, ever. That scared her. She didn't want trouble for me. So far as I know he never came back."

"He has never spoken to me."

"Good. Stay away from the bastard."

"Whoa, that's my Dad you're talking about."

"Ellie, he does not deserve any respect from you. He's worthless. If I could ever prove what he did, I'd put him in jail. 'Course it's a little past statute now."

"What are you telling me? It doesn't sound good."

"No, it isn't. Think about it now as a woman. Your mother was a widow at nineteen. She was beautiful, alone, vulnerable, defenseless. He was her brother-in-law, a man already with children scattered among the young women of the town. Probably wanted her when his brother was alive and now saw his chance. She told me one of her cousins took photos of her face the day after the night visit. The guy came in through a window she forgot to lock. She told me there were bruises all over her body. She wouldn't let me see those photos. She was convinced the family would disown her if she went to the police. She knew I would report it, even five years after the fact, so she wouldn't tell me who it was. She loved you with all her heart. You know, right?"

"Of course. My poor mother. Kind of hurts to know I'm the daughter of a rapist."

"Alice is probably looking down on us right now saying, 'Tommy, why did you tell her?'"

"So many secrets. This is a very sad, ugly story. Like so many others in my town."

"Life is different now for most folks, isn't it? I mean, restoration will re-establish some rights that should never have been taken away. There is a strong contingent trying to have a reservation again. I struggle with how it can be a good thing."

"Life might be better in Newport than in the 1950s, but things aren't much different for our people no matter where we live. Getting some of our land back now when we're a restored tribe may help us recapture our cultural ties like language and crafts, maybe even establish some businesses to bring jobs for our people."

"I hope it's true. Now, since we can't go out for lunch, I'll pick up chowder and dessert from Lou's Dog House. I took an official day off to spend with you. We can eat right here, or in the staff lunch room, whichever you prefer."

"I prefer not to be anywhere anyone could accidentally overhear our discussion, so I guess the safest place is right here in your office. I must be home by six. I have a meeting at seven. May I use your phone while you're gone?"

"Sorry, all the calls from my office are recorded. Don't imagine that works for you."

He's gone and back in 20 minutes. Not enough time for my whirling mind to calm. I have more questions. As we settle in around his conference table, I say a silent prayer I can trust this man.

"I'm wondering how you met my mother and why no one talks about her dating a cop, a white cop."

"I wasn't a cop. I was a college student taking a year off to make more money. I came to the coast to work on a crab boat, met your mother at a restaurant and didn't go back to school for almost two years."

"In Newport? The restaurant where you met her, I mean?"

"Yes. She worked at a fish plant on the bay front. Though she usually ate in the lunchroom at the plant, she decided to get out of there on a nice, sunny afternoon. I knew right away it was my lucky day."

"So, you started talking to her? Tell me…"

"You still ask lots of questions, don't you? The two of us could never answer enough questions for you. Your grandmother told me you had too much white blood and made you ask so many questions."

"Wait! You know Grandma Kline, too?"

"I know her. It was Alice's mother who said it."

"Oh, Grandma Ruby. I barely remember her. Mama said she moved away after Mama and John were married. I've never understood why Grandma Kline always comments about my white blood. I need to ask her."

"You do know Ruby was white, don't you?

"What? Shocked, I stare at my arms, feel my face. Yes, I remember, but it didn't sink in I am part white like Grandma Kline teased. It's not unusual for our people to blame anything bad on white people or white people's blood. Wow, so many things I haven't thought about as an adult. Not really a secret, but also not something I was taught to be proud of."

He concentrates on his soup. I can't eat. I take a small bite before the questions in my mind regain control. "Where did you come from? Where did you grow up before you started college, I mean?"

"Baker area. My family had a large cattle ranch at the base of the Wallowa Mountains. I didn't want to be a rancher. I always wanted to be a cop. Never thought of doing anything else. Alice figured it out pretty fast and argued against everything I suggested otherwise."

"Why did you want to do something else after you met Mama?"

"I didn't. I wanted to marry Alice and make the three of us into a family. I knew I couldn't take you two away from Siletz, or the coast. You being exposed to your culture was so important to her. I thought I could continue as a fisherman, or perhaps become a teacher--whatever would work in this area. She was absolutely convinced I couldn't get a job in a Lincoln County police agency if I had an Indian wife and child."

"And here you are in Lincoln County."

"Yes, without my family."

"Didn't you marry later? Mama mentioned you were married or had a child. Something."

"Yes, I married. Unfortunately, my wife always knew there was some-one else before her in my heart. When she couldn't take it anymore, she left me for another guy. She's happily married to him. Our daughter attends school over in Monmouth. Plans to be a cop."

There is another long pause before he continues. "Ellie, I know what happened to your son. I am so sorry. I wanted to call you right away, but it didn't seem like the right time to hit you with my story. I kinda thought you might call me after a while. Then I realized you were so young the last time I saw you. Probably wouldn't remember me, or at least not my last name."

"You're right. All I ever knew was 'Tommy.' So why did you call me?"

"I heard you moved back and were looking for details on Jean's murder. I thought you might want some help."

"Where did you hear that? Oh, the newspaper article."

"Yes, I also talk to the sheriff. He seems to know a lot about your activities. I was surprised one day to hear him say, 'Hey, I see your little girl's back at the rez.' Didn't have any idea he knew I'd lived here before, or he knew about you and Alice."

Now, I'm losing trust again. Does Tommy care or is this another guy trying to gather information for Sheriff Kramer? And where is the sheriff getting all this?

"How long have you lived in Newport?"

"A little over a year. I got transferred here, promoted, when the former lieutenant retired."

"So, you think the sheriff knew you before? How would he know about me, about my mother?"

"I wasn't sure. I checked around. Finally realized he was the kid who hung around with young Andrews, the Newport Cubs' main guy. I saw him down on the docks around the boats when I worked there. He made a few comments one time and I had to make sure he hurt for a while. Makes sense he would remember."

"You beat up the sheriff?"

"He was a smart-mouth kid. I knew calling Alice a squaw, even when she couldn't hear him, was not happening in my world."

"Yeah, seems to be one of his favorite words."

"Are you having trouble with the sheriff, Ellie?"

"Some. He's such a dullard I don't think he will cause me any harm. Other than following Chance around, threatening to put him in jail, he hasn't done much."

"Why does he want to arrest Chance?"

"Because he's Indian, I guess."

"Look, if you ever need any help with Kramer or anyone else, you call me. Be careful of Andrews, too, if you see him. There was a third kid who hung out with them then. Didn't ever hear his name. I remember he always wore cowboy boots. Kind of odd in a fishing village."

"I don't trust a lot of people, Tommy. I wouldn't want to call you here and have the person answering your office phone tell others. It's too dangerous."

"How about a code name? You don't have to give your real name because our phone system doesn't have the ability to see the call-in number. What name do you want to use?"

"There's only one name both of us will remember and will cause you to answer the phone immediately."

"True. Be sure you use your mom's name and I'll know it's important."

35

I hurry to Grandma Kline's house when I return to Siletz.

"Grandma, did Mama have many boyfriends after your son died?"

Her response, a long time coming, is in the form of a question rather than the information I anticipate.

"You asking me who was your father, Ellie?"

"No, Gram. I know who my father is, but a man told me yesterday he wanted to marry my mother and she sent him away."

"This old woman have one good son and one bad. Very bad."

"It's OK. Don't worry. I figured it out a long time ago."

"You see Tommy?"

"Yes, Tommy Jensen. What's the story there?"

"Your Mama love my boy, John Simpson. After he die in woods she very young and sad. She was hurt real bad by my other son; police won't come. She keep baby and love you very much. Then she working, cleaning fish and meet nice white boy."

"Tommy?"

"I call him Tommy Whiteboy. He laugh. You were little girl, maybe three then. Mama happy like before John die in woods."

Our conversation is interrupted by a whistling teakettle. I hurry to the kitchen and return with steaming cups of hot water and Gram's favorite tea bags.

"If she loved Tommy so much, why did she send him away?"

"Hard to live in two worlds. She want him to follow dream. She want you to remember to be Indian. She can help you, but she think she will be in Tommy Whiteboy's way."

Ah, poor Mama. She gave up her love to make sure I learned my Indian ways. Then as a bratty teenager, I ran off and got married. Left her here alone.

"Hmmm. Pretty much what the lieutenant told me."

"Where you see Tommy?"

"In Newport. He asked me to meet him at his office."

"Office? Why he have office in Newport?"

"You remember people talking about a new state police lieutenant over there? It's him. Tommy is that lieutenant."

Grandma's toothless smile spreads across her face as she claps her hands together without spilling her tea.

"Good. Tommy Whiteboy will help you find bad people who dig us up."

"I don't know, Gram. He was with Mama a long time ago. Things happen. He may not be the same guy you knew."

"Why he call you?"

"I'm not sure. He knew all about me and wanted to be sure I knew who he was."

"He ask questions?"

"No, he assured me I could talk to him about anything. I can call him for help. We have a secret code, so I can call him without people in his office knowing."

"Why you not trust him?"

"I didn't. ..." I start to explain. Grandma's laughter fills the room. She really knows me.

36

CHANCE IS GRUMPY WHEN HE ANSWERS MY PHONE CALL, SAYS he is concentrating on his project. I know, without being there, his desk is covered with information he has collected on the history of grave robbing, and the work being done by the cemetery protection group Grandma Kline told us about. He has been up since early morning assembling a comprehensive report for today's meeting at my house and now I'm about to tell him the meeting is postponed.

"I'm at the Portland airport. Flying out at nine to Anchorage." I shout into the phone so he can hear me above the terminal noise.

'Where, Ellie?"

"Anchorage. I found Harrington's widow. She's willing to talk. I want to get there before she changes her mind. Let Roger know. He didn't answer the phone."

"He'll be pissed you went alone."

"Yes, he will. This could be big. The woman kept all Harrington's notebooks and files. I'm anxious to see them."

"Good news. How did you locate her?"

"Simple. I talked to Mitzi and found out her ex-husband's sister's friend was married to the guy who was hired to fill the vacancy when Harrington died. So Mitzi called her ex-sister-in-law who called her friend to ask about the Harrington woman. The friend is now divorced from the deputy. She remembered the widow had married a Cordova commercial fisherman who skippered the *Patriot*."

"Good lord. How can you keep this straight? And how does it put you in Alaska?"

"I checked at the docks in Newport and a guy knew the *Patriot* was in Dutch Harbor for the season. He gave me the owner's name and I checked at the port office for his address. Fishermen are often the best source of information."

"Have you talked to the woman? Does she know you're coming?"

"Of course. She knows where Harrington's records are and will make them available to me."

"I hope this gets us someplace."

"Be careful with Roger. I spoke with a fisherman who says he's Roger's brother. He said not only did he and Roger go to school with Hank, but Jack Kramer was almost as good at football at Newport High as your father. Apparently, there was a lot of competition and jealousy on Jack's part."

"Jack Kramer---the sheriff?"

"Yep. Interesting our friendly cop neglected to mention it, don't you think?"

37

It's a nice walk from the historic Anchorage Hotel to the Barker home near Resolution Park. The petite young woman with large brown eyes who opens the door is too young to be the woman I am here to see. I offer my card and ask to see Donna Barker.

"You must be Mrs. Carlisle. Please come in. I'm Teresa Harrington. My mother's waiting for you in the family room."

I surrender my coat to Teresa, then follow her down a narrow, cedar lined hallway, through a small, modern, kitchen into a light-filled room with a magnificent view of Cook's Inlet and beyond. In the distance, the Aleutian chain draws my attention. I gasp at the long-awaited scene.

"Are you alright, my dear?" Turning, I see the soft voice belongs to a shorter, matronly version of Teresa.

"Oh. Yes, I'm sorry. This is my first sighting of the Aleutians. I've waited years to see them."

"Do you have Aleut heritage?" The question comes from Teresa and I see disapproval in the mother's eyes. Her look reminds me of Grandma Kline's irritation at my many questions.

"No, I'm Siletz. My uncle served here in the Army Air Corps in World War II on a crew which flew supplies to the troops on the islands. I've always wanted to see the Aleutians. It's a beautiful view from here."

Teresa says, "Let's sit at this table so we can look at my Daddy's papers. You sit on that side, so you can see the bay."

I sit.

"This is my mother, Donna," Teresa explains as the older woman takes a seat at the far end of the table.

"Hello. And thank you for seeing me, Mrs. Barker."

"I don't know much about any of this. Teresa has tried to solve the mystery, or what she believes is a mystery, of her Dad's death for years, so I thought she should be here."

"I hope you don't mind, Mrs. Carlisle. I think I may have important information if you want to know about Daddy's death."

"Ellie. Please call me Ellie. I'm glad you're here, Teresa. I had no idea you were investigating Deputy Harrington's accident."

"It was no accident." She points her finger at me and adds, "THAT I'm sure of."

"Tell me why."

Teresa pulls a photo from a file.

"My father's cruiser. He went off the road into the slough. It appears he was driving on a straight stretch of Highway 229 and angled off the road, flew over and plopped into the water."

"Okay." I study the photo as Teresa continues.

"You see the car's sitting on the highway in this photo. Daddy had already been removed and taken to the hospital. We don't have photos of the car in the water."

I want to ask a question, but I wait for her to finish.

"See anything wrong with this picture?" Teresa asks.

"Yes, I do. I'd prefer to hear your analysis and theories, your proof, before we begin a discussion."

"Oh. In the photo you're holding, it appears the left side of the car is damaged, like something sideswiped it. See, there about the back, passenger door up past the driver's door."

"Yes, I see it."

"Then, in this photo, you see the skid marks on the road," Teresa continues. "It looks like he tried to stop. The marks angle and then stop at the very edge of the road right where he flew into the slough."

"Explain to Ms, to Ellie, why you say 'flew' Teresa," Donna interrupts.

"There are photos of the slough here and the bank where the police reports say Daddy's car drove." Teresa used her fingers to emphasize quotation marks around the words "into the slough."

"Hmmm."

"See, there are no tracks, nothing indicates he drove into the water," Teresa says as she hands three more photos to me.

"And these photos I thought showed such tracks," she says. "Recently, I enlarged the photos. See? These are drag marks. All the vegetation is lying uphill. I'm convinced these were taken after the tow truck pulled Daddy's car out of the water."

"You should ask Jack, dear. He would know since he took the photos."

"Who is Jack?" I ask, fearing I know the answer.

"Sheriff Kramer, down in Newport."

Teresa rolls her eyes.

"Mom thinks he's wonderful. I think he's a snake who would walk over anyone to get to the top. And he's there now, isn't he, Mom? Right at the top. He's the sheriff, like he bragged he would be."

Donna sighs. "We do have company, Teresa."

"Sorry. Mentioning the man's name sets me off."

It's probably best I don't let her know yet I can't stand him, either.

"So, anyway, the official report says Daddy fell asleep, drove into the slough and drowned."

"She has never believed it," Donna says. "Teresa was only twelve when Dan died. She's spent the rest of her life trying to solve what she thinks was a murder."

"What do you think, Mrs. Barker?"

"We have Jack's report. He sat with me after Dan's funeral and went over everything. I have no reason to question any of it."

"If your daughter has found evidence to the contrary. ..."

"She hasn't. Jack says none of what Teresa has saved proves anything different than the original report. He's sorry she misses her Daddy. Jack thinks she read too many Nancy Drew mysteries when she was young."

Her shallow laugh hurts my teeth.

"Mom, why can't you see. ..."

"Does it bother you that Teresa continues her investigation? She believes her father was murdered."

"Not really. It keeps her connected to Dan, I guess. She was the last of us to see him alive. I wasn't home when he was called to work. He planned to spend the evening with Teresa."

"Yes, and he was not sleepy, Mom. He worked the swing shift the night before, remember? He got home at 11:30, slept all night and didn't get up until ten or so that morning. He felt great. We were going to a movie later. Then Jack called to say the sheriff wanted Dad to come in to cover for a guy who didn't show up. Daddy was not sleepy," she explains while glaring at her mother.

I push my chair away from the table and walk to the window, giving them time to simmer down. When Donna leaves the room, Teresa joins me at the window.

"Stunning view, isn't it? So peaceful."

"Yes, although I am imagining it with military planes flying in frightful weather." In a lower voice, I state, "An interesting theory you have."

I turn toward Teresa. Our eyes meet briefly before she says, "Let me tell you why mother is so defensive about Sheriff Kramer."

38

AT THE HOTEL AFTER 10 P.M, I AM HAPPY TERESA INSISTED ON driving me back. She assured me it was almost on her way home and not wise for a woman to be out, even in a taxi, late at night in downtown Anchorage. The hours at the Barker house melted away as I absorbed the details of Teresa's suspicions. We scoured Deputy Harrington's notebooks for names and details, especially those Teresa considered loose ends.

Donna stayed at the table, obviously annoyed, not adding to the discussion. She left once to make sandwiches and salad for dinner, otherwise stayed firmly glued to her chair at the end of the table, watching and listening. Teresa's brief whispered description of the romantic involvement between Donna and Kramer immediately following Harrington's death kept me wary.

I agree with Teresa, Kramer took advantage of Donna's vulnerability to dispel any notion she might have about Dan's death being anything other than an accident. The day of Dan's death, Kramer assumed control of the investigation of Jean Kline's murder, but I didn't mention to Teresa that Kramer took over the investigation prior to calling Harrington into work.

This wasn't the time to give anything away. Not on this trip and certainly not while Donna listened.

In the car Teresa shared another reason for driving me to the hotel-- there was more to her suspicions she couldn't share in front of her mother.

Now, lying in my hotel bed running the day through my mind, I think her theory that Jack Kramer killed her father seems plausible. She says Kramer ached to become sheriff of Lincoln County. He was a Newport hero, one of the best football players at the high school. He and Hank Andrews set individual state records and led their team to three state championships. Hank was a good student. Jack was not. Hank's parents owned the Toledo sawmill. Jack's mother struggled with minimum wage restaurant jobs. Jack didn't know his father who was rumored to be part Indian. Kramer was Jack's mother's maiden name.

While Hank went off to Oregon State to continue setting records, Jack was stuck in Newport. His mother died of lung cancer a few months later. When the sheriff offered him a deputy's badge, he saw his opportunity to make a name for himself and began his upward climb, or so Teresa deduced from the conversations she overheard in her teen years while Jack lived with her mother.

"He is dangerous, Ellie. I heard him tell Mom his plans, bragging about what he could do to anyone who got in his way. I think she is afraid of him. For some reason the power intrigues her. Maybe that's what she liked about Daddy. Maybe the uniform and the badge are attractive to women with little personal strength. Do you think so?"

"It's certainly possible, Teresa. I don't know much about weak women and I don't personally like cops much."

Except for Roger, and I can't begin to explain that to anyone, especially after discovering he knows the sheriff. He has a lot of explaining to do.

The telephone rings in my hotel room and startles me from a restless sleep. I can't find the phone in the darkness, so I feel around in the general direction of the nightstand until my fingers wrap around the receiver.

"Ellie? Roger. Hope I didn't wake you."

"Roger? How did you find me here? What's wrong? Did something happen? Is. ..."

"Hey, slow down. Everything's fine. Chance told me you were in Anchorage. Took a few calls to track you down. That's why I worry, you know. Anyone could find you."

My heart thumps out of rhythm. Because Roger is concerned about me? Probably because his comment reminded me of the death threats.

"What time is it? It's dark in here. Hold on while I find the lamp."

The darkness extinguished, I return to the phone.

"There. It's better now. I can see."

"Yeah. No problem. It's only a long-distance charge."

"Why did you call me if you didn't want to stay on the phone?" I grouch, living another frustration with males.

"Sure, I wanted to talk to you. To ask what the hell you were thinking running off to Anchorage alone. Chance didn't think it was such a good idea."

"You're taking Chance's advice now? That's new."

"No. Maybe when it comes to you since I always make the wrong move."

"Seems to me you've never made a move, Roger."

Oh, no. What am I doing? I can't go there.

"I distinctly recall you bounced from room to room to avoid talking about our feelings, miss."

"I remember you tried to do more than talk."

"Weren't you complaining I never made a move? You confuse me, girl."

Out of bed! I can't talk to him while I'm in bed. Oh, crap! I forgot about my book.

"Ellie? Ellie, where'd you go? What was the noise?"

"Must be static on the line, Roger."

"Right. Sounded like you fell out of bed."

"Fine. My book fell on the floor. Now what was it you called about?" I ask as I pull a straight-backed chair over toward the nightstand and sit on it.

"I wanted to be sure you were safe, plus I was curious about what you found out today."

"Safe as ever. I spent the entire day with Donna. She married a commercial fisherman and…"

"Chance told me about the convoluted way you found her. Good work. What did she say?"

So, you probably know I talked to your brother. Wonder why you didn't mention it?

"She didn't say much. She believes his wreck was an accident, as the official report says. However, her daughter Teresa has a completely different opinion. She's spent all these years trying to solve the mystery she believes surrounds her father's death."

"What mystery?"

"She thinks her father was murdered; her mother disagrees. Donna had a romantic liaison with Kramer immediately following Harrington's death and she believes the reports and explanations he gave her. He lived with her for a few years before he left her for someone else. Yet they're friends and in constant contact."

"Odd."

Not nearly as odd as you not telling me you've known Kramer most of your life.

"Yes, and Teresa assured me her mother probably called Kramer as soon as she hung up from my call. Teresa thinks Kramer knows everything."

"That's not good."

I want to see his face when I ask him about Kramer. I need to wrap this up before I slip and mention it.

"We didn't discuss anything about Jean's case. I listened all day to Teresa's theories and looked at what she considers proof of her father's murder."

"What did it accomplish?"

"A lot. We can talk about it when I get home, Roger. I need to sleep. I have to be up early."

"And, you're coming home. ..."

"My ticket is for Friday morning at eight. I should be in Siletz by 7 p.m. if the plane is on time. Why?"

"Curious. Need to know when to start worrying," He laughs and adds, "When's the next meeting? I have things to tell you, too."

And one of those things better be a good explanation of why you haven't told me about the sheriff.

"Why don't you call Chance to see what day looks good to him? It will probably be an all-day session, so make sure his calendar is clear. I can meet on Sunday if it works out better for you two."

"I'll call him. Ellie didn't those women ask you what you came all the way to see them about?"

"No, they didn't. From the moment I walked in the door, the conversation was about Dan Harrington's wreck. ...or his murder, if you consider Teresa's focus."

"I would think they'd be very curious to know what you're working on."

"Didn't surprise me. Teresa's so sure her father didn't fall asleep and drive off the road she assumed it's why I'm here."

"What about her mother? What if she called Kramer? He must have told her about our investigation."

Our? It's MY investigation.

"Maybe. A dead Indian wouldn't interest her, Rog. Donna grew up in Newport in the '50s."

As did you, mister. I'm beginning to see why you aren't interested in protecting dead Indians.

39

BEFORE I RIDE THE ELEVATOR DOWN TO WAIT IN THE LOBBY for Teresa, I call Chance to catch him up on yesterday and all I'd shared with Roger.

"I'm eager to go through all those papers and notebooks when she brings me the copies, Chance. There is a lot to think about. If Dan Harrington's death was not an accident and may be connected to Kramer, the sheriff may be even more dangerous than we knew."

"Are you sure she's going to tell you everything, Ellie?"

"Yes. She trusts me and knows I don't like Kramer. We'll have to go through those notebooks and reports more than once, I'm sure. We spent a lot of time with them last night. In the car, Teresa mentioned there are entries that show her father and Kramer didn't get along. I'm hoping there will be something useful regarding Jean's death."

"Good then. Can't wait to read them. Is Teresa the only kid?"

"No, she has a younger brother, Kent, who doesn't remember Dan and has no interest in Teresa's theories."

"Ok. I have a meeting in a few minutes. Call me if you need anything."

"Chance! Don't hang up. Did you mention anything to Roger about me talking to his brother at the dock?"

"No, left it out."

"Let's keep it that way. His secrecy puts what he's told us about Vivian's stories, your Dad's possible criminal behavior—*everything*--in doubt. Be very careful when he calls you."

Saying goodbye to Teresa at the airport all I can think of was, "The copies are mine. Nothing more to keep me in this beautiful city with its views of six mountain ranges."

The return flight to Portland is interminably long and boring with a layover in Seattle. I call Chance from the airport, then check into my motel room. I hope to have several hours, perhaps a day, to study Harrington's notes before Roger tracks me down.

I pull out a notebook and start reading, but I can't identify Harrington's contacts with only 'CI' listed for names. He was kind enough to number all those confidential informants, though CI#1 and CI#2 are no help without a list to identify them. So far, I haven't found a list and there are only a few folders left to wade through before I head home. I'm growing tired of fast food and this musty room.

Harrington's comments swirl in my head as I drive home. So many references to 'D' through a period of five or six years, but nothing to point to a specific person. Perhaps another deputy, or perhaps someone in the Newport Police Department? I'll break out the references to see if I missed anything.

I sneak into Siletz at dusk, straight home to piece together the 'B' references in Harrington's official notebook (ONB) and his personal notebook (PNB). Now to see what's useful:

2/18/46: 'B' home. Attitude. Sheriff wants info. (ONB)

3/8/47: Jensen. No info. Nervous about talking to me. W/young widow. Trying to fit in. Will call if he hears anything. (PNB)

"Whoa! What's this? Jensen. Lieutenant Jensen? I'll be talking to Tommy about this. Wonder what Harrington thought Tommy might know?

4/10/47: Graveyard report. Upper Farm above Siletz. 'B' will check. (ONB)

4/15/47: Grave robbing. 'B' "Reports unfounded. (ONB)

4/16/47: Doubt 'B' checked on grave robbing problem in cemetery at Logsden. People up there don't like him. (PNB)

7/8/47: Graveyard rumors. Siletz Cemetery. People sad, scared. No CI. (ONB)

7/15/47: Definite grave robbing problem. Need better laws. 'B' and sheriff laugh it off. People afraid to talk. (PNB)

3/21/48: More grave robbing. Check with CI#3. Rumors. Will ask old lady on Government Hill. TC. She's scared. Won't talk. (PNB)

5/8/48: CI#3 TC. Grave robbing in private cemetery down river. Bones scattered. Photos. DA—no investigation because there are no laws. 'B' to follow up. (PNB)

5/15/51: Jean Thom murder. Dewey Creek. Marshall Franklin, fisherman, Tillamook. Notify kin. Kline, 'Grandma'. Lives on Govt. Hill. Photos. Report prep. Responders: 'B', sheriff, private ambulance. (ONB)

5/16/51: Anonymous TC to dispatch. Rumors in Siletz: Jensen kicked out by Alice Simpson. May be father of Jean Thom's baby. Probably unfounded. Jensen left couple years ago. School at Monmouth. Will contact. Also contact Alice.

5/19/51: Tomorrow off. Promised Teresa movie and ice cream. Dispatcher asked me why 'B' had taken over Thom murder. Hasn't. Will discuss with him when I work next. Check for bones from bonfire. Not in the evidence room? (PNB)"

Damn. Only a few tidbits to follow."

40

I HAVE HAD ENOUGH! STRANGE GOINGS-ON IN THE NIGHT.
Rose's inflated stories. We've confirmed Lee was in Klamath Falls—in his
own vehicle—the night the shoot-out occurred in my front yard. Rose
admitted to Chance she lied to us, but she won't say why. I asked him to
bring her to my house after work and to drop the boy off at Marge's house.
We need answers.

Rose arrives bubbly and excited. Chance told her we expect a big
break in the case and want her here for the meeting. But Chance is searching in his back pockets, his jacket pocket and outside in his Jeep. When he
returns, he asks Rose for her apartment key, "I can't find my wallet. Maybe
I dropped it in your bathroom, or maybe the parking lot. I'll be right back."

"What have you been up to lately, Rose," I ask as we wait for Chance.

"Nothing. Why do you ask? Did you hear something about me?"

"Always hear things about you. Just wondering what you do all day.
Never see you at the store anymore."

"Got fired at the store. Late too many times, I guess."

"Must be tough. Did you have to apply for welfare?"

"No, I. ..."

Chance comes through the door just in time to save her from my prying questions. He carries a medium-sized cooler, large enough to hold about twelve cans of beer.

"Did you find your wallet?"

"I have my wallet. Found this under the boy's bed right where he said it was. Remember the conversation, Rose?"

There is no answer. Rose is sitting on the couch, sobbing into a pillow. Now we will get answers.

I know the story about her boy saying she had money under his bed, but I am shocked to see bundles of cash poured onto the couch beside Rose. She doesn't look at the money, or at either of us.

"Now, young lady, what is going on with you?" I ask.

Rose sits up with a start, her hand over her mouth. "Chance?"

"Sorry, Chance is eager for answers, too, but I will be the one asking the questions. You'd better tell the truth the first time because I haven't an ounce of patience or pity left, Rose."

"I can't."

"You can. Start with the answer. Who gave you all this money?"

Her stare is disconcerting. I see there is someone she fears more than she fears me. What has she done? No wonder she thinks Grandma's a fooler. She's been up to something and discovered Grandma doesn't really know everything.

"What did you have to do to earn all this money, Rose?" Maybe she'll feel more comfortable if I pretend she did something useful for this pile of cash. Not that I believe she did, but if it works, it works.

Silence.

"Did you show the men where our burial sites are, Rose?"

"No. They already knew. Oscar told them years ago, made maps for them."

Curse the god who thought we needed Oscar on this earth.

"Okay. Tell me who the men are. Who gave you this money, Rose?"

"He will kill me, Ellie." No tears now. This is real. She is afraid for her life.

"The man who gave you the money will kill you if you talk about it. Did he mean if you tell the police?" I ask.

"He didn't say the police. He said, 'Girly, if you breathe a word of this to Ellie Carlisle, I will slit your throat and leave you on your old grandma's porch like a useless dog.'"

Girly. I cannot control the shudder that takes control of my body. He's back! Stunned, I hesitate too long, and Chance takes over.

"Hell, no. You are not going to keep this information from us any longer, Rose. This guy must be arrested, taken off the streets. Now!" He slams his fist onto the old chest in front of Rose. It's solid wood so he may have some broken fingers.

"He is the police, Chance. He has people everywhere. Who do you think set up the whole lie about Lee, the shooting over here? I've tried to get away, but somehow, he always finds out where I'm going. He shows up in the middle of the night sometimes to remind me he can kill me."

"How did this happen, Rose? Where did you hook up with a dirty cop—and why? Just for the money?" Chance asks.

But Rose has turned toward me again, staring with those huge black eyes. Willing me to help her or maybe daring me to push for the answer. She knows I know.

"Chance. Let it go. I have other questions for Rose. Okay, tell me the names of the others involved in the grave robbing. It's a good place to begin."

"The cop is in charge. He spearheads the whole thing, mostly from somewhere by Portland."

"The cop?" I ask.

"Yeah. There are other top guys, but they don't do the digging. He calls one guy a lot, but he never uses names and those guys don't come here."

"Who digs, Rose?"

"None of the guys are from here. He brings them in from other places. Has some pretend to be digging in Paul Washington Cemetery, but they are just a cover for the guys digging in the older family graveyards in other places on old rez family land.

"I got in trouble for being involved with Lee. Part of the money was for me to rent my apartment, so the cop can use it for a secret office. He doesn't trust Lee. That's why he set up the shoot-out and made me lie to you. Supposed to get Lee arrested and in jail, but you didn't call the sheriff."

"Speaking of the sheriff. Do you know how Roger got the sheriff's reports? We can never get an answer."

"Said he had them ever since the murder. Kramer gave him copies then, after they talked about what could be included."

"Why would he tell you these secrets, Rose?" Chance asks.

"The money was supposed to keep me quiet. He reminded me all the time."

"When will he be back, Rose?" I need to get her safely away.

"He's pulled everybody out for a while. Said you're getting too close. He talks about you a lot and then gets mad and cusses and throws things. He's not as organized or nice as he used to be. He scares me to death when he gets like that."

I don't want to know any other details. The heat in my face is not only from anger. I am so embarrassed and disappointed in myself. This is what results from allowing personal emotions into an investigation.

"Rose, does your dad still live on the rez in Montana?" When she nods, I begin to formulate a plan to get her to him—to the canyon like Grandma said—where no one will get past her father or his tribe.

41

WHAT WAS I THINKING? STUPID, STUPID, STUPID! I STOOD there in front of my people at a General Council meeting and promised them I would stop the grave robbing. I would solve Jean's murder. I would get Mark out of prison. Grandma Kline. I promised Grandma Kline. Why? Over confidence? No, just plain ego. Too many years away from the reservation. Grandma's right, I have forgotten myself and our Indian ways.

This isn't one of my Chicago cases where the bad guys are proud to be criminals and do their dirty work in public. This is a damnable Indian Reservation where greedy, disrespectful white men steal the bones of our loved ones. Where one of my own blood told the diggers where to find our sacred burial grounds. How did I think a smartass woman could stop these ghouls?

So many ignored clues. Too much trust. No, not trust, too much looking away from what my gut told me. I violated my usual emotional barriers and let my thoughts be led astray by a handsome, evil cop.

It's time to re-evaluate every clue, every suspect and find the key to this whole mess. I do have a theory, shaky for sure, but my theory means one of these guys will have to turn against the others.

42

I DIDN'T GET MUCH SLEEP LAST NIGHT. BY THE TIME I ARRANGED to get Rose and her little boy safely to her father in Montana, and spent time berating myself for my failures, it was nearly daylight again. Chance's early phone call surprised me.

"Ellie, I'll be at your house at 8:30 tomorrow morning. Be ready to go to Portland. We have an appointment with Hank at noon."

Stunned, I can only stutter into the phone. "With…with…your adoptive Dad? With Hank Andrews?"

"Yep. I guess the only way I can answer your question, or Mark's, is to ask some questions of my own. I called and asked him to meet me at the Benson Hotel. I've reserved a small conference room, so we can have all the privacy we need."

"Wonderful, Chance. Didn't he wonder why you were bringing me?"

"No. Didn't want to give him possible excuses to decline. He can learn about you when he meets you."

"Okay. Anything to talk about before tomorrow?"

"No, we can discuss on the way. Have breakfast in Corvallis. See you in the morning."

"Yes. Let's not mention this meeting to anyone, especially Rose and Roger."

"Even Roger? Guess you'll explain tomorrow. It's all good. I asked Hank to keep it to himself, too."

While I'm in the kitchen for a fresh cup of tea, the phone rings again. I suppose Chance forgot something, so I answer, "Yes?" into the receiver.

"Miss Carlisle? Is this Ellie Carlisle?" The voice is deep and growly.

"Yes, it is. I'm sorry. I thought I knew who was calling."

"This is Hank Andrews. I understand you know my son. I'm meeting Chance tomorrow and I suspect you will also be there."

Too shocked to respond, I fumble to pull a chair out from the table before my knees give out.

"It's alright. I've heard about you from Roger Wood. Understand you and Chance are close and work well together. We'll talk tomorrow. I wanted to ask a favor, if you don't mind."

"A favor?"

Expecting him to ask me to stay out of the room while he and Chance discuss personal issues, I am surprised when he says, "Please don't tell Roger about this meeting."

"That won't be a problem, Mr. Andrews. I discussed the very issue with Chance. Roger won't hear about it from either of us. But he does seem to always know what we're doing."

"More than you know, I'm sure. Looking forward to meeting you."

He hung up without a goodbye. Abrupt and to the point, as I imagined he would be.

The phone rings again. Donna Barker. She begins sharing information with me so quickly all I have time to say is "Hello." She talks fast, but what she says is so important I grab for my pen and paper, any paper, so I don't miss anything.

"Donna, why are you in such a hurry?"

"I don't want anyone, not even my daughter, to know I hid one of Dan's reports. I discovered it after I married Jack. He is a dangerous man and I don't want him to know. But I lied to you and there are things you must know."

"Ok. I have made a few notes. Anything else?"

"No. Now promise me you won't let Teresa know, either."

"Promise. Thank you so much, Donna."

It is awhile before I can put the phone down. This information confirms so much, makes me angry, and breaks my heart. I didn't want to be right this time. When I replace the receiver, I glance at my hastily written notes and feel sick in the pit of my soul.

Portland area. Wood spearheads. No names other than Kramer.

43

"What brings you here, Ellie? I was surprised to receive your Alice message. Pleased, yet surprised. You sounded distraught."

"Sorry about the message, Tommy. I was distraught, or at least needed someone sane to speak with," I explain as we seat ourselves in his comfy office chairs.

"What's happened?"

"I have come to some conclusions. These reservation mysteries are taking me down paths difficult to believe. I need someone to tell me if I'm misinterpreting the clues or simply losing my mind. Also, I have a meeting in Portland tomorrow with Chance and his adoptive dad, Hank Andrews. I'd like more clarity when I arrive."

Tommy, the ultimate policeman, careful not to tread on another's jurisdiction says, "I thought you were working closely with the other cop? Can't he put this together for you? Not that I don't want to help."

"The other cop is part of the problem and it worries me."

"Start from the beginning."

"First, Tommy, you need to know this guy, this other cop, is drop dead gorgeous. There, I got it out on the table. This is the beginning of my confession and confusion."

"Never had such a problem myself, with pretty PIs falling for me, I mean. How far has this gone?"

"Oh, no affair or anything. Just my silly imagination. Some flirty talk and hand holding at a burial ceremony. Enough connection that I'm struggling to separate it from peculiar activities, clues perhaps, which I otherwise would immediately investigate. Ordinarily, I would not bring this type of problem to another police officer. Tell me if I'm out of line coming to you as a friend and confidante."

"You're fine. We agreed to honor Alice by being friends and stepdaughter-stepfather as if Alice and I had married. As we should have. Tell me how you met this guy, all the information. I have all afternoon."

I fill Tommy in on the way Roger Wood and I met and how he's been involved in the investigation right up through the incident at his grandmother's gravesite, and the ceremony that followed at the other reservation.

"Don't know I would have tried that way to educate him. But it's over and done with," Tommy says.

"I don't know if it worked, if he's a good actor, or a bad actor in the sense of being a dangerous man."

"So, there is danger involved in your concerns?"

"Yes. I strongly suspect more danger than I ever anticipated."

I continue my story, sharing information about the death threat phone calls to me and to Grandma Kline; Sheriff Kramer's statement they didn't get Jean Kline's killer, the sheriff's file and the fake shoot-out at my house, Grandma's dead dog, too many strangers associated with suspicious activities on the reservation lately, and Roger's stories about Hank Andrews buying and selling Indian babies, possibly including Chance, and more robbing of our graves.

"Especially difficult to handle is that I've learned from a young girl my son had organized his cousins to fight against grave robbing. Just before the wreck in which he died, he had an argument with his father who tried to warn him of the danger he was in. There is a possibility the boys were murdered, Tommy!"

"Definitely danger signs can't be ignored, but you share these as facts you would know how to handle. Kind of a one step at a time investigation challenge. Little different, I imagine, from a criminal case in Chicago. What aren't you telling me?"

Where do I start? Is this all only a feeling? Am I misinterpreting Roger's comments and activities? Rose didn't say Roger's name when she talked about the cop, though I know it's him.

"From the beginning, Roger Wood has fought against investigating the grave robbing. He agreed to work with us to determine who murdered Jean if we would help him investigate whether Hank Andrews is Chance's biological father. He didn't want to hear about anything related to grave robbers. He said he didn't see any connection to the murder, though he seemed to keep close track of that part of our investigation, even as he downplayed its importance."

"Okay. I'm listening. I'll keep my questions until you're finished."

"His quick temper has always bothered me. He's controlling to the point he called all over Anchorage until he found where I was staying, after he threw a fit with Chance when he found out I had gone to Anchorage to do an interview without his knowledge or permission. He's overly concerned about me. I find his actions unprofessional and recently more faked than sincere."

I eagerly accept the Pepsi Tommy offers. Nerves always constrict my throat. Makes it difficult to give a speech. I'm finding it difficult to speak intelligently right now while trying to make sense of my concerns.

"Even more troubling is I learned from one of his brothers, Roger grew up here in Newport and was part of the high school football team that included Hank Andrews and Sheriff Kramer. He told me Roger's been friends with Hank for years and is following up on Vivian's allegations. He's never mentioned, despite ample opportunity, that he has also kept in close contact with the sheriff for many years. It's not a lie, exactly, but certainly provokes questions and suspicion when added to his fight against finding those who disturb our graves."

"Does seem odd he wouldn't mention it."

"Speaking of odd. Tommy, I found references to you in a log book kept by the original deputy assigned to Jean's murder."

"Probably Dan referring to asking me about grave robbing rumors. Only topic I can think of. He only asked me once. I told him I didn't want to be involved because I was with Alice. Wouldn't be good for it to appear as if I was working with the police right then. There was something else?"

"A rumor from someone you might be the father of Jean's baby. He noted Alice sent you away years before and that you were in school in Monmouth."

"Good lord. I forget what people report as fact on the reservation. So ridiculous. Dan was a good friend. I was sad to hear he died in the accident. His little girl is grown now?"

"Yes, she is. Would make an excellent PI. Another issue has popped up to further confuse all this. I was in Anchorage to interview Dan's daughter. She believes her father was murdered by Jack Kramer. She had her Dad's log book, copies of all his reports, and a private notebook with some very interesting entries. I have copies of all except one. Her mother called to tell me she had hidden a report that detailed the grave robbing. It mentioned a cop named Wood, from the Portland area, spearheaded the thefts and Deputy Kramer was involved. Oh, and there were several entries in the logs about someone named 'B'. I'd love to identify the guy."

"Okay. Interesting. Still fact reporting. Let's get to what's bothering you."

"I haven't met Hank yet, but I believe this strange group of friends, who don't seem to like or trust one another, was involved in Jean's death. I also believe Jean's death has something to do with the grave robbing. Numerous clues point to the three being involved in grave robbing. One of them is probably making the death threats. There were times during the calls I heard a familiar tone, but I was not able to identify it."

I stop to take a drink and catch my breath. Pouring this information out makes it real and even more frightening.

"Why would you recognize the voice, Ellie"

I forgot I haven't told him about the threat, the main reason I was glad to leave the rez with Russ right after my high school graduation.

"Because when I was a little girl, I used to sit in a tree on Government Hill and watch people working in the cemetery. Sometimes I went there just to enjoy the peace and quiet when no one was around. One evening, it was near dark, I couldn't get down because a truck came in and three men began to dig in a grave below my tree. I was very quiet, but one of the men looked up and saw me. He yelled at me to get down, then grabbed my arm and dragged me near the open grave. 'You see that hole, girly? If you tell anyone what you have seen, I will find you and put you in a hole just like it. I'll bury you alive, girly. Do you hear me?' Then he pushed me away and said, 'Get the hell out of here.'

"I ran all the way home. I told Mama, but she said, 'Don't tell. You can't trust anyone.' I threw it in her face so many times in my teen years. Especially when she didn't want me to leave with Russ. I remember yelling, 'Why should I stay here with liars and grave robbers when you won't even tell me who my father is?' Poor Mama."

"But, Tommy, the worst part is last night Chance and I interrogated Rose, Marge's daughter. It's a long story, but she has been seriously threatened by the man spearheading the grave robbing in Siletz burials. He called her "Girly" and threatened to cut her throat. She would not utter his name, but I know it's Roger!"

"Why don't we discuss one guy at a time now? See what you know for sure. Tell me what confuses or frightens you. What is your bottom line opinion? Start with Kramer. By the way, you do remember I knew Kramer and Andrews back in the day, right? Don't think I ever met Wood, but I knew some of his brothers. Bunch of brats in those days. I didn't have any desire to be around them. Quite a bit older than them."

"Of course. We discussed that. Oh, I see. You don't want to be a suspect."

I laugh and assure him he's not being considered, but a suspicion has flickered. I think he can tell my thoughts.

"To add to all the confusion, Oscar, my rapist father, came to my house a couple of days ago. I didn't open the door, just asked what he wanted. He said, 'There are things you must know, Ellie.'"

"But I shouted back, 'I know what you did to my mother. That's all I need to know. Go away.' He insisted I open the door, so he could tell me what was so important. I refused. I am curious what he knows. Even Oscar might have clues. I'm not curious enough to let him in my house, though."

"Why don't I pay him a visit? I'm sure he'd be happy to see me," Tommy says.

"Sure, if you want to. I keep my doors and windows locked and my .38 at hand even more now."

"I'll extend an invitation to him to stay far away from you, like he was told about Alice."

"Thanks, Dad." I love the sound of my words and seeing Tommy's quick smile.

"So, regarding Sheriff Kramer," I continue. "First, he hates Indians, or at least claims he does. He threatened Chance. He told us he was the lead investigator on the murder case and they didn't get the real killer, which means he knows Mark was, and is, innocent, but hasn't done anything about it. He called me a 'Squaw' to provoke Chance into a fight, so he could arrest him. Kramer seems quite familiar with the reservation roads and lands. It's possible he forced Dan Harrington off the road after stealing the murder investigation assignment from him."

"Okay, Ellie. Add this to your list. In high school, Jack Kramer was known as 'Bull'. Most people continued to call him that even after he was a deputy. He might be the 'B' person in Dan's notes."

"Excellent! Those notes make it appear though "B" had calls and was assigned to investigate grave robbing on the reservation, he either didn't do the work or labeled the complaints as unfounded or false. There may be more. I will reread the notes."

"Now, for Roger Wood. I've told you my concerns. But there are also some clues from Grandma Kline that fit Roger. The young man who came only at night to date Jean, drove a truck like the one driven by the sheriff, but with a different logo on the driver's door. The guy looked tall and blonde."

"Any guy would look tall to your Grandmother."

"Yeah, true, but Grandma only saw him seated in his truck, so she decided he was tall, based on where the top of his head was in the cab. Plus, he had blonde hair and Roger said he had blonde hair when he was young. The truck could have been one of the Wood Fisheries trucks since they were a big deal in those years. There is a logo on all their equipment now. Probably the same one."

"Yes, I remember. I think all the Wood boys drove those pick-ups. The money family of Newport then."

"And Grandma remembers Jean's guy promised to buy her a large home in the city. Away from his family, especially his mother who was already irritated she had one squaw daughter-in-law and didn't want another one. I checked the date of his father's death and Roger was already an owner of the company, training to be a cop, on the date Jean died. He could have flaunted his money with big promises. Plus, I found out from a woman in Washington that trying to get information on a reservation should be old hat to Roger. She said he worked as a sheriff's deputy near one of the tribes up there for several years. Another lie he carried out to get in tight with our investigation. I am convinced he was only here to stop me from investigating the desecration of our cemeteries and private burial grounds."

"Everything seems plausible so far. Wonder what you'll find out about Andrews tomorrow?"

"I suspect a lot! I already know he got, or maybe bought, baby Chance in Alaska. Why are you looking at me like that?"

"Tell me what you know and then I'll answer."

"Vivian found a note in an old jacket of Hank's. There was also an airline ticket for a trip to and from Anchorage the day before Hank arrived home with the baby. He supposedly has a cousin in Alaska named Ruthie. Chance says he's never heard of her. Of course, Mark's girlfriend's name was Ruthie and she does live in Alaska. I doubt it is her because someone on the rez would have mentioned by now Chance was her son. And Mark's. Wouldn't they? Wouldn't Mark have mentioned it when he told us he and Ruthie planned to be married after her graduation?"

"Maybe not. That is the kind of secret to keep tied to the reservation. Mark wouldn't tell outsiders and wouldn't have had to tell rez people. Word would have spread quickly. He turned Ruthie away when he was arrested, remember? She would have made difficult choices, an abortion or to move away on her own, away from her family and community without telling anyone she was pregnant. Perhaps adopting the baby out. Have you checked the records for Chance's birth date?"

"Yes. We only have the date on Vivian's papers. It's nowhere near Jean's murder date. I haven't determined why he's convinced Jean was his mother, except Vivian told him so. There is no certified Oregon birth record."

"You do realize if Chance is Ruthie's son it means Mark is his father. How will he like that? You told me he didn't want to visit Mark at the prison."

"He didn't, Tommy. Once they met, he seemed okay. He's more concerned now with Mark's belief Hank is his biological father. If I give him another possibility he might be more receptive. I'll wait until we have some proof."

"My money is on Mark. Chance looks so much like him, plus I haven't mentioned I called Alice after Jean's murder because I knew she would be upset. During a long conversation, she told me Ruthie was pregnant. We never talked about it again."

"Tommy! Now, aren't you straight off the rez school of secret keeping! Very interesting. Reminds me as I'm being prideful no one will give answers to Roger, the whole village is keeping important information from me. I learned only yesterday my ex, Russell Carlisle, comes to Siletz quite often. I had no inkling he didn't return to Montana after Logan's funeral. He called me a couple of times. Other than brief answers to questions about Logan, I've wasted no time on him."

"Where's he staying?"

"Staying? You mean like living?"

I laugh as I recall Tommy and my mama arguing about those two words. One of my few memories of him in our lives.

"White people live somewhere," Mama always told you, "But Indians stay."

"Yes. I realized after I left Siletz I'd picked up a few local words. Most of them have stayed with me. Like Enit. That one puzzles people."

"I don't know where Russ stays. Didn't care enough to ask when Marge said he'd been to visit her. She said he works for some export company and travels around a lot. Nice he's finally quit drinking. He got a job after he didn't have a child to support."

"Sorry you had it so rough."

"Russell Carlisle is an old-style white guy who thought he'd got himself a squaw to support him and his son. The good-looking guitar playing, romantic persona evaporated before we'd been married six months. By then, I was married, not to the man I'd fallen for, but to his cruel, drunken other self who left right after Logan was born. I never saw or heard from him again until the day of Logan's funeral when he blubbered on his knees in the mud at the gravesite."

"I hope you can work through the bitterness. It's not healthy."

"Ah, who's bitter? Facts are facts and the fact is Russ is a poor excuse for a man, let alone a husband or father. Another big rez secret kept from me for a long time is Russ came back to Siletz on the very week of the wreck. Grandma told me Logan was determined to find him and give him the what for. Now I've learned on the day our son died in the wreck, Russ warned Logan not to pursue the grave robbers as he might be killed. I have to talk to Russ whether I want to or not."

"I'd rather you not, Ellie. It sounds like Russ could have information of a possible criminal threat, or action. Let me handle it. The wreck happened on a state highway. I'll pull our reports and do a follow-up."

"Thank you. Please let me know what you find out. Can we take a short break, Tommy?"

"Let's have lunch. I can grab some hamburgers and we can sit on a log at the beach and relax a bit."

Sounds like a good idea, so I stand and take his arm. We garner a few glances as we walk out through the reception area, but today I don't care. I have a Dad to help me solve my problems. Rez rumormongers be damned.

44

Typical Oregon coast winter day, windy and pouring buckets. Glad I don't have to do the driving to Portland.

I couldn't sleep last night after spending most of yesterday with Tommy. We discussed, pondered, compared and determined little more than we had before lunch. It was too windy to sit on a log, so we ate our hamburgers and fries in the front seat of his truck with the powerful Pacific waves for entertainment.

I have suspicions, maybe some circumstantial evidence, but no real proof Jean's blonde boyfriend was Roger Wood and that he killed her. I have no proof the three men robbed graves in years past and are involved now, nor proof Mark and Ruthie are Chance's biological parents. If one of the three, Kramer, Wood or Andrews, cracks a little, the pieces may come together, and I will have a witness. I'm hoping Hank Andrews will crack today.

As I get into Chance's Jeep, he asks, "Where were you yesterday, Ellie? I came by, called a couple of times. Roger called me twice trying to find you. Started to worry about you. I drove by before dark and saw your car here and the lights on."

"I was in Newport, conferring with Tommy, getting his perspective on this mess we're trying to untangle."

"Did he have any good ideas?"

"He listened and did have a couple of useful clues. Mostly it helped to spew and try to make sense of it all."

"What clues?"

"He knew Kramer's nickname during his high school years was Bull. We think he may be the 'B' in Dan Harrington's notebooks. That's a good clue. I think it is probably correct. Those notes fit Kramer's probable actions. Non-actions would be more appropriate, I guess."

"What other clues?"

"One pretty good one. It pertains to Hank and I'd prefer to let it play out today, if possible, Chance. I'm hoping Hank will be the key to our mini mysteries, so we can solve the large ones."

"Me, too. I am nervous about how he will react to my questions. He sounded calm on the phone. Possible he might work himself into a tirade before he gets to Portland. Maybe not so easily with Mother not around. At least I know he won't take his belt off."

"He called me yesterday."

"Who called you?"

"Hank."

"When? Why?"

"He called right after you hung up. I thought it was you calling back. He knows we are working together and suspected I'd be at the meeting. He was okay with it but asked we not bring Roger or tell him about the meeting."

"Holy. ...! Wonder what that's all about? Did you tell him you had already mentioned the same thing to me?"

"Sure."

Waiting for Chance to register and receive the keys to the conference room, I scan the lobby hoping for a quick peek at Hank Andrews. I am apprehensive to meet him. Perhaps seeing him interacting with someone before he makes it to where we are standing will help. But we're the only people here other than the desk clerk. I watch the door.

As Chance turns to tell me the room number, a deep, growly voice rumbles a greeting from directly behind me. "Hello, Son."

Hank must have arrived first and gone into the restroom. Darn. I turn and am astonished. No one ever prepares me for the good looks of the men I'm to meet. Chance never once mentioned the rugged, handsomeness of his father. He has a kind face and appears to be even more apprehensive than Chance or me. I step aside because at this moment I am standing between two potential powder kegs.

A moment's hesitation and then both extend their arms to shake hands. Chance's hands, large, brown, a little soft from desk work, Hank's the rugged, tanned and hard hands of a man struggling to survive on a commercial fishing boat. The father, tall and slim; the son, shorter, though taller than most Siletz men, stocky and strong shouldered. They face one another, waiting, wondering.

Finally, Chance introduces me and invites his father upstairs to the suite. He's ordered lunch. I offer to eat in the restaurant, so they can visit. They decline my offer in unison. Thank goodness.

In the room, the table is set, complete with a beautiful centerpiece of holly and carnations, a gentle reminder it is December already. Two Christmases since I lost my son. A knock at the door announces lunch has arrived. A big pot of chicken and dumplings, with a green salad and side dish of buttery corn kernels. Sparkling water and coffee are available on a side table. Chance has outdone himself.

"Our favorite dish, Dad. Do you remember we always wanted Mother to make chicken and dumplings when you came home from a fishing trip? I thought it would be fun to have it today."

"Yeah, thanks."

Not much enthusiasm in Hank's response. Chance is trying hard. Hank hasn't relaxed at all. We continue with no further conversation until the dessert arrives and Hank finally talks.

"I'd rather have my dessert later, Chance. This food was good, but my nerves are shot worrying about why you called me here."

"Sorry. I know. I should have done this another way. My stomach is rolling, too. How are you, Ellie?"

"Not much better. Let's wait for dessert."

Seated in a conversation area with Chance and Hank in facing recliners and me on the couch, we wait again, this time for Chance to start the show, or meeting, or whatever this is. He drinks coffee from his cup and begins, "Hank. Dad. I'd like to hear the true story of who I am, where you got me, and why you hate me so much."

Wow. Nothing like laying it all out there in one sentence. Hank's face goes two shades whiter, then several shades redder.

"Who the hell ever said I hated you? Dumb shit. Why would I go to all the trouble to get you just to hate you?"

"That's been the question most of my life. Why don't you start at the beginning, back when you went to Alaska to get me?"

Hank sits up straighter and stares at Chance.

"Oh yeah, I know. Be sure to keep it on the straight and narrow. I'm tired of the games, the lies, not knowing who I am."

Hank sinks back into his chair, breathes out loudly, then says, "Once upon a time..." and Chance bursts out laughing. He reaches across to shake his Dad's hand again, their shared sense of humor cooling the tension.

"As you've heard all your life, Chance, your mother and I wanted a family. We were not able to have a biological child. This affected Vivian deeply. She spent a lot of time in bed, or on the window seat staring off across the water. I suggested adoption, but she felt it would be announcing her failure as a wife, as a woman or something. I never understood how she felt. Guess it would be difficult for any man to know."

Chance hasn't moved since he first leaned forward, intent on Hank's every word.

"Growing up I was very close to my cousin, Ruthie. We went to Newport High School together, in the same grades because she skipped an early grade. Beautiful girl and very smart. We spent a lot of time together. Our houses were on the same street. Our moms were sisters and quite close. When Ruthie fell in love, I became her cover when she needed to fool our families."

"Why, what was she doing?" I ask, only to move the story a little faster.

"She met, somehow, a nice guy from the Siletz Reservation. I liked him, or I would never have helped her. We prevented both our mothers from finding out. There were strict rules, prejudice, against dating Indians, Black people, anyone other than white."

He looks at Chance, probably wondering how this distinctly Indian man was taking the facts. Chance sits in the same position, his demeanor unchanged.

"Anyway, something horrible happened to the guy's family. A relative was murdered on the reservation and he was convicted. Sent to jail forever. You know his name, of course, because of your involvement in the investigations. Mark Thom. That's him. Ruthie's boyfriend. Her fiancé. They planned to be married as soon as Ruthie and I graduated from high school.

We were nervous about the uproar which would follow their news. We were excited. A few of us knew, and were excited, a baby was on the way."

Chance's expression still hasn't changed.

Hank continues to look at Chance and says, "Mark immediately forbid Ruthie, any of us, to have anything to do with him or his case. He thought it would protect Ruthie and the baby. I left to play football at Oregon State and Ruthie went to Seward, Alaska to live with an aunt on her Dad's side who knew about her problem. I met Vivian in Corvallis during my freshman year in college."

Now I know for sure what's coming. It appears Chance is still waiting, unaware of the punchline that will change his life forever.

"I married Vivian and we moved to River City. I didn't hear from Ruthie for months. Vivian knew I had a cousin in Alaska, though she didn't know anything about the murder or the trial. Then Ruthie called. Vivian hadn't come out of the spare bedroom for a couple days, so I answered the phone.

"Ruthie was crying, saying she had a little son and was forced to give him up for adoption as she had no job, no way to care for him and her relatives didn't want to raise another kid. She wanted us to take him. Even though Vivian didn't want to adopt, I thought a baby was what she needed."

"Did you ask her?"

"No, Ellie, I knew what she would say. I was often gone for several days on the boat. She wouldn't wonder where I'd gone. No chance she'd go to the dock. She never left the house. I flew to Anchorage, drove to Seward where I met Ruthie and picked you up, Chance. Had a few diapers and a change of clothes and several bottles of milk. Not even formula, regular milk. She got an Oregon birth certificate made out with our names on it somehow. I still wonder how. So, that, my son, is your true story. I can tell you the day I walked into our house and handed you to Vivian was the happiest day of either of our lives," Hank declares as he wipes a red hanky across his eyes.

Chance stands, "You're telling me that Mark Thom is my real, my biological father? And that he knows this?"

"Yes, he is your father. I have no idea what he knows. I've had no contact with him in years. Didn't discuss him with Ruthie."

"It sounds like the whole reservation was aware. Why Grandma Kline waited all these years for me. Why I look so much like Mark. Ellie, did you know?"

"No. I suspected. Waited for verification before I mentioned anything. Now you know."

"Yes, now I know, and I hope Mark didn't know when I met him the other day. We'll have things to talk about one way or the other." Chance pauses. "Thanks, Dad. You've answered most of the questions that have eaten at me for years."

I'm surprised, probably not as much as is Hank when Chance stands to hug him and bursts into tears. I exit to the bathroom to give them some long overdue connection time.

When I return to the room, the men are back in their chairs, involved in a lively conversation that sounds to be covering a multitude of Chance's childhood issues.

Hank says, "It's something you'll have to discuss with Vivian, Chance. I could never understand why she was so convinced you were in danger of being kidnapped. I can tell you I deeply regret the way I reacted and how I treated you. We have much more to talk through. It's my fault. I never hated you, son, I loved you. Love you."

"Yeah. We better talk it all out and then start over as adults," Chance says. He walks toward the kitchen, patting Hank's shoulder as he passes his chair. When he heads to the bathroom, I take the opportunity to speak to Hank about my reason for being there.

"There are some questions I hoped you might answer for me today to help with our investigations, Hank."

"Ellie, I'd be happy to, except there's something I'd like to do for Chance before we get to your questions."

"Oh. I'll wait then."

"A couple of doors down, there is a woman waiting to talk to her son. Please bring her here. I hear you knew her years ago."

Numb with anticipation, I grab the keys and hurry out the door. Knocking on the door of the nearby room, I have no idea what to say to Ruthie or how Chance will react to meeting her. Does he understand what it must have taken for her to give him up? Guess I'll soon know.

The tiny woman who answers the door is stunning. Mark's description of her when we were at the prison was accurate, of course. As a child, I wished my hair would turn red like hers. She is one of those redheads whose hair makes her seem to glow. She will be shocked to see her son who looks like the Mark she last saw decades ago.

"Ellie? I remember you as the little girl who loved Mark so much. How nice our lives bring us together, again. I hear you have been a big part of Chance's life. Thank you, so much." She reaches to take my hands in hers. "Let's go to my son now."

"He's heard his story from Hank, but he doesn't know you are here."

At the door, I step back and watch as Ruthie lightly knocks.

"Ellie, what are you. ...Oh, who are. ...? Ruthie? My mama?" Stuttering, reaching to embrace Ruthie, Chance scoops her up and carries her into the room.

"Hey, Dad, look who I found at the door. A stray redhead."

45

RUTHIE WENT TO CHANCE'S HOUSE AND I FINALLY HAVE TIME to review the notes I took from my visit with Hank. The three of them had a great time getting acquainted or reacquainted at the hotel. Chance kept changing which one he wanted to touch, to hug, to squeeze. Ruthie didn't talk much as the tears flowed. For a long time, they tried to decide what Mark's reaction would be to their reunion, to the realization Chance is his son. Ruthie is sure he'll be proud and happy. Chance isn't so sure. He remembers the lectures, the responsibility he must accept or reject and the consequences of rejection.

"Man, he's intimidating enough as a cousin. I don't know if I can handle what his expectations will be as a father," Chance says.

His comments were met with laughter from the three of us who know Mark from a different era.

I rode back to Siletz with Hank who decided it would be good for Chance and Ruthie to have alone time driving back. It is late when we arrive at my home. Hank plans to get a room in Newport and will call me in the morning. He's unhappy with the rumors and assumptions about his involvement in the murder, though he refuses to discuss grave robbing until after he consults his attorney.

My answering machine is full of messages from Roger. By the third time he asks, "Where are you, Ellie?" I am irritated. He's become a stalker. I do not have to answer to him. The fourth message, "I have information Deputy Lofton is in a care center, unable to remember anything or to talk. His family has a 'No visitors' order on his door," makes me so angry. He just won't quit getting in the middle of things. His reports are a disaster. Where did he get this information about Deputy Lofton's location? How does he know Lofton's condition and there is a sign on his door?"

The next message is from Tommy Jensen. "Ellie, Tommy here. I received a call today from my ex-wife informing me an old friend of ours, former Deputy Jim Lofton, was in a terrible accident yesterday. Alive, but in a coma in the Medford hospital. OSP investigating, but it looks like he just ran off the road. The ex remembers he was involved in the murder case against the Indian kid from Siletz years ago. I thought he might be someone you are looking for."

46

The phone call came in early morning and I'm a wreck. I was expecting it to be Hank, but it was Marge. Her only words were, "Meet me at Grandpa's grave at eleven." She hung up with no further explanation. She didn't, probably wouldn't, answer when I called back.

Hank did call. I am to meet him in Newport at one, so this better be a short meeting with Marge.

What can she possibly want to do at Grandpa's grave? She didn't sound upset, so it can't be she's discovered another disturbed gravesite. No, she sounded like her usual self. Most times she shows up at my door. I can count on one hand the times she's called me in my whole life. She's never asked me to meet her somewhere. Maybe she heard we met with Hank and Ruthie.

I make my daily 10 a.m. call to Grandma Kline, am assured Grandma is up and doing fine this morning. Her new dog, Monster, yaps in the background.

I finish washing the breakfast dishes and the phone rings again. This time it's Roger saying he is spending the weekend with his son in River

City. He'll be back in time for Monday night's meeting at Chance's apartment. I don't mention Marge's order or Hank.

It's 10:30. I grab a coat and make sure my gun is safely loaded and hidden in a readily accessible pocket. This is insane. I trust Marge with my life. That's the point, I guess. These days, I'm trusting everyone with my life because I don't know who or where the enemies are, even among my own tribe. I am constantly prepared for trouble.

There are more cars than usual on the streets this Saturday morning as I drive past the two small grocery stores on Gaither Street. Further along, a large sign promotes a sale at the grange hall. A line of motorcycles roars in from the north and parks at the tavern as I turn east.

Marge's old, white Chevy is parked near the front entrance of the tribal building on the Hill. She's sitting behind the wheel. I decide to pull in beside her. At the last moment, I make a sharp right turn onto the lane that winds through the cemetery. Marge must have a reason for wanting to meet me at Grandpa's gravesite or she would have suggested the parking lot. Best to follow directions.

I park off the edge of the lane, leaving room for a car to pass, and walk to Grandpa Kline's tombstone, every nerve in my body at full attention. I sit on a stump at the edge of the family plot where I can see across the cemetery toward where Marge has parked. I remember chastising Chance right here, months ago, for wanting to ask Grandma about her dead daughter.

I'm waiting, scanning in all directions, ready for what? I don't know, except Marge may get out of her car and walk over here. Or she might be a plant and someone else will show up. She's on my list of possible traitors, but for no real reason. Oh, I'm so tired of being paranoid.

Now I see Marge moving slowly toward me, stopping here and there to brush dried grass clippings from a tombstone or to right a tipped vase. Her pace quickens when she enters a more secluded area, shaded by towering conifers. She's coming through the last stretch, past the WWI hero's grave, down a little dip in the terrain and across the final section where the Simmons family is buried, moving quickly for such a large woman, her broad shoulders swaying in rhythm with her feet. Her arms swing at her sides, pushing her forward with determination.

Even as paranoid as I am I still find I'm so jealous of her long, straight, black hair. Not a touch of gray. She's older, but my hair is already naturally frosted.

I know from years of adoring my older cousin what others describe as Marge's "mean look" hides a soft and sensitive soul. However, the uncertainty of this meeting, combined with the death threats and suspicion a tribal member is involved in the grave robbing, keeps me on alert with everyone, even Chance.

"Hey!"

Marge steps between a tree and my perch, leans against an old hemlock and bends her right leg up to push the flat of her foot against the trunk for balance. She crosses her arms over her chest and looks over at me.

"Hey, yourself. Why are we here?"

"I think it's time you met the bastard who raped me."

"Why now? Wait, you were raped? Is Chance *your* son?" Can't let her suspect I'm aware she's lied about not knowing his parents.

"No, he's not my son. He's not Jean's son, either. I can't tell Chance his story. He can't face Mark's claim Hank Andrews is his father, so I don't know how he'd handle the whole truth."

"So, it's true? Hank is his real father?"

"No, he's not. Chance's story has no good starting point. Anyhoo, I want you to hear my story and get this guy to talk."

Guess now isn't the time to interrupt her with questions or to tell her I met Ruthie and know Chance's real story. I don't know why we are talking in a cemetery, under a tree. Guess she's paranoid, too

"I'll take you to the house where it happened. He goes where no one will bother him while he gets drunk. Maybe we'll get lucky and find him there."

"What then? We can't just walk in and confront him."

"Why not?"

She glares at me. It's obvious she has a plan and doesn't intend to let me change it.

"Tell me what you have in mind, Marge."

Her foot returns to the soft earth. She straightens up and walks over to place her hands on my shoulders and begins to share her plan in a soft tone, barely above a whisper.

"We go there, tonight. If his car is there, we wait until the lights go out and we think he's asleep or passed out, and then we go in. I will confront him. Make him admit what he did to me all those years ago. He will admit it in front of you."

Marge's grip tightens with her increased emotion.

"Then what?"

"Then you make him admit he killed Jean. Maybe he knows who is digging in our graveyards."

"Marge, if he's drunk, nothing he says can be used in court."

"That's your problem, Ellie. I will take you to him. I'll make him admit what he did to me. What you do about the murder and the grave robbing is up to you." She steps back, places her hands on her hips, never taking her eyes from mine.

"Alright, Marge. I'll help you only if you agree to leave your gun at home, and if you promise not to tell Chance where we're going. Let's see what Kramer has to say before we tell Chance anything."

"I didn't. …never mind. Yeah, sure. Sounds good to me. Tonight?"

"No! I must think this through. Make sure we're not messing up a confession in our hurry to get him to incriminate himself. But I have an appointment in Newport at one, Marge. Let's talk again, soon."

47

Hank's truck is in the state police parking lot in Newport when I pull in before 1 p.m. anxious to find out why he picked such an unusual place for a meeting. He better not say Tommy has anything to do with the murder or the grave robbing. I am not eager for another disappointment.

No one in the truck, so I march right into the lobby, ready for battle, or whatever awaits me. Life has too many strange turns these days. Some pieces of the puzzle are falling together. I'll keep working until I have concrete answers.

"Go right into Lt. Jensen's office, Ms. Carlisle. They are waiting for you."

They? Tommy and Hank? Though my instinct is to run back to my car, I summon courage and a professional PI attitude and open the door to Lt. Jensen's office. He may not be "Tommy" today.

"Hey, here's my girl. Have a seat. Hank and I were just discussing you."

I bet you were. I'll sit, but I'm not your girl today. Not until I know why the man I think is involved in the grave robbing and perhaps a multitude of other nefarious activities does some explaining.

I smile, sit and hope to present a stern demeanor.

"Ellie has only a few drops of patience, so let's get right to the point, Hank. I'll let you share your story and then I'll follow up," Lt. Jensen says.

I turn toward Hank as he says, "Right up front, Ellie, I'm an undercover FBI agent. I need to hear what you have developed in your investigation of the murder."

"What?" I think I shouted. I didn't expect this, or a question right off. "Is this legit, Tommy? That he's FBI, I mean."

"Yes."

"Start at the beginning then. I'm not sharing any investigation information with you until I hear the story of how you became an FBI agent. You must know how little trust tribal members have in your agency." I sound nasty, but I don't care.

"OK, Ellie, here's what happened to me. I left Newport to play football at Oregon State, as you've heard. My second year there, an FBI agent showed up and invited me to lunch. Didn't think I had a choice except to go. Said they heard complaints about grave robbing over on the Siletz and couldn't find any laws that allowed them to make an arrest, even though they knew who was digging. They had set up a dummy corporation in Wenatchee to buy stolen grave goods. They had photos of me on the one night I went with Jack Kramer. The agent said there had been a murder, which I also knew. They did have jurisdiction, sort of."

"Sort of?"

"I was glad to hear there were no laws. Sneaking around the reservation at night on the back roads looking for little cemeteries was a favorite pastime for several of the guys I went to school with in Newport. One was much more involved than the others and had identified a buyer in another state for bones or collectibles like knives, beads, or old guns they might dig up."

I try to hide my disgust. "You replied 'sort of' about the murder."

"Sort of because during the years the tribe was terminated, the FBI had little jurisdiction. When they are restored, we might have it, again. There has been no reservation land here during termination. I think the selling of grave goods is disgusting. I agreed when I was a kid. I only went one time, but I heard all the stories from Jack. He was too involved and couldn't say no. When he became a deputy sheriff, he had to be careful not to get caught or he could lose his badge. He became very good at participating in the dark and making sure it was not while he was on duty."

"There was a so-called 'leader' who could rat on him and cause him to lose his badge. Someone even more devious and evil than Jack Kramer? Terrifying."

"The leader, as you call him, was much smarter than Jack, Ellie. He went to school and became a cop, climbed the ladder so he could keep abreast of the new laws and what was being investigated across the state. Even managed to pass the physical tests despite an old injury. Made quite a name for himself. He's running scared now, making dumb mistakes. There's a woman involved. Now may be our best chance to finally get him."

So, my suspicions are right on. Tommy must think I'm a total fool. Probably told Hank all about my recent confession.

"When Chance said you were meeting us in Portland, I hoped you would be the last piece of the puzzle," I explain to Hank. "That you would confess, testify against Jack Kramer and clean up this whole mess. The more pieces came together, the more I knew someone had infiltrated our investigation. Knew every move we made.

"Rose was my first suspicion. There was someone using her. I worried about Chance. Seemed possible it was the two of you because there were times when Chance seemed too angry at you. More like bad acting than anything believable. Determining who made threats, why he knew so much. That was the difficult task."

"So, you know why I'm here?" Hank asks.

Oh crap! I realize I've twisted one side of my hair into a knotted mess. I push it away from my cheek and answer in my best professional voice.

"Yes! You want to know what I can tell you about Roger Wood because I am the woman who has made him begin to make mistakes."

"True, though not the major reason. He's running scared because nothing has worked to frighten you away. He's drinking heavily, putting pressure on Rose to help him get you alone. I assigned a guy full-time in Siletz to make sure no one attempted to kill you."

"What? Who could come into Siletz and get enough information of any use? I didn't need protection, by the way."

Hank glances at Tommy like he hopes he'll take over the conversation, Tommy shakes his head, declines the offer.

I don't know what's up; someone better speak soon.

"I found the right guy. Told him to find a way to let you know. He was never successful in having a conversation with you. He talked to Rose, but she was terrified of both the guy and you. The Lieutenant paid him a visit, then decided you would never believe him if he told you."

What is Hank talking about? Who did Tommy. ...? Oh no. One look at Lt. Jensen's red face and I know my security guard was Oscar, my rapist father.

I stand and walk toward Tommy and growl, "Why didn't you tell me?"

"You wouldn't have believed me, or him, and he was able to do his job even without you listening to him. You'll not want to hear this, but Oscar recognized Roger when he first came to town because Oscar was the one who told the kids years ago where to find all the cemeteries."

"I know about Oscar giving the information to Roger. Part of what we learned from Rose." And Katie, too, but I don't mention her name. I feel dirty knowing this man is my father. Now, looking at Hank, I ask, "You know Roger was the father of Jean's baby?"

"No, why do you think so? Do you know for sure?" Hank looks puzzled.

"Clues. Grandma told me the young man who came to get Jean at night, who made all the promises he had lots of money. He had blonde hair and was tall. Roger slipped once and mentioned he had blonde hair when he was in high school. Neither you nor Jack Kramer were blondes, especially Jack, and Roger was the third guy in the group. He came to me wanting help to prove you, Hank, were selling Indian babies, and protested long and hard every time we mentioned Jean's murder. He didn't see any reason to investigate grave robbing or the murder. He also seemed to forget his original reason for coming to Siletz. I finally got suspicious. The baby selling story from Vivian didn't fly with me, by the way."

"Yeah, but my ex did a great job of setting that up with Roger, didn't she?" Hank says. "Since he wanted to get to Siletz to find out what you knew about the grave robbing he fell for our baby selling story. By the time he realized it wasn't true, he probably thought he was in tight with you and Chance.

"The money had nothing to do with Indian babies. Her attorney got excited about nothing. My old man sold the mill before I met Vivian," Hank continued. "I invested the money and decided when I got married I would live on my fishing income and leave the mill money for emergencies and any children. Had to dip into the mill money a few times because I couldn't say no to Vivian or Chance. Wanted the best for those two."

"Neither of them knew about the other money?" I ask.

"Not until recently. Explained it all to Vivian, except the FBI payments, so I could get her to plant the story with Roger. I'll have to figure out what I can share about the FBI. She and I finally had a good conversation.

Things are better now. Still divorced but speaking. I'll work out a settlement with her. Decent thing to do. Chance agreed when I called him last night. He asked me to tell you these details because he couldn't be here today. Taking Ruthie to Salem."

"Oh, that will be an interesting meeting with Mark."

"So how are you two planning to get Roger to confess?" Tommy asks.

Hank looks at me. It's time to tell them my plan to get Sheriff Jack Kramer to confess the entire scheme, including Roger's role in both the murder and the grave robbing.

"My cousin Marge was raped in the days following Jean's murder. I have agreed to go with her to confront the man she hates with a passion." I pause to see Tommy's reaction. One eyebrow shoots up. "She wants to get him to confess and have him arrested. He hangs out in a little house in Seal Rock, she says. Even though she didn't mention any names, it clearly is the sheriff."

"Jack? She said Jack raped her?"

"Yeah. No. She didn't say his name. It seemed obvious."

"I suppose anything is possible. Did she describe the house, or give you the address?"

"No, I'll get the address and call Tommy—if Jack says enough to get himself arrested."

"You're sure she meant Seal Rock?" Hank asks.

"Yes. Why?"

"I have a cabin in Seal Rock which overlooks the ocean. I haven't visited in years. Jack had nowhere to go when he came back on weekends from training. I was in Corvallis going to school. No time for trips to the coast, so I gave him a key to the cabin. He even lived there full-time until he had a few paychecks. I never asked him to return the key. Several people have had keys over the years."

"That's Kramer," Tommy says. "What about Roger?"

"I hope to get Kramer's confession and promise him a deal if he gives info on Roger," I explain. "But I have to ask--who has a cabin overlooking the ocean but never goes there?"

"My Dad had it built when I was a kid. 2439 Seagull Lane. So many memories. When we got Chance, I didn't want him close to the reservation, so we never went there as a family. I doubt he knows it exists."

Strange. He adopted an Indian boy but doesn't realize how racist his remarks are.

Tommy says, "I think we know the address Marge has in mind."

"I will call you, Lieutenant Jensen, with the date and time," I call out as I head out the door. I don't want these law guys starting a discussion about this not being a job for a PI. This is my investigation.

48

Once again, I've had a day of angst and confusion. Early this morning, Tommy called to report on his conclusions about the wreck that killed my Logan. Blood alcohol tests did show all the boys had been drinking. There was no evidence of foul play. Yet another Siletz tragedy played out in conclusion to a night of teenager's drinking and driving. Tommy spoke to Russell and determined he and Old Joe were speculating about the danger to Logan and the boys. No facts just wanted to give Logan some fatherly advice. Nothing developed regarding Logan's mention of a man he was to meet that night.

'Let it go, Ellie. There's no way to figure it out."

Yes, I will let it go because I know without a doubt the man was Roger. I won't forget, though. Someday, somehow, I will find proof Roger Wood killed my only child.

Now, as I pull in behind a black Mercedes convertible and turn off the engine, I hope the thunder of the crashing ocean waves and the wind smashing through the trees masks the sound of my Jeep crunching along the gravel driveway.

"Nice car for a fisherman," I say.

I can't let Marge know I've figured out who the rapist is. She still thinks I believe it's Hank Andrews. Hell, truth be told, she still thinks I believe all the hooey about Chance being Jean and Hank's son. So I pretend that this car is Roger's when I know Sheriff Kramer has to be the rapist.

Marge doesn't respond. She's been in her own strange world since we left Siletz and traveled here to Seal Rock.

Hidden from Highway 101 by a small, thick forest of coastal pines, we move quickly, silently toward the ramshackle cabin. The bluish glow of the full moon, filtered by fog, dimly lights our way.

We flatten ourselves against the cabin's outer wall of ragged and weathered cedar shakes and inch toward the only north facing window. No lights shine in the house. That doesn't mean he is sleeping.

The couch faces the ocean. He sleeps there a lot. I've learned this from Marge over the weekend as I continued to question her about her plan, her need, to make the rapist confess.

Telling me about being terribly violated, she shuddered. She'd promised Grandpa Thom she would quit drinking and finish high school. She couldn't take a chance of getting arrested when she hitchhiked back to Siletz on Hwy. 229 late one night after getting into a row with friends carousing around Toledo, drinking and raising hell. A guy came along, offered her a ride home. She'd seen him around Siletz. It seemed safe. Suddenly he whipped the truck around and headed back towards Toledo. At the junction of 229 and 20 he turned west and raced toward Newport. She begged him to stop, to let her out. He kept driving. Too fast for her to open the door.

Terrified, she waited for her chance to jump and run. At this cabin, before the truck stopped, he reached across, grabbed her arm and locked a handcuff around her left wrist. She struggled, but saw the other end was firmly attached to his right arm. He was ready, eager and excited to find her. Marge had walked into the predator's trap.

It was not the first time she'd been raped. This was different. He was a madman. He attacked her, beat her. "She lied! Jean lied!" he screamed over and over. His deep, raspy, maniacal voice pounded into her in rhythm with the beastly, tearing thrusts that still haunt her nights. Marge thought the ripping and tearing would kill her. Her body eventually healed, though she says her spirit died.

Marge said she struggled to push the memories aside, then for too many years hid in beer bottles. Lately, she has fixated on getting the confession so long in coming.

My plan is to slide against the wall, then duck down and crawl along the ground under the window until we are safely on the far side. From there, we may be able to see into the living room. With luck, we will determine if he is asleep on the couch. I will face south toward the back door with my .38 ready to fire. Not exactly what I'd promised Tommy, who expects us to wait for them at the driveway's entrance. He'll be here soon enough.

The soft sound of cloth scraping on wet wood sends a chill through me until I realize it is the sound of my own jacket. Moving downward, I remove the jacket, slither up again and press against the soggy, rotting wood. I sneak a peek at Marge. She's doing something inside her jacket. Too late I realize she did not leave her gun at home.

We duck and crawl to the far side of the window. Popping up again, I stand ready to defend against anyone who comes to the door. Marge creeps back toward the edge of the window and I follow. Stretching to see as much as we can, we risk exposing ourselves.

Moonlight flowing through the undraped windows into the room's blackness bounces off a shirt and floods over a table littered with empty bottles. Marge whispers, "He's on the couch!"

Seeing him there, in the room, on the couch, is too much for Marge. She falls to her knees, spewing her stomach's contents, reeling from the pain of pent-up anger and hatred. She doesn't get up, so I move onward, afraid that he heard the retching. I'm counting on the door being unlocked.

Gun in hand, I open the door, let my eyes adjust to the darkness, and listen for his sounds.

Before I can say a word, Marge steps in front of me and yells at the sheriff, "Now you will die. You'll know what it feels like to be helpless. To beg for your life."

When she turns on the flashlight my carefully crafted plan melts away. The body lying on the couch is unrecognizable, his face gone. Probably a .45 bullet to the head. I step to Marge's right side as she says, "Shoot him, Ellie."

"I think he's dead."

As I step forward to check for a pulse, I see the fancy cowboy boots.

"Oh. Oh, no! Roger. Who did this to him?"

Tommy arrives in time to save me from collapsing to the floor. Bent over, I see the gun lying on the floor.

"Where is the sheriff? Marge, it was the sheriff, right. Roger didn't rape you. You said it was the sheriff."

"The sheriff's in jail, Ellie. I called in the FBI to detain him until I can get there to question him."

I grab Marge's shoulder and pull her toward me. "That's Roger there, Marge. Look at me and tell me. Now. Who raped you?"

"Jack Kramer. Why is this guy here? He ruined everything,"

Tommy stands in front of Marge now, reaches out to lift up her right arm and takes her gun out of her hand.

"You won't be needing that now, Marge. I'll have someone drive you home. Ellie will be going with me to the courthouse."

49

CHANCE IS AT THE COURTHOUSE IN RESPONSE TO TOMMY'S
call. He hugs me, but without much enthusiasm. Mad at being left out.
Guess I can't blame him.

"I will be talking to the sheriff, Ellie. You and Chance wait here,"
Tommy says.

"But, I want—"

"Of course, you do. But you've done your job. It's a police matter now.
Don't leave this room. I'll come to get you."

So, we sit. I sulk because there are questions I must ask the sheriff.
Chance sits as far away from me as possible in the tiny law library. So difficult to wait. Random thoughts rip through my brain. Why did Roger shoot
himself? Or did someone else shoot him and leave the gun as a decoy? Did
our attempts to show him how wrong grave robbing is cause so much guilt
that he couldn't handle it?

I believe Roger fathered Jean's baby. I don't believe he killed her,
though he did threaten to bury me alive. The bastard. Poor Roger. I am a

mess since I saw his boots. Oh my god, his head. I wipe a sleeve across the tears falling down my cheeks.

"Did you love Roger, Ellie?"

"What? No, Chance. Of course not. Maybe. Oh, who knows? He was evil. He's gone now. I am so confused."

"Ellie." Tommy comes into the room shouting my name. I jump out of my chair and see Chance stand to block his way.

"Sorry. Calm down, Chance. I'm just on edge. Kramer won't talk unless Ellie's in the room. We've tried everything."

Turning to me, Tommy says, "I know Roger's death was a shock. For all of us. Can you do this?"

"Yes, I can. Let's go." I don't want to miss this chance to question the sheriff.

As we're walking, Tommy cautions Chance to stay out of the interrogation room and tells me I am not to speak no matter what Kramer says or does.

"He's cuffed and shackled and there are state police in the room. No deputies."

"Yeah those deputies would probably rescue him," Chance says.

"State police have taken over. All deputies and corrections employees are on temporary leave with orders not to leave Lincoln County. Kramer's been in charge for too long. We don't know who to trust yet."

At the door, Tommy puts a hand on my shoulder. "Kramer doesn't know about Roger. Be careful. Don't let his comments get to you. Sorry to do this."

"I'm OK. I want to hear his story. His lies. Whatever."

Glancing through the two-way window before I enter the room, I see Kramer sitting calmly. His demeanor changes when I walk in.

"You bitch. What lies have you told them? Roger did this, didn't he? Fell for your Injun ways and spilled his guts."

I want to scream at him, but I take a seat without comment. Further enraged, he yells, "C'mon, you hateful squaw. Tell them that the grave robbing was all Roger's idea. Tell them how he found the buyers. Tell them how he stole my Jean, knocked her up and left her because his Ma didn't want an Injun brat for a grandkid."

The officers try to push him back onto his chair, but he's frozen in anger only inches across the table from me. His rant continues. He spills it all. Even that he ran Deputy Harrington off the road. So much emotion that I begin to feel sorry for him, or at least to accept that Roger might be the most evil of the two, odd as that sounds. And now Kramer is back to Jean again. No matter where his tirade rambles, he always finds his way back to Jean.

"He stole her. My beautiful Jean. She was mine, but he made promises and she wanted money, fancy stuff like his family had. She called me, though. She knew where to go when he deserted her. She was really mine again."

With this he smiles and sits down.

Now, Tommy steps in with a question.

"She called you?"

"Yeah."

"What happened?"

"I met her at the green bridge down by the blueberry field. We were going to talk."

"Where did you go to talk, Jack?"

"She started screaming right after she got into my truck. Saw something she shouldn't have and just went crazy. I just wanted her to shut up."

"What did she see?"

"Nothin'. Doesn't matter. I'm done here." He starts to stand, but Tommy stops him.

"Not yet. Ellie has some questions for you."

What the hell? He told me not to speak and now I'm supposed to come up with questions? Well, here goes.

"Jack, I have to return to Siletz to face Grandma Kline. You know what she wants to hear. Why did Jean have to die?"

The rage appears to be gone. The sadness in the sheriff's face is difficult to witness. His body slumps in his chair.

"Grandma. You've got it all, don't you Ellie? Your family. Grandma Kline. The respect of the tribe. And now you've brought me down. Ruined the one chance I had."

"You ruined that years ago, you idiot. Your father is a useless rat, but you chose to work with him and rob the graves of our relatives. Knowing it was you will kill Grandma. What am I supposed to tell her? Give me the answer, Jack. Tell us why Jean and the baby had to die if you loved her so much."

I'm so angry I'm sobbing. Not very professional, but this is family business now.

"Tell Grandma that there was a lot of stuff on the floorboards of my truck when Jean got in. She kicked some bags to make way for her feet. Just as I started to turn onto the Dewey Creek road, she pushed another bag and a skull rolled across her foot. She started screaming that she would tell; that I would go to prison. I couldn't think with all the screaming."

"What did you do, Jack?"

"I slapped her to shut her up. Her head smashed into the back window. She was knocked out. When I got up into Dewey Creek forest, she came to and started yelling at me, saying I was evil. I grabbed my hunting knife and stabbed her bastard child in her gut. When I saw the blood, I kept stabbing and stabbing. But she wouldn't quit screaming until I choked her. I thought she was dead, but I heard a truck coming so I had to get out of there.

I hid my truck farther into the woods and waited until the guy left. Fisherman, I guess. I went back and threw the bones from my truck into the bonfire and hid the skull by the creek. Then I found a hiding place to wait until the sheriff showed up and with all the cars and guys there no one noticed that I came from the wrong direction. Except Harrington. Had to get rid of him."

"This is what I'm supposed to tell Grandma? What about the fact that you knew Mark wasn't guilty, that you let him get convicted of a murder your committed? How much do you think she can take?"

Now he straightens up from his slump and proclaims, "Tell her I will sign a full confession and Mark will be set free. Will that satisfy the old woman? I don't care what she thinks, anyway."

"Liar. You made the wrong choices when you figured out who your father was. Two of a kind. Sign your confession. Do what's right for once."

I could feel his eyes burning into my back as I left the room.

Later, Tommy came out looking exhausted but relieved.

"He's signed his confession, plus it was all tape-recorded. We can use that if he changes his plea later. Search of his house turned up boxes of bones and skulls. Guess the tribe will have to find a way to identify them unless he'll provide some kind of records. But for now, it looks like he'll be off to prison. We'll hold him here until Mark has been released and away from Salem. But I'm curious, Ellie, what sent you down the path of questions about your grandma? How did you know the sheriff would be sad that Grandma Kline would learn he was not only a graverobber but the man who had murdered her daughter and the baby?"

"All the clues finally came together, Tommy. There could only be one answer. I guess he knew before I did since he made the remark telling me to remember who I am. That was a reminder that I am Oscar's child. Jack is one of the thirteen siblings. He's my brother."

50

When the prison doors opened for him, Mark told me, he found Ruthie and Chance waiting. Tommy had called the warden to make all the arrangements. What the new family discussed with one another remains their secret. They drove straight to Siletz for two wonderful days with Grandma Kline at my house. When they left, Grandma announced she was ready to join Grandpa now one grave robber is in jail and the other is dead.

After yelling at me for not including him in my plan, Chance took a leave of absence from work and moved into my spare bedroom to spend final time with Grandma. She was supposed to have the extra bedroom but chose to sleep in the recliner to enjoy the warmth of the wood stove we kept burning day and night for her.

I treasure my last moments with her. Wrapped in the old Pendleton blanket, Grandma sips tea, listens to the news and strokes her ragged cat. One day she calls in a strong voice for me to turn off the television and sit with her. Holding Grandma's gnarled, brown hand in my own younger, healthier version, I hear her say, "It's time. I need to talk to Grandpa now."

My heart is breaking, but I know not to argue. "Do you want me to call Chance? He went up to the office. What about the others, do you have any final words for anyone? Don't you want to wait for Mark?"

"No. They can remember what I say for hundred years. Mark knows my heart. He is good boy." She chuckles, then looks back at me. "You did good. Don't be sad. Think good thoughts like Jesus say."

"I still struggle with that, Gram. How do I worship Him and still honor my tribal culture and beliefs? The old ways teach us Grandfather Creator says to respect Mother Earth. ..."

"I do," Grandma whispers.

"Jesus says love one another and be baptized in His name."

"I do it. Girl think too much."

I hug Grandma to my chest and promise to search for answers.

Soon, she grows quiet. Through tears, I watch her soul fade away from her tired eyes. The little body grows still beneath the blanket as I hold her close.

When Chance returns, he barges through the door to find Grandma cradled in my arms. For the first time, I think he understands the love and pain of the honor wail for the dead.

51

Snuggled onto the little bench beside Logan's grave, proud and comfortable in my regalia, I pull Grandma's tattered shawl tighter against the gentle, sodden breeze whirling over the hill to kiss my cheeks. I raise a corner of the soft wool to my nose to savor the lingering scent of my beloved elder. The sweet tang of tea and huckleberry honey tickles my nose. Drum sounds drift on the wind, keeping pace with my heartbeats.

The past months have been difficult. I often seek refuge here at my son's gravesite, speaking mother words in my heart, building more strength to continue without him. Earlier today, I brought a flower from Grandma's garden and laid it beside Katie's fern frond. I can come to Logan's grave now with only my mother love to affirm; the bitterness, blaming others for his death, and my suicidal thoughts resolved. My son is cherished in my heart and in precious memories.

Solving the murders and stopping the grave robbing brought peace and happiness to Grandma Kline in her final days despite learning of Jack Kramer's involvement, and gave me a renewed energy for life. Helping Chance learn about our tribe's culture and heritage and watching him mature remains a welcome challenge. He's not Logan but he was a lost boy who needed me--still does even with major pieces of his life restored.

Snippets of conversation and occasional laughter ring across the cemetery from the community hall where relatives and tribal leaders from throughout the northwest are gathered following the afternoon's beautiful tribute and burial ceremony for Grandma.

I hear footsteps approaching and look up to see Chance walking toward me as I stand. He looks exhausted. Poor kid. This has been so difficult for him. Even for those used to numerous deaths on a reservation, this has been a very difficult year.

"Hey, El." He puts his arm around me and pulls me close, so I can rest my head on his chest as we stand, looking down at the headstone which features Logan's artwork.

"I wish I could have had more time with him," Chance says.

"I hate to think of the mischief you two would have created." I reach up to pat his face. "Yes, I think you two would have been like brothers."

Chance takes my hand in his and we turn to walk to the hall. Along the way Grandma's scraggly cat ambles past us. I haven't seen him since Grandma passed. We think he went out the door when Chance heard the wailing and rushed in. We watch as he makes it to Grandma's gravesite, sits near her stone. Moments later we look back and the old cat is gone.

At the door of the community hall I hear the roar of many voices and the clatter of dishes for the potluck dinner. An aroma of salmon swirls in the air from the pits outside the kitchen door where the fish bakes on cedar stakes. "Are you ready to go inside?" Chance asks.

"Yes, I think so. I'm hoping someone will have another mystery for us to solve. We didn't determine who killed Grandma's dog, so we know there's at least one mystery—and one more bad guy around here. Of course, identifying the criminals doesn't guarantee another band of looters won't violate our graves in the future but our tribal leaders are more aware now. They will take precautions to avoid a repeat."

"Ellie, I'm not good at saying thanks. I came to Siletz as a last resort, hoping to find myself, my reason for being. At a young age, I planned to end my miserable, confusing life. When I learned about my connection to this tribe, I thought I'd give it another try."

Shocked, I reach out to him. He lays a hand on each of my shoulders and holds me away, so he can look down into my eyes.

"I owe my life to you."

He pulls me to him, kisses the top of my head and reaches for the door, then draws his hand back.

"Almost forgot. A bird dropped this in front of me at the river early this morning, I saved it for you."

He pulls a small, blue feather from his pocket and lays it in my hand.

Struggling to breathe as tears form, I whisper, "From my angel son. Enit!"

needs editing!

TELL THE WORLD THIS BOOK WAS		
GOOD	BAD	SO-SO
		X

Acknowledgements

THE INITIAL WORDS OF THE STORY I FIRST ENVISIONED WHILE walking down a hallway at Siletz High School sixty years ago were typed on a portable typewriter loaned by my friend, Beverly Youngman. My imagined story has changed so much over the years, but I treasure that friendship and the generosity of her grandparents and her Aunt Babe on the many days and nights I spent in their home as a teenager.

When it takes a major part of a lifetime to complete a story, there are many friends and loved ones whose support was constant, but who passed on before the book was published. I especially want to remember Nancy (Olson) Anderson, Patricia 'Patsy' (Harrison) Pullin, my Aunt Phonola (Van Pelt) Smith, John Trudell, Robert 'Bob' and Marjorie Lasher, Nilak Butler, Robert and Maxine (Ben) Rilatos, Carl and Verna (Miller) Kentta, and my cousins Robert "Bobby" Simmons, Edwina "Tinker" (Simmons) Brown, and Robert "Robbie" (Marzan) Smith.

Through the years people shared their homes, their advice, their editorial skills, their knowledge and/or their passion for justice. They are my mentors, my heroes. Naming every person would fill pages, but I must mention Selene Rilatos, Valerie J. Brooks, Barbara Sullivan, Bruce Ellison, Darelle "Dino" Butler, Paul J. Ciolino, Harold and Monteen Nash, Ray Thomas, Larry Weaver and Mary Wells, Jeffrey Van Pelt, Don C. Johnson, Rosemary Camozzi, Kate Herse, LeeAnn Dakers, Cindy Snider, Mary Etta Schneider, Margie Fell, Marie Girard, Ishbel Munro, Trish Jordan, Robert Kentta, Jane Cracraft, Bonnie Cubit, Michele Longo-Eder and Ivan Kelley, D.C.

Three contributed words to this book: Michael Darcy's description of the emotions felt during a Run to the Rogue were given to my character, Old Joe Logsden. Joe's name was suggested by Kathy (Robinson) Pokorny and Grandma Kline's name was suggested by Jason McWain.

Nothing would be accomplished in my life without the constant and consistent presence of my immediate family, my daughters, Nancy and Tari to whom this book is dedicated; my sons-in-law David Cary and Gene Messman; my grandsons and their wives, Brinton and Ashley Cary, Ty Cary; Kyle and Krista Utterback; Eric Utterback and Leann Coleman. I look forward to seeing grandson Shane Utterback again. My great-grand-daughters, Presley, Sutton, Chevelle, Cheyenne, Addison and Kailey, and great-grandson Keaton, continue to teach me the real meaning of life.

A special thank you to all the writers and librarians I have met over the years. Again, too numerous to list, but gratefully remembered and appreciated.

About the Author

GRACE ELTING CASTLE WAS RAISED ON THE SILETZ INDIAN Reservation in Siletz, Oregon. She is a fierce protector of Native culture, traditions, stories, natural resources, sacred items and burial sites. She was an outspoken advocate for the passage of the Native American Graves Protection and Repatriation Act (NAGPRA) and was often the lead investigator for Native American defendants. A member of the initial committee for restoration of Siletz tribal rights terminated by the U.S government, she later helped the tribe regain their largest burial ground, as well as the surrounding acreage known as Government Hill. In 1985, she led a successful drive to strengthen Oregon's law against robbing of Native American gravesites.

Grace is a retired professional investigator, a nationally-recognized writer/editor and an award-winning newspaper reporter and photographer. She edited and co-authored the critically acclaimed investigative textbooks *Advanced Forensic Civil Investigations*, *Advanced Forensic Criminal Defense Investigations* and *Corporate Investigations*. She represented the National

Association of Legal Investigators (NALI) on the planning committee for the 1998 "Wrongful Convictions and the Death Penalty Conference" in Chicago and was a speaker at the event. In 2001, she co-sponsored and co-chaired the first national conference for investigators working on wrongful conviction cases. She participated in the re-investigation of countless wrongful convictions during her years as the Executive Managing Director and Innocence Project Coordinator for Paul J. Ciolino and Associates in Chicago and continues the battle to reform our system of justice.

She is a past president of the Oregon Association of Legal Investigators (OALI), past regional director of the National Association of Legal Investigators, Inc. (NALI) and past editor of their educational journal, *The Legal Investigator*. She has also served as editor of the National Association of Process Servers' newsletter, *The Docket Sheet*; as editor of the Pacific Northwest Legal Assistants' newsletter, and for over a decade as editor of *PI Magazine, the Journal for Professional Investigators*.

A deep interest in the history of her paternal families, the Dutch and French Huguenots, of the Hudson River Valley of New York state, resulted in her serving in several offices, including president and editor of the Bevier-Elting Family Association of New Paltz, NY. She served on Historic Huguenot Street (HHS) committees, and in 2008, she published a 244-page book, *Answering the Call, An Elting Military Tribute*. She is a member and past president of Paul Washington Auxiliary to the Veterans of Foreign Wars 732, Siletz Oregon.

Contact: grace@graceeltingcastle.com